THE
BLACKSTAR
LEGACY

THE VEILGUARD SAGA

2

TRAVIS STARNES

Maps available at

https://tstarnes.com/book-series/veilguard_saga/

Signup to get free previews of upcoming books before they're released at

http://tstarnes.com/preview-notification-newsletter/

Contents

The Document

"Faster. You have to react faster," Rowan said as his sword passed within inches of Osric's face.

Osric danced back and feinted left, then quickly changed direction, trying to catch Rowan when he was off balance, on his back foot. Or so it had seemed to Osric. Rowan's wrist pivoted, turning to parry the attack, but then Osric moved. The attack had been a second feint. He ducked under Rowan's guard and struck, his practice sword connecting solidly with the ranger's side.

"Damnit," Rowan said, stepping back.

The stag-folk stamped their hooves in appreciation, their way of cheering. Osric stepped back, a grin spreading across his face as he lowered his weapon in an overly fancy bow.

During the past month, waiting for the Sage of Avendell to translate the ancient document they'd found, he had not spent his time idly. Although Osric had learned a lot about fighting 'on the job' as it were, he had no formal training. Osric had been brought up to be a blacksmith's apprentice, and knew more about forging a blade than wielding it.

That time of his life was over, and it looked as though he would never make it back to Eldham and Master Ironhand. Ever since finding the ancient artifact and the quest that had begun from that discovery, Osric's life had changed. He'd been in more life-and-death situations in that time than most soldiers would go through in their entire lives. He'd fought warriors of a secret order known as the Brethren and creatures from the other side of the veil, monsters outside of his understanding.

And he was sure to be fighting more before long. Jasper, who, besides being a cleric of Heathus, had studied the veil nearly as long as the sage had, both as part of the Brethren and on his own

1

after leaving them, had told him he thought they were close to having the whole document translated. If the sage was right, it should tell them how they could stop the veil from breaking entirely. Considering the creatures he'd seen that had already slipped through, Osric was certain that the veil breaking was something he did *not* want to happen.

So, he took the time to practice with Rowan. The ranger may have been more proficient with a bow than a sword, but he still knew a sight more than Osric did, having trained with the Greenwood Rangers for years before being allowed into their ranks.

"It's about time you finally got through my defenses," Rowan said, rubbing his side where Osric might have whacked him a little too hard.

Osric wasn't one of these hulking giants, but he'd spent a lifetime, or at least his lifetime, at the forge, hammering away at iron and steel, and sometimes he forgot his own strength.

"Thanks," Osric replied, catching his breath. "I've been working on that move."

"It was a good strike, but remember – in a real fight, that opening you created could have been deadly."

"What do you mean?"

"When you ducked under my guard, you left yourself exposed," Rowan explained, demonstrating the movement. "A more experienced opponent could have seen that and struck while you were vulnerable. I didn't happen to catch it this time, but I did notice it just after the opening closed. You won't always be so lucky."

"I see," Osric said, his enthusiasm dampened slightly. "I'll work on that."

"Don't be discouraged. You're improving rapidly. Just keep in mind that in battle, one mistake can be your last. Don't get so wedded to an idea that you don't adjust for the realities of the combat at hand."

Osric nodded, processing what Rowan had said as he glanced up, trying to catch a faint sign of the sun, to determine its position in the sky and how far it had traveled.

Rowan followed his gaze and chuckled. "Go on then. I know you're eager to see her before she finishes for the day."

"What? I don't know what you're talking about."

"There's no use denying it. You've been watching the sun's progress all afternoon."

"Am I that obvious?"

"Only to anyone with eyes," Rowan teased. "Now go. You've had enough for today, and I'm sure Talia could use a break from her studies as well."

"Thanks, Rowan," Osric said, already hurrying out of the practice area, waving at several of the stag-folk as he passed.

They'd quickly taken to coming to watch Rowan train Osric, and on lucky days Valen, or one of the others who'd actually engaged in combat on the borders of their lands, had offered their own pointer or two. Most of the denizens of Avendell were magical creatures with no use for weapons or even language, but the stag-folk were surprisingly similar to most of the people he'd known back home in Eldham.

Well, a little similar, at least.

The walk through the forest was peaceful. The ethereal light filtered through the canopy with the occasional glimpse of shimmerlings as flittering lights further away, and a creature Valen had called a glom silently ghosted by in the distance. The creatures of the forest seemed enchanted by the presence of humans and were never far away. They kept their distance, except for the stag-folk, and there were always more just out of sight.

Osric couldn't fault them for being skittish. The majority of the humans they'd dealt with were interlopers. Brethren scouts, treasure seekers lured by tales of fabulous wealth beyond their imagination, and mages who could feel the power of the place and desired to be a part of it. Then there were the hostiles who wanted to hurt the inhabitants and take from them.

Osric gave himself a rueful headshake. It was a marvel how quickly he'd grown accustomed to the otherworldly beauty of the place. What had been unbelievable the first time they'd come here had now become ... expected.

As he approached the clearing where Talia practiced with the druids, Osric slowed his pace. He didn't want to disturb their lessons, but he couldn't resist watching for a moment. Talia stood in the center of the glade, her 'concentration' face in place as she wove intricate patterns in the air.

Osric leaned against a tree, smiling slightly as he watched her work.

"Caught you staring again," a voice said behind him.

Osric didn't jump. He'd gotten used to Grace's idea of fun, sneaking around, getting close before she revealed herself.

"I'm just watching," Osric said, not turning to look at her.

"Sure you are," she said, coming to stand next to him. "You've been 'just watching' a lot lately."

"It's not like that."

Grace arched an eyebrow. "Whatever you say, Osric."

Ignoring her, Osric turned his attention back to the clearing, where the druids were wrapping up their session. Talia lowered her hands, the light fading from her fingertips, and she wiped her brow, clearly exhausted from the exertion. As the druids began to disperse, she caught sight of him and waved, a tired smile on her face.

Osric waved back, feeling an inexplicable warmth in his chest. He could hear Grace snickering behind him, but he didn't care. He felt … happy.

He knew it wouldn't last. Once the document was translated, they would be back on the road, chasing after whatever they said would fix the veil. Assuming the sage and Jasper were right about what it contained. He pushed the thought down. For now, he would savor these last moments of peace.

He approached the edge of the clearing as Talia made her way over, still looking a little worn from her practice but smiling nonetheless.

"Did you finish your training?" she asked.

"Yeah. I scored a hit against Rowan."

"Really? That's great."

"He says I did it in a way that opened myself up to getting hit back, so … still more work to do. You look pretty tired."

"It's nothing. Just … stretching my limits," she said, brushing a stray lock of her wild red hair from her face.

Talia had been pushing herself harder in this downtime than any of the rest of them. She'd always loved magic. He hadn't even known his friend was learning from Elder Miriam, but it had become clear on their adventure together how important it was to her. When she'd learned that she was damaging the world, the veil, every time she used magic, it had been a serious blow to her. So when she had the chance to learn how to use magic without damaging the veil, she'd jumped into her studies.

Pushing herself hard.

"You're really getting good at this," he said.

Talia laughed and said, "You say that every day, Osric."

"And it's true every day."

She rolled her eyes, though she couldn't hide the pleased expression on her face. "It's not just about weaving spells, you know. The real challenge is learning to be gentle with it. It's all about precision. You have to feel their tension, their give. One wrong tug, and you could tear something, break something."

"How do you know which ... threads to pull?"

He didn't really understand magic. Talia had tried to explain it to him, Elder Miriam had explained a bit, even the sage and Jasper had tried. But Osric was more comfortable with steel and sweat than with pulling fire or whatever from the air around them.

"It's all about recognition. Each type of energy has its own ... signature, I suppose you could call it. Once you learn to identify them, you can start to manipulate them without damaging the overall structure."

She demonstrated, her fingers moving in intricate patterns. For a moment, Osric thought he saw faint lines of light tracing her movements, but they vanished as quickly as they appeared.

"See? If I were to just grab at the energy," Talia continued, making a sudden grasping motion, "it would be like yanking on a thread. You might get what you want, but you'd damage the whole in the process."

"I can barely wrap my head around it."

Talia gave a shrug. "Well, I've had good teachers. The druids here, they understand magic in a way that's so different from what Elder Miriam taught me. It's like ... they're part of the weave themselves."

"I'm still impressed."

"Thanks," she said softly, shyly touching his arm and looking down at the ground.

For a moment, they stood there in silence. Osric wasn't sure what to say and apparently, neither was Talia. Their moment was broken by a call from some of the stag-folk, yelling at the three of them to come back to the sage's hut.

Talia and Osric exchanged a glance. It meant they must have done it. They must have finished translating the document.

Osric and Talia, followed closely by Grace, hurried to the sage's hut. Word must have passed, as many stag-folk were also headed in that direction. Osric saw Valen, and realized that he was finally starting to be able to tell some of the stag-folk apart. Something he'd never thought possible.

He was tired and a little sore from his training, but this was the moment he'd been waiting for, so he pushed ahead, forcing Talia to keep up with him.

When they got to the cabin, the door burst open and Jasper came rushing out, probably having seen them through the window.

"You're here! Excellent. Come inside. Come inside."

Osric exchanged glances with Talia and Grace, the three of them amused by Jasper's exuberance. The man could be a contradiction, sometimes deadly serious and other times jovial and giddy, without much care for decorum. He was quite unlike anyone Osric had met before.

Inside, they found the older sage seated at a desk in the small cabin, a chair next to him where Jasper had spent nearly every waking hour since their return to Avendell.

"We have indeed 'done it,'" the sage said, giving them a small smile as he looked to Jasper and then back to them. "Although I would temper Jasper's enthusiasm somewhat. While it does tell us a great deal, it raises as many questions as it answers, as is often the case with such ancient knowledge."

"But what does it say? Why did he want us to find this so badly? Why'd he send the ring through to the future? What did this guy expect us to do once we found it?"

Jasper looked to the sage, clearly excited to be the one to tell it. The sage gave him another smile, and then a small nod of permission.

"It's a long explanation," Jasper said, pointing to the few chairs in the room as Rowan came in to join them. "The man who wrote this document was a high master of the Calaphium, which seems to be a highly placed position. He oversaw something called the Nexus Tower, a place that ... well, it controlled the flow of magic in Peridia. In a way."

"Controlled magic? How?" Talia asked, her interest piqued as it was any time magic was mentioned.

"At the top of the tower, there was an artifact of some kind. He called it the Blackstar. It was a magic lodestone, drawing magical energies to it. It absorbed stray magical energies, loose magic, and redirected them into the veil, repairing the damage caused by the use of magic."

"Wouldn't that make magic less effective?"

"Probably," the sage said. "Our records show that the people who rebelled against the Calaphium, and caused it to fall, were mostly motivated by complaints that the Calaphium controlled magic. Limited its use. Some documents even indicated that they thought the Calaphium were making magic 'worse.' I'd always written that off as just complaints, finding a way to blame them for the veil crumbling, but it seems I was wrong. They were, indeed, weakening magic, pulling energies out and putting it back into the veil. This would make it harder to use the veil, as the more damaged the veil becomes, the easier it is to access its energies."

"But it can help us repair the veil?"

"Yes," Jasper said. "But it's not that simple. When this man, this high master, saw what was happening, it prompted him to write this document. He was apparently in a unique position to witness the veil tear apart firsthand. Which is also where part of our problem comes from."

"But if this thing was repairing the veil, how did it come to the point where the veil tore apart?" Osric asked.

"When their capital, a place called the Great Citadel, was destroyed, it sent a wave of energy across the veil, creating ruptures everywhere. It caused the energy that normally pushed into the veil to push back into this artifact. That destroyed it, breaking it into pieces, which released even more energies," the sage said. "It, in effect, did the opposite of what it was designed to do. It became a focal point. The high master described it; the tower became surrounded by dark, malevolent realities that merged with ours, becoming stuck in ways they couldn't have predicted."

"Like the creature in the lake?" Rowan asked, referencing the monster they faced on their last adventure, that had become stuck in their reality, tortured by it.

"Similar, but it wasn't a thing, but parts of reality, all battling against each other to exist where they shouldn't be," Jasper said. "It allowed beasts to come through but not be torn apart like the creature in the lake. The high master wrote that these things, beasts from nightmares, things that haunted children, were all around the area, making it their home."

He knew the survivors, the remaining members of the higher orders of the Calaphium, had retreated deep into the Great Forest," the sage said, taking over. "My ancestors, who would eventually form this part of the forest. He also had some contact with them, enough to know they were attempting to close the veil. But the high master was certain that their efforts were only a stopgap. He could see what was coming ... their success would be fleeting at best."

"But I thought you told us they managed to close the veil when they established this place?" Talia asked.

"They did, but he knew it wouldn't be permanent. With the Nexus fractured, they couldn't strengthen the veil anymore. And they couldn't make a new one. The Calaphium's power had waned too much. It was only a matter of time before magic would once again wear down the veil, tearing it open as it did during the Great Rupture."

"But he had all the parts, right? Couldn't they repair it?"

"He didn't," Jasper said. "When it broke, it tore open the veil and two parts of it flew through those openings. He knew they were somewhere in Peridia, but he didn't know where and couldn't leave his tower to find them. He mentions that he'd keep looking for them, but if he found them, there's no way to know."

"That's why he sent the ring and the document," Talia said. "It wasn't just a warning. It was instructions."

"Yes," the sage said. "The high master's only hope was to explain how the Nexus worked, how it could be reforged using the existing pieces, and that someone else not trapped like he was could find the pieces. Since he knew how dangerous it was to send something through a tear in the veil, he tied the document to the ring with a thread of the veil itself and sent both through, creating two chances for the document to be found. If the document got through to my ancestors, fine. Otherwise, they could find the ring, which was bound to the document, leading them to it."

"But the document got lost somewhere in the world, and the ring flew into the future. For me to find it in the forest," Osric pointed out.

"True, it didn't go as planned, but it did work. Just … a bit late." Jasper chuckled softly, spreading his hands. "The ring led you to the document, and it is now here in the hands of their descendants."

"So now what? Can't we just … recreate this Nexus thing now that we've got the document?" Grace asked.

"No, I'm afraid not," Jasper said. "The high master who wrote this document was only a caretaker, responsible for maintaining the Nexus. He wasn't alive when it was forged and has no knowledge of how it was originally created. He only knew how to repair it once the pieces were found."

"So, we go find these pieces and bring them back here to be reforged," Rowan said.

"Partially," the sage said. "Even with the pieces, the reforging will likely have to happen at the Conclave in Celestia. The kind of artificing required is beyond the skills of anyone here in the forest."

Osric knew nothing about Celestia, the capital of Aeloria and to whom they all owed their allegiance as citizens of the kingdom, but it might as well be located in the heavens. It seemed like a far-off and impossible place to reach.

"So we gather the pieces, take them to the Conclave, and convince them to fix it?" Talia asked.

"Convincing them might not be as easy as you think, from what I've heard about them, but that's a problem for later. Right now, our first task is finding the pieces," said Jasper.

"And we do know the location of one of the pieces. Two disappeared into the veil, but one remained in the tower with the man who wrote this letter," the sage said.

"Except, we don't know where the tower is," Jasper added.

"So this was all … for nothing," Osric said, sagging in the chair.

"Not entirely," the sage said. "There is still a chance. But it will not be easy."

"As opposed to how easy the rest of this has been," Osric said.

"This will be difficult in a different way, and it will fall only to you, Osric," the sage said. "In the deepest part of the Great Forest, beyond where even the stag-folk roam, there is a place, a small pond hidden from the world. Within that pond is the point where the veil is weakest. This place … it's like my grove here, but far stronger. The energies are raw, wild. A place where the barrier between our world and others is thin, fragile. Unlike the rips in the veil, however, this one is controlled. Main7tained."

"Maintained by who?" Talia asked.

"The Veilguard. I think," the sage said. "It's hard to communicate with them, so I cannot be sure I'm right, but I think they use this as a way to access our world more directly. Watch us. Follow us."

"And what will happen when we go there?"

"You've been chosen, Osric. By the gods of the Veilguard. They have shown you favor before, guiding you, protecting you. In places like this pond, where the veil is thin, a direct answer may be possible. Or a type of direct answer. They might communicate with you. You can ask for their guidance."

It was a frightening thought. He knew things were different now, that he wasn't just a blacksmith's apprentice any longer, but this? This was different. Getting that close to the gods was a terrifying thought. It scared him to his very core.

And yet, what choice did he have?

"Alright. I'll do it."

The Pool

A month was a long time, and they had settled into the safe and amazing world of Avendell in that month. Not quite put down roots but spread them out. Gotten comfortable. He had enjoyed his time, putting off the thought of what would happen when the Sage finished translating the document. Now that it was done, they had to abandon the safety they had known and go back out into a world that had tried very hard to kill them the last time.

It was worth the danger, of course, but he was feeling bittersweet about it. His life in Eldham had been a happy one, but living amid the magic here had been ... amazing. Something he didn't think he'd ever get to experience again.

Everyone else was quiet as they packed up their things, preparing to leave this place behind, perhaps forever, and Osric couldn't help but wonder if they were feeling the same things.

It didn't take him long to learn the answer to that, at least personally, as Grace said, "I'm not going."

She had been quiet since leaving the Sage's hut, but Osric had thought it was the same introspection as everyone else. He was, frankly, shocked at her revelation.

"What do you mean, you're not going? We need you," Talia said, sounding as much offended that she would abandon them as surprised.

Grace shrugged. "I've stayed too long already. I'm not here to save the world. I need to get back to what I do best."

"If the world burns, Grace, you burn with it," Jasper said. "It won't matter how much you steal if you're dead."

Grace let out a short laugh, though there was no humor in it. "Then I'll wish you all good luck. Besides, if I stay with you lot, I'll probably wind up dead anyway. You've got your mission. I've got mine."

"Don't you want to be part of something bigger?" Osric asked. "This ... this is more than any of us. You know that."

"That's not going to work on me. The only thing you get from joining something bigger is getting used and tossed aside when you're no longer useful. That's the way the world works."

"That's a terrible way to go through life," Talia said, shaking her head.

Grace rolled her eyes, picked up her pack, and put it on her back. "It's what life gives us. Letting people in only gives them the chance to take advantage of you. I'm no one's chump."

"I know we can't make you come with us, but you've become important to us, Grace. We'll need every bit of help we can get, and I don't think we would have gotten this far without you. If you want to go, though ... I wish you good luck," Osric said, and then paused, looking directly into her eyes. "You know, though, the Brethren won't forget you. They'll come looking."

"Why would they care at all about me?"

"They know you were with us, at least for a while. They're angry about the document, and if they didn't want us to have it, they certainly don't want us to get this Blackstar thing. They're not going to just let you walk away. At the very least, they'll want information from you so they can find us, and they're not known for asking politely."

"I can handle myself," she said confidently, but it was clear to Osric that his words had hit home.

The 'I don't care' attitude was an act. She definitely cared about the Brethren tracking her down. Not that she would admit she was afraid. Grace had a chip on her shoulder that was larger than she was.

"I'm sure you can."

The two of them looked at each other for a long moment.

Finally, she said, "Well ... Bye."

As she walked out of the hollowed-out tree the group had been using for shelter since they arrived back in the forest, Jasper said, "Grace, there's greatness inside of you if you give yourself a chance. You could be better than you are."

Grace froze in place, not looking back at them, but for a moment, Osric thought she was going to change her mind. Turn around.

Instead, she said, "Whatever," and was gone.

"Think she'll come around?" Talia asked quietly.

Osric shook his head. "I don't know."

He watched the exit out of the tree, half expecting her to suddenly turn around and come back. Except she didn't. He sighed, looking at the others. Everyone had resumed packing their things, the atmosphere heavier than before. Grace leaving had been a sobering dose of reality. They'd been a band of adventurers bound together by a quest.

A quest that was now over.

He shouldn't have been surprised. None of them had planned on being on a quest together, it had just kind of happened. There was no reason to stay together, go on this new quest together. It was only a matter of time before more of them started to drift away, just like Grace.

Osric turned to Talia, who was quietly stuffing her belongings into her satchel.

"Do you think more will leave?" he asked quietly, so only she could hear him. "We all just kind of ended up together. Is this going to fall apart?"

Talia paused in her packing and looked up at him, her eyes soft. "Cinder and I won't leave. We're in this for the long haul. You're stuck with us."

The wolf raised his head at the sound of his name, tail thumping against the ground. A faint smile tugged at the corner of Osric's lips. It was comforting to know that not everyone had one foot out the door.

"Jasper probably won't either," she continued. "He's too invested now. He was a member of the group and is clearly harboring anger toward them. And he's spent years ... decades, trying to learn about the veil. He won't give up an opportunity like this."

"Well, that's four."

"Don't be so negative," Talia chided, giving him a playful nudge. "People can surprise you, you know?"

"I hope you're right," he muttered to himself, as much as to anyone else, before standing up and hefting his pack onto his back. "Is everyone ready?"

"Ready as we'll ever be," Jasper said.

They filed out of the hollow tree and started down the forest path behind Valen, who would lead them to the pond and the weak point in the veil. There was a lot of day left and it would only take them a few hours to get there. After that, who knew where they'd end up?

They'd walked for a few minutes when there was the sound of someone running through foliage behind them. Hands went to weapons as they turned around. There shouldn't be any danger, not in Avendell, but after the journey they'd been on, none of them were prepared to take a chance.

Osric wasn't sure what he expected to burst through the trees, but it hadn't been Grace, who skidded to a stop when she realized she'd caught up with them, slightly out of breath. Without a word she started walking down the path, as if she were waiting on them.

A smile spread across Osric's face as they all fell in step with her.

"I'm really happy you decided to ..."

"Shut up," Grace cut him off, but there was no real bite to her words.

Osric's smile widened. She might never admit it, but he knew they'd gotten through to her. Or at least Jasper had. She put up a front of never caring about anything, about being apathetic to the world. But Osric knew that was a lie. She cared.

She cared a lot.

They had walked a lot of places over the last two months, covering what felt like the entire Great Forest, but this might be the most amazing walk they'd taken yet. The deeper they got into Avendell, the more amazing the forest got. Osric was lagging a little behind the group, looking at the marvelous creatures that followed the procession led by Valen and several of his stag-folk brethren, through the strange, almost luminous trees around them.

It was a spectacular place.

14

As they walked, Talia and Jasper had engaged in something of a philosophical debate over the nature of magic versus worship of the gods. They'd been going at it for weeks, since a few days after they arrived back in Avendell. They were both stubborn, but Osric thought they kept going not in an effort to win, but because they each liked the test of their wills and minds. Rowan and Osric had always stayed out of it, both of them more interested in what they could see and feel, or so it seemed to Osric. Grace was ... well, Grace. She'd join them sometimes, but more to throw a pole into the spokes than to actually participate.

That girl thrived on chaos.

"But surely there must be some universal truth that underlies the nature of magic itself," Jasper was saying. "After all, the gods created the world, taking all of the energies around us and making ... everything, including the veil. The very energies that you harness to cast your spells. So in a way, it is no different than asking the gods for favors."

"Magic is just magic, Jasper. There is no universal truth, not in the way you mean. It's ... a mechanical process, in its own way. I don't ask anyone to cast spells and hope. I do specific things and get expected results when I do. It's a craft, learned and practiced."

"So you feel nothing when you're casting your spells?" Rowan asked. "You don't feel anything ... greater? Some presence or power beyond yourself?"

"Magic isn't like that, Rowan. It's learned and practiced, not some mysterious blessing."

"So it all just ... comes from inside of you?"

"No. The way I understand it, we're not pulling power from within ourselves, but rather shaping what's already here. It's a tool."

"See, that's exactly why I don't bother with either gods or magic," Grace said. "The moment you start depending on higher powers, or the universe, or whatever it is at the moment, you lose your edge."

"There's nothing wrong with having faith," Jasper said quietly. "The gods provide guidance and purpose."

"And rules. So many rules."

"Structure creates order. Without it ..."

"... we'd all be free to make our own choices," Grace interrupted. "How terrible."

Osric was only half listening. He didn't really know anything about all this. Yes, he had some kind of connection to the gods, or at least the ones that made up the Veilguard, but he didn't pretend to understand any of it. He just ... did his best to deal with each problem in front of him. It was all so much; he was still grappling with his role in all of this. Who needed to think about the nature of the universe when they'd been tasked with saving the world?

The debate continued and settled into familiar patterns, both of them confident in their own beliefs, with Grace occasionally mocking one or both of them. They seemed to enjoy it, so who was he to tell them to stop?

Rowan must have felt the same, because he slowed his pace, falling back to walk beside him.

For a moment, they just walked in silence next to each other, before Rowan finally asked, "So the Sage seems to think you've got a special connection with the gods, Osric. Or at least with the Veilguard. Do you ... feel it?"

"I was just thinking about that and I don't really know. I mean, I've never spoken to the gods, never had some grand vision. It's more like ... I've been guided at times by Cinder or their message to the Sage that I was coming, but that was kind of external. Not directly connected to me."

"But you can heal, like Jasper does. You put your hands on someone and—" he made a vague gesture with his hands, "—and they're mended. Not everyone can do that."

"Yeah, but I don't even know what I'm really doing when that happens. With Jasper, it's different. He asks Heathus directly. Me? I'm praying to all of the Veilguard, hoping something works."

Rowan clapped him on the shoulder and said, "You're selling yourself short, Osric. Maybe you're praying to all of them because you matter to all of them. Maybe they're listening, all of them. That's something even Jasper can't say."

"I guess what I really wanted to know is if you feel anything from Wyndra, when you heal someone? Or ... anything at all?"

There was something in Rowan's voice. A sincerity, or maybe a desperation, that suggested this wasn't just a theoretical debate, something to pass the time the way Talia and Jasper argued. He was looking for a specific answer. There was something bothering him.

"Honestly, I don't know. There's something, yes. An energy that passes through me when I try to heal, but it doesn't feel directed. Like, I don't sense a guiding hand or voice, if that makes sense. I can't tell you which god is behind it, or even what they think of me. It's not something that happens to me, it happens through me. It's like I'm a weathervane being struck by lightning."

"Oh," he said, disappointed.

"I'm sorry, Rowan. I wish I could give you more. I mean, I've seen the power work, but ... if there's a greater meaning to it, I haven't felt it."

Rowan nodded, looking down at the forest floor as they walked.

"I've worshipped Wyndra my entire life. Trained under the Greenwood Rangers to protect her lands and keep her balance. Never once have I doubted that my faith was worth it." He paused, glancing up toward the trees that towered above them. "But knowing about the veil now ... I can't help but wonder why she's let things come to this. Why she hasn't stepped in to set it right."

"Maybe she has. I mean, she's part of the Veilguard, and they are the ones actively trying to rebuild it, or whatever."

Rowan shook his head. "It's not just the veil, though. It's all the creepy things that have come with it. The creatures in the woods, the abominations and twisted monsters. They tip the balance that Wyndra taught us to protect. If balance is her will, why are those things allowed to kill, to destroy? Why hasn't she prevented it?"

"Maybe she's focused on fixing the veil, as it's the bigger threat," Osric suggested. "And maybe they all have rules, boundaries they can't break. Or maybe they trust their followers to be the ones to act. I mean ... I think about Cinder, the ring, all these pieces pushing me, nudging me along a path without a direct hand. Maybe she expects the Rangers to do the same."

"Maybe," Rowan said, but it was hard not to hear the doubt in his voice.

Osric felt for him. It was a confusing time, with everything they'd learned about the world, but he did know how he could help the ranger. Maybe, once they got this Blackstar thing and repaired the veil, they could work with the other rangers and rid the forests of those creatures.

For now, though, their duty was clear.

It took hours to get to the pond, most of it filled with restless chatter. Everyone was nervous about what was going to happen once they got the answers from the Veilguard. What the next phase of their quest led to. Considering how close they'd come to death already, Osric knew he was nervous, and it seemed the rest were too, even Jasper and Rowan, who had seen a lot more than the rest of them.

The forest got darker the further they went; the trees larger and the canopies thicker. And yet, it never became hard to see. It was as if the entire forest glowed, just enough to keep everything just visible.

They'd all started to relax, letting their camaraderie calm their nerves, when Valen slowed and then stopped.

"This is where I must stop," Valen said, still looking down the path rather than at them.

"Why can't you continue with us?" Osric asked.

"Ahead lies a place of communion. The gods, our creators, reside there. It is forbidden for my kind to enter. This is a place only for those chosen by the gods," he said, shifting to look at Jasper and then back to Osric. "You bear the blessing of the Veilguard, Osric Yarrow. Your group has earned the right to tread there."

"Ohh," Osric said.

"Thank you, Valen, truly, for bringing us this far," Jasper said, keeping his senses about him better than Osric had.

"You honor me, Jasper Mowbray," he said, bowing his head slightly, causing the small trinkets and fine chain woven around him as decoration to sway slightly. "You have only to head down this path a ways and you will find the place you seek. I will wait here and guide you out once your purpose is complete."

Osric gave Valen a small smile and squared his shoulders, taking the first step toward their destination, leaving the rest to follow. If he was the one selected by the Veilguard, then it was up to him to go first, even if this whole thing terrified him some. They walked the path in silence for several minutes until the dense foliage ahead parted, revealing an open space that stopped Osric in his tracks.

Before them lay a perfect circle of cleared earth, the trees and even bushes stopping, as if they were afraid to intrude on this ground. In the center, as though drawn with meticulous precision, rested a pond, again a flawless circle, exactly in the middle of the clearing, as if someone had sketched the outline of two different-sized cups, one within the other, upon the ground.

It was unbelievably perfect.

Jasper inhaled deeply beside him. "I can feel them ... the gods. Their presence lingers here, close by."

"I don't know about gods, but I can feel the magic here. The energy ... it feels like it's crawling along my skin. Like little pricks in my skin," Talia said, almost whispering, as if she were afraid to disturb something reverent and precious. "It pulls at me."

"Funny," Grace said, never one to fear being irreverent, wiggling one foot. "All I feel is this rock in my shoe."

"Show some respect," Jasper said harshly.

Osric didn't look at them. He was focused on the pond. He didn't know about what Jasper and Talia felt, but he knew he felt something. Deep in his stomach. Like a twisting.

He was jolted out of his thoughts by a push against his knees. Looking down, he saw Cinder, who lowered his head and butted the back of his knees again, as if pushing him forward. Osric took a step forward and felt the gentle pressure of Cinder's muzzle, again urging him onward. Another step, and another, each encouraged by Cinder, until his boots met the water's edge. The air around him grew warmer the closer he got to the pond, the sensation both frightening and comforting. It was a warmth he recognized, like when he got near the forge on a cold day, the heat settling and calming him.

Straightening his back, he took a step into the pond, feeling the ground squish under his boots. Cinder wasn't pushing him on any longer, but he still felt pressed forward. Or was it pulled forward. He stepped in deeper, letting the water rise to his waist, feeling its warmth wrap around him, like a heated bath. Again, it felt almost ... welcoming.

Osric turned to the others, intending to reassure them. "I don't feel anything here, really, I ..."

A force struck him, driving the words from his throat as his vision twisted and spun. The clearing around him faded into shadow, only for his senses to be swallowed by a vast, desolate landscape.

Osric found himself standing at the base of an ancient tower, spiraling high above him. Not a peaceful tower. The ground shook under his feet, making him feel as if he was going to fall over. The source of the quaking was easy to see as jagged mountains clawed their way upward through the ground, all around the tower. Cracks appeared in the earth, widening as if the world itself was tearing open, reforming the landscape.

Through these tears in the ground, from them, pitch-black, grotesque shapes slithered and clawed their way into existence. Creatures of nightmare that defied reason, spilling out into the newly formed mountains, howling and writhing as if enraged by their own presence.

He was only able to watch them for a moment as the scene lurched, and he found himself ascending, shooting upward to the tower's summit, through a wall into its sealed peak. Inside, three men stood around an object, a twisted three-pointed star, lying flat on its side so each tip pointed in another direction, suspended in midair. Floating.

It gleamed, a strange, dark radiance swallowing the light, and within its depths, Osric felt the pull of endless black, a yawning void stretching into eternity. The men weren't as entranced. Instead, their faces were contorted in terror, mouths opening in screams that never reached his ears. Again, the reason for it wasn't hard to see.

Above them, above the deep black artifact, the air warped and split open with a tearing shriek as a wound in the veil appeared, pulsing with raw, unbridled energy. It was like the other tears he'd seen, but ... more. What was certain was that knowing what it was did not make it any less frightening.

Especially considering the other things that were happening.

As the veil tore, the star-like device quivered, trembling faster and faster, as if unbalanced, wobbling like a child's toy, although one that was large enough that it could crush a man when it became too unbalanced and fell over.

It never reached that point. As it seemed about to flip over in its violent thrashing, fractures spread across its surface, hairline cracks erupting into jagged fissures, emitting a deep blue light from within. It pulsed erratically, thrumming with a dangerous, unstable power, shuddering until, with a violent snap, it ripped into three parts in a blinding explosion of light.

A wave of energy pulsed out from the broken pieces as it ruptured, throwing the men around it against the walls of the tower hard enough to break them. Shatter them. The wave passed through Osric, but he felt nothing. With the explosion of energy, two of the shards were pulled, sucked into the veil, disappearing into the hazy, unseen beyond, swallowed whole.

Then something unexpected happened. As the shards passed through the veil's edges, it rippled and then closed around the pieces, almost as if the pieces pulled the tear shut behind them. The rip was gone, as if it had never happened, aside from the carnage left behind. The third piece plummeted to the ground, striking the floor of the tower with a bone-jarring impact. The force sent splintering cracks across the stone, spidering outward, ripping the tile as though it were paper. As it hit, it released another burst of energy. This one Osric felt as it swept over him, sending him stumbling backward.

He felt himself falling, tumbling backward. As he fell, he saw ... something. Not a vision. More like a single image, although this one was both less and more cryptic.

It was a frozen image of Jasper standing over a young girl, his expression cold and angry as he looked down at her. The girl, in turn, looked up at him frightened, her eyes wide with dread, as though she wanted to flee but was rooted in place.

Osric felt something else as he looked at the image. Not only was it different from the first vision, being a single image, it also felt different. Osric wasn't sure how, but he knew it wasn't given to him in the same way. He didn't know enough about magic, or gods, to know why or even how it felt different.

Just that it did.

Almost as soon as he had that realization, the image faded as Osric's awareness snapped back to the clearing. He was falling, the edge of the pond rushing up to meet him.

Strong hands caught Osric before he hit the ground. Coming to his senses, Osric looked up to see Rowan pulling him from the water and dragging him onto the dry ground. Water dripped from Osric's clothes as he tried to get his bearings.

"What happened?" Talia asked, kneeling beside him.

"I had a vision," Osric said. "A long one."

"How?" Grace asked. "You stepped in the water and dropped like a stone."

"Really? It didn't feel like that. It was ... much more than that," Osric said, pushing himself up to sitting. "The Blackstar. I saw it shatter. There was ... a tower. It was surrounded by mountains that felt like they were tearing through the ground, out of the farmland all around it. The whole landscape was changing, twisting into a few mountain peaks surrounded by hills. There were these horrible creatures coming out of the rips in the ground. They kind of reminded me of that beetle thing we faced in the temple. Inside the tower was a perfectly black, three-pointed artifact that had to be the Blackstar. I watched as a tear in the veil opened above it and ripped the artifact into three pieces. One dropped in the tower while the other two were sucked into the veil, pulling it closed behind them, like the document said it did."

Rowan and Jasper turned and looked at each other. It wasn't just a look. It was concern, even worry.

"What?"

"That sounds like the Claws," Rowan said, almost dejectedly.

"The Claws?" Osric repeated, confused.

"It's a mountain range," Rowan said.

"Kind of a mountain range," Jasper clarified. "It's a cluster of peaks and jagged hills, not really a full range. Not something ever created by nature. Instead, they thrust up from the plains as if something from deep below forced them to the surface, just a few peaks with a ring of hills around it, like you described. Locals say the place is haunted, a cursed land."

"People don't go there," Rowan added. "Anyone who's been stupid enough to try has never come back."

"Well, that's where we have to go," Osric said.

"You heard the part where it was said: no one ever comes back from there, right?" Grace asked.

"I did, but the alternative is to let the veil tear open and destroy everything. Either way, we're dead. At least in those mountains, we have a chance."

"I knew you'd say that," Grace said.

"We will make it," Jasper said. "Osric just spoke to the gods themselves, who blessed him with a vision. They will watch over us."

Osric nodded along, glad that he was reassuring them. He only wished he believed it himself.

Back into the World

They spent the rest of the day retracing their steps back to the Sage's glade. Even with Jasper's proclamation, the mood had turned somewhat darker, if that was possible, as the fullness of their task became apparent. Rowan and Jasper spent most of the walk describing what they would face when they reached the Claws.

Osric had seen it in the vision the gods had given him, seen the images of what the place looked like and felt the hate from the place, but Talia and Grace had no idea what was in store. The descriptions were enough to give even Grace pause, and had affected the mood of all of them.

When they'd searched for the temple, they'd been blind, groping about in the dark, not knowing what they were looking for or how they would end up. Osric wasn't sure if he didn't prefer that more. This time, knowing exactly the kind of obstacles that lay ahead of them, he had time to think about it. To worry.

That wasn't the only thing on Osric's mind. The dangers of the Claws, the vision of what had happened to the Blackstar and how it had shattered, that all made sense. It was where the Veilguard had always been leading them, in a way.

The vision of Jasper was something altogether different. For one, it hadn't come from the entire Veilguard, that much was clear. For another, it was hard for Osric to see how it was connected to their quest. It felt more personal than that.

But was it a warning? A clue about something? Only one person knew the answer to that.

They'd decided to spend the night in the safety of the Sage's grove one last time before they headed out of Avendell and back into the world that had tried so hard to kill them the last time.

It had been a long day, for Osric as much as any of them, but he found it difficult to fall asleep.

Finally, he gave up and made his way toward the few small huts built for the druids who did not want to live inside the massive trees, one of which had been given to Jasper for his use. Osric wasn't jealous about it, since he liked the tree, but it was a good sign of what the Sage and the other humans living in the forest thought of Jasper.

Osric raised his hand to knock on the wooden door of Jasper's hut, hesitating for a moment. The small building stood quiet, its lantern extinguished. He glanced back toward the tree-dwelling he was supposed to be sleeping in, wondering if he should just go back and drop his concern. But he couldn't. He'd tried and all it did was make him restless.

The choice was made when his knuckles lightly rapped the surface, almost of their own accord. Moments later, the door creaked open, revealing Jasper with a faintly curious expression. His robes, usually pristine, were slightly rumpled, and his graying hair seemed even more disheveled than usual.

"Osric?" Jasper's voice held a hint of surprise. "I thought you'd be resting or making plans for tomorrow."

Osric gave a half-smile. "I should be, but something's been on my mind. I wanted to talk to you about it."

Jasper studied him for a moment, then stepped aside. "Come in."

The interior of the hut was sparse but comfortable. A modest cot occupied one corner, a table covered in neatly arranged scrolls and a lit candle stood near the center, and a worn leather bag hung on the wall. Jasper motioned Osric to a chair as he moved to his own seat near the table.

"The vision I had at the pond ... there was more than just the Nexus and the Blackstar."

"Something about me."

It wasn't a question. Jasper was smart and had worked out that Osric being here meant something.

"Yes. There was ... something else. I didn't want to bring it up in front of the others."

"What exactly did you see?"

"What I saw, it was … it felt different from the other visions. Like it was meant for me to see, but not to scare me. This wasn't like the visions I've had before. It felt like someone was trying to warn me. Or maybe warn you. I believe it came from Heathus."

"You could tell which god spoke to you?"

"Sort of. I can't see them, or hear them, but the feeling that comes with their visions changes. Some burned with anger, others felt like gentle guidance. A few seemed uncertain, like they were testing the waters. Based on what you've told us of Heathus, his care for family, his protectiveness, it felt like that."

"How can you be certain? Dark forces could plant false visions to divide us."

"It wasn't that. I felt that darkness in the temple, and this felt nothing like that."

"But what did you actually see?"

"A young girl with blonde hair. She was with a younger version of you, and she was somewhere I didn't recognize. She clearly admired you. Then I saw her again, a little older version of her. A little taller. She was afraid, not of you, of something else. You both were looking at something in the distance, and you seemed worried, too."

He knew what Osric was talking about, that much was clear. Osric could see it in his eyes. Not just his eyes. Jasper's fingers traced the worn edges of a bracelet Osric had noticed on him before but hadn't really thought of until now. Though he tried to hide it, there was also pain on his face. Something so deep it was almost physical.

Jasper sat back, his hand still touching the bracelet, but when he spoke, he managed to keep the pain out of his voice. "No. I don't know what you're talking about."

Osric didn't reply at first. He just stared at Jasper, studying his face. His eyes.

"Why did you just lie to me?"

Jasper froze, his hand stilling over the worn leather. For a moment, it seemed he might say something, but the words didn't come.

"You know exactly what I mean," Osric pressed. "I get it, you don't want to talk about it. Whatever happened, whoever she is, it's clearly something that hurts you. But this wasn't some random vision. Your god wanted me to see it. That has to mean it's important."

"I … can't talk about it. Not right now."

Osric studied him again, and then sighed. "Alright. I'm not going to pry, and I won't tell the others if you don't want me to. But if it becomes important, if it puts them, or this mission, in danger, then you need to say something. And if you don't, I will."

The words hung between them for a long moment. Jasper's expression softening, his hand dropping to his lap.

"I will," he said.

Osric wasn't a counselor or a reader of people. He was a blacksmith's apprentice, but even he could hear the regret in Jasper's voice.

Osric nodded, rising from his seat. "Good."

"Osric," Jasper called, just as Osric reached for the latch to the door.

Osric paused, glancing back. Jasper was looking at him, but also into the distance … as if he were looking through the walls of the hut.

"Whatever happened with that girl … I made the choices I thought were right at the time."

"I hope so," Osric said. "I really do."

With that, Osric stepped out into the night, closing the door behind him, leaving Jasper to his secrets.

It took the better part of a day to get out of Avendell and back into the Great Forest. Instead of heading north through the forest, they decided to head straight west and catch the Great Road north to the Claws.

Although they'd been in Avendell for over a month, the last time they'd been in the forest, it had been crawling with Brethren looking for Osric and the ring. Of course, things might have changed now that they'd found both parts of the document, but Rowan felt it safer to be out of the forest, just in case.

The Greenwood portion of the road was patrolled by the Farvale Guard in the south and the Greenwood Levy in the north and widely known to be one of the safest sections of the road that circled the lake and central island that were the heart of the Kingdom of Aeloria.

It still took days to get through the forest to the road, and thankfully, they'd avoided any run-ins with the Brethren along the way. Osric hoped that meant they'd given up after so much time had passed and had gone home.

He also knew how unlikely that was.

The sun was just setting over the horizon, and dusk had fallen, turning everything into a deep blue when they finally broke through the tree line.

And then they froze. Osric and Rowan were in the lead, and both pulled up short as the road came into view. Even at night, the Great Road got a lot of traffic. Merchants and guardsmen, travelers and farmers would be coming and going.

What they didn't expect to see was an elderly man, two women, and a handful of children surrounded by ten men in leather armor, brandishing clubs and short swords.

They hadn't heard anything before coming out of the forest, which wasn't unusual. The tree line had a way of absorbing all but the loudest sounds. Now that they were in the open, however, Osric could hear them clearly.

"... toll or we'll take it out of your hides. Or do you ..."

They stopped mid-sentence as Osric and his group came into view.

"What's this?" Rowan asked.

Their expressions changed when they looked at Rowan and took in the clasp holding his cloak closed. The symbol of the Greenwood Rangers.

"Ranger," one of the bandits said, disgust in his voice.

"Walk away now," Rowan replied, colder than Osric had ever heard him speak.

"You're all by yourself, Ranger. None of your Ranger friends here, just a kid, an old man, and a couple of girls. There are ten of us. You Rangers are finished. Done for."

"You heard him. Walk away!" Osric shouted, pulling his sword.

"Look, Dorun, the kid thinks he's a man," one of the other brigands scoffed.

They were ignoring the travelers now, who were still frozen in place, like if they didn't draw attention to themselves maybe the men would forget they were there.

The only thing that gave the brigands a moment's pause was Cinder coming up next to Osric, baring his fangs and growling. They were committed now, though. Not even a wolf appearing out of the forest and joining their targets could dissuade them. Osric had been in a lot of fights in the last month and a half, enough to know they wouldn't back down. Not now.

Talia and Grace fanned out, Talia so she had a clear line of sight for her weaving and Grace for ... whatever it is Grace would end up doing.

Osric and his friends might not be the ones to make the first move, but they weren't going to let the bandits draw first blood. As soon as the brigands began to move toward their group, they sprang into action.

As always, Cinder was the first to react, his growl turning into a snarl as he lunged forward, a blur of muscle and dark fur. The closest bandit barely had time to react before the wolf's powerful jaws clamped down on his arm. The man cried out, the sickening crunch of bone audible even over the commotion. Cinder pulled him down to the ground hard, smashing him into the worn cobblestones.

Grace, always fast, wasn't far behind him. The bandit she got close to swung clumsily. She sidestepped it easily, her short sword flashing in under his blade, piercing his side. The man let out a strangled cry, pulling himself off the sword and stumbling back, to put room between himself and the nimble thief.

He didn't make it far when an arrow came streaking in over Grace's head. The first one smashed high in his chest, the impact causing him to stumble back another step and drop his sword.

He might have still survived if Rowan hadn't sent a second arrow, which thumped into the man barely a finger's width from the first.

The bandit looked shocked as he crumbled to the ground, as if his last thoughts were of disbelief that his life had ended so quickly.

The rest of the bandits hesitated, glancing between their fallen companions and their still-standing leader. They'd clearly not been prepared for this, expecting unarmed women and children.

The man named Dorun sneered and said, "What are you doing? Kill them!"

The bandits surged forward, whatever organization they had forgotten. The bandit Cinder had pulled down managed to get his arm free and scrambled to his feet, but Cinder wasn't finished with him, managing to bite into the man's shoulder, his sharp fangs punching through the leather and flesh as he tried to get up.

Only a wild swing of his sword forced Cinder back, giving the bandit a chance to stagger backward, away from the animal.

Another man, seeing Grace focused on his now-dead comrade, swung his cudgel at her. Something alerted her to the danger because she managed to dodge backward at the last moment, avoiding the full brunt of the weapon, only being clipped on her off arm.

Grace and Cinder had been the only ones to move into their range, forcing the other bandits to charge forward to meet the rest of them. Osric had learned from his experience when he had dashed in too early, left his friends exposed and Talia had been badly injured in Farvale.

This time, he kept himself between Talia and Jasper and the attackers, knowing that those two could hit the enemy from a distance, but were safer if the enemy could not get to them.

Rowan, too, although Rowan had proven that he could defend himself and didn't need Osric to do it for him.

The bandit nearest Osric lunged forward. A month ago, Osric would have probably been hit by the attack or forced back, but the training with Rowan paid off as he brought his sword up to intercept the weapon, blocking and deflecting the swing.

Another bandit moved past Osric, just out of his reach. Not that it mattered since he was already engaged in fighting with his friend. This bandit was making a run for his own attack, going toward Rowan. The man's charge was wild and Rowan dropped, rolling out of his way and yet somehow didn't lose his footing. Worse for the attacker, his sword sunk into the tree Rowan had been standing near, costing the man any follow-up.

They weren't done yet, another bandit coming in on the heels of the first one Osric had intercepted. Osric couldn't get his sword back in time, but he'd trained for this, too. Osric dropped his shoulder, allowing what had been planned as a low swing to smack into his pauldron and deflect down into the cobblestones. Osric brought his arm up, swiping an elbow at his attacker. That move would not actually hurt anyone, but had enough force to push the man back, giving Osric a little breathing room.

"Heathus, grant us strength," Jasper called out, holding the amulet around his neck.

Light streamed from between his fingers, and Osric could feel something, a warmth or strength entering him as Jasper brought Heathus's blessing on them.

Osric pushed the blade he'd blocked, forcing the man to slightly lose his balance, and pulled the blade back hard, the sword slashing down, across the man's midsection, catching flesh and eliciting a cry of pain.

Their leader, the man called Dorun, came at Osric as well, seeing him as an obstacle between his men and the ranged combatants. Osric had gotten his sword free and was able to pivot back now that the man he'd parried and then injured had been forced back.

Osric barely managed to deflect the blow as Dorun swung down with massive force, the impact making his arm strain, but not causing him to stumble or lose his footing.

To Osric's left, two more men tried to get at Grace. She'd moved too far forward and was in the midst of several of them. She twisted away from the first attacker's blade and then rolled away from the second. It was hard to follow with how fast she moved and how quickly she managed to change direction.

Feats that Osric could never manage, let alone get back to his feet the way she did, ready to fight again.

All of this happened almost simultaneously, in an instant, as Talia's hands were moving behind him, twisting and turning in a delicate pattern. Finally, she finished, her hands thrusting forward, sending three shimmering shards out of them, streaking past Osric and smacking hard into Dorun's chest, each hit causing him to stagger backward.

"A mage," Dorun said in warning to his friends.

In spite of what was happening to the veil, magic was a rare thing for the average person to see and was wildly feared. Which is why, at his warning, several of Dorun's men turned to start making their way toward Talia, having identified her as the biggest threat.

Not that Osric and his friends were going to make it easy for them. Rowan had already notched an arrow again. The arrow flashed past Osric to one of the men trying to get around him to Talia, smacking into the man's shoulder, punching through his leather armor. The man staggered and tried to recover, until a second arrow found its mark, punching through the man's throat.

He gripped at the shaft, gurgling, as he fell.

Cinder wasn't far behind. Another bandit tried to get past the wolf, making his move for Talia. Cinder ignored the man he'd been trying to take down, in favor of going after the bandit that was trying to slip between him and Osric, whipping around and clamping down on the man's ankle. He only got a piece of it, ripping flesh but not latching on tightly, only causing the man to stumble, but not dragging him to the ground as the animal would have wanted.

Osric wanted to join them, move to block Talia from danger, but of all the men facing them, Dorun was clearly the most dangerous. Osric parried him, and then parried again as Dorun pressed him. The third parry put Osric's sword on the inside of the bandit's reach, allowing him to slash back diagonally. Not a strong swing, but the tip cut in under the man's leather chest piece. A shallow wound, but it caused the bandit to wince and favor his other side.

Grace fared better. Surrounded by three men, she danced among her attackers, pivoting past a swing of a cudgel and then a swipe with a sword, catching one man in the hip and the other in the shoulder. Neither hit was deep or fatal, but both caused injury as she tried to keep all three men off balance.

Her luck only held out so long as the third man managed to catch her with his club against her back, sending Grace stumbling forward, off balance. She managed to recover before his friends could take advantage, but from Osric's position, it looked as if she was moving slower, hurt by the hard impact.

Rowan was also struggling now, trying to fire his bow, a shield for his allies, while still retreating and trying to avoid the man trying to kill him. He'd managed to dodge out of the way twice, but the third time, the blade found its mark, leaving a deep wound on Rowan's off arm.

For a moment, Osric worried that they'd bitten off more than they could chew, outnumbered as they were.

Jasper, however, saw Grace's predicament and moved around Osric to support her, as was being pressed hard, putting her in danger. The bandits hadn't expected him, his mace catching one of the men in the back, returning the favor for the hit made on Grace.

It didn't take him down, but it was a new threat they had to adjust for, taking some of the pressure off of Grace.

Talia, bless her, managed to ignore all of the men trying hard to get past Osric and Cinder, her face scrunched in concentration as her hands moved, tracing intricate patterns. As she finished, golden energy coalesced around her fingertips before radiating outward, touching each of her companions.

Again, Osric felt energy entering him, although different than the blessings Jasper had called down on them. He felt his muscles working harder, his movements speeding up as she pushed the energies of the veil into them.

Rowan's next two arrows were released faster, Talia's magic affecting him in the same way. Another bandit tried to get around Osric, but was hit twice. Neither shot was fatal, but the man was struggling as the shafts inhibited his movements. Each of his attempts to attack pulled on them, causing him to grimace in pain.

Cinder made another attempt at the bandit he'd missed latching onto the first time, gripping onto the man's other leg. This time, he firmly clamped down on the leg and pulled back hard, yanking him to the ground as he dragged the man back, away from Talia.

The man slashed at Cinder, forcing him to let go, but Cinder seemed ready for it this time. As the bandit tried to push himself off the ground, Cinder leaped forward, his powerful jaws clamping over the man's throat. When the wolf yanked his head back this time, the throat came with him, ending the man's life.

With Jasper helping her now, Grace managed to put a little distance between herself and some of her attackers, giving her a chance to dart in for another attack. She made two quick slashes into either side of one of the men. The cuts were not fatal, but the more they were cut, the slower they moved, and the easier they were to dodge.

As if to prove that, the man tried to retaliate, his clumsy strike missing Grace entirely.

Dorun took a step back to give himself some room and took another powerful downward strike. One of the things Rowan had drilled into Osric again and again was that meeting power with power was not always the best option. That sometimes it was better to give way to the power, let it flow past you. So Osric didn't parry the blow.

Instead, he sidestepped, using his blade to just guide the strike down and away from him, which left his weapon inside the bandit's guard, before lurching forward, pushing the blade deep into the man's chest, punching through Dorun's chest piece. The man's eyes went wide, as if he couldn't believe this boy had just killed him.

The shout of pain he let out, however, was enough to distract Grace, who looked to Osric, uncharacteristically concerned, opening herself to being cut by one of the bandits circling her. She did manage to get out of the way just in time to keep it from being fatal, but the blade still cut a dark red slash across her leg.

It could have been worse. The third bandit also tried to make a play for Grace during her moment's distraction but was intercepted by Jasper. His mace caught the blade and almost ripped it out of his hand.

With their leader down and most of their friends now dead, the remaining five bandits clearly wanted to run, to extract themselves from the fight.

The only man still near Osric tried a final, desperate lunge to get to Talia, still hampered by the arrows protruding from him, but unwilling to back away and leave Talia with a chance to kill him.

Osric intercepted him easily, deflecting the wild thrust and responding with a precise cut that opened the bandit's sword arm from wrist to elbow. The man dropped his weapon with a cry of pain, stumbling backward.

Behind him, Grace had recovered her footing. Despite her injury, she was still able to dodge between the two remaining attackers not distracted by Jasper. As one swung high, she ducked under the blade and drove her short sword up into his armpit, cutting vein and tendon, his weapon dropping from his hands.

He was out of the fight and, judging by the amount of blood pouring down his side, would be dead in a moment. Grace turned her attention to the other man, rolling out of the way of a blow that would have smashed her face in, but instead crashed harmlessly into the paving stones.

As she came up, her sword darted out, sliding under his chest piece and into his body. The man went rigid as organs were pierced, clutching at his side as he tried to pull himself free of her weapon, only to fall dead on the ground a step later.

The third tried to turn and run, but his timing was poor, lowering his guard for the escape just as Jasper's mace was sailing in, trying to force him back, away from Grace.

The hard metal end of Jasper's mace caught the back of the man's head without any obstacle, cracking his skull open and sending him tumbling to the ground, his body sprawling.

With everyone else gone, Rowan finally allowed himself to deal with the man who had been chasing him across the battle area, trying unsuccessfully to stop Rowan from shooting any more arrows.

Rowan didn't bother shooting this time. Instead, after dodging another wild slash, Rowan stabbed forward with the arrow still in his hand, un-notched, punching it through the man's throat.

The battle had lasted less than a minute, a sprint of violence and gore, but it was done now. All of the bandits were down, dead or dying on the road they'd hoped to exploit for their gain.

As Cinder began sniffing around the bodies, maybe to determine if any were still a threat, and Grace began her normal looting of the dead, Osric stepped over his fallen opponents and up to the terrified travelers.

"It's okay; we aren't going to harm you. Is everyone okay?"

The children looked too stunned to speak, but the elderly man said, "We owe you our lives. Those men would have killed us all."

"We are happy to help. People like that shouldn't prey on other people."

"Perhaps we shouldn't stay here," Jasper said. "The bodies will draw scavengers, and it's an ill thing to linger near the recent dead."

"That's a good point. It's almost dark, and we were going to camp soon. We were headed north, but we could go south with you a bit and camp with you for the night, to make sure you can continue your journey safely in the morning," Osric offered.

"That would be very kind of you," the man said.

"Let's go. Grace, leave them be."

"Yeah, yeah," the thief said, pulling something off one of the dead men before following behind the rest of the group, apparently already finding everything of value.

Osric did not begrudge her taking from men who would have so easily taken from others; he just wished she was a little less brazen about it.

Doubts and Dreams

They traveled south down the road for thirty minutes, until after the sun was well down over the horizon and the sounds of the night started their song. Smaller animals and insects came out to look for food under the cover of darkness, and larger animals looked for the smaller animals.

Finally, Rowan led them off the road a bit to make camp, to give their group a little bit of cover from any additional bandits that might be traveling the road.

In a few minutes, a campfire was crackling softly, its warm glow pushing back the growing chill of the autumn night. Temperatures were already starting to drop as winter neared, and it would not be long, maybe another month and a half or so, before snow would begin to cover the trees and ground.

The travelers sat, pressed together more in search of security than for warmth, looking at their saviors, who must have seemed a strange group indeed. They were eating the small amount of extra food the group had been able to share. As they did, they kept a close eye on Cinder, probably wondering why anyone would let a wild animal sit so close to them, especially after having watched it rip a man's throat out less than an hour before.

"Thank you again for your aid," the old man said. "We left Wolfridge a week and a half ago and made good progress at first, but ... the road has become dangerous. Those were not the first men to try to stop us. We'd already been forced to forfeit much of what we managed to get out of the capital, but we were able to get away. This time, we were not so lucky."

"Why did you leave Wolfridge?" Osric asked.

The old man exchanged glances with his companions before continuing. "The baron's new policies, well ... those of his advisors.

From what I hear, no one has seen the baron in five or six weeks, since he returned from some big expedition. He marched out with fifty knights, loud and big as the world. When he came back, there was no fanfare, just word that he returned and his advisors started issuing new rules. They claimed the rules were for security, but ... the guard presence in the city has doubled. They monitor everyone's movements and people have been ... disappearing."

"Including my husband," added the woman, who squeezed the children tighter as she spoke. "Our family's inn, three generations we ran it. Then, one morning, guards arrived with papers. Said it now belonged to some trading company I never heard of. That we hadn't paid some tax we'd never heard of. When my husband stood up to them, they arrested him. We've not heard from him since."

"That doesn't sound like the place my mentor told me about," Osric said.

"What really concerns me is those bandits," Rowan said. "This stretch of the Great Road used to be one of the safest in the realm, patrolled by the Greenwood Levy all the way to Farvale. If the guard has increased as you described, why are there so many thieves loose, plaguing the road?"

"We thought the same," the old man said. "It's why we felt it would be safe for us to choose this route. But we haven't seen a single patrol since leaving Wolfridge."

"Maybe that's where all the new guys came from," Grace said. "Pulled in from the patrols instead of hiring new guards."

"But no patrols at all?" Rowan asked. "What about the Rangers? We don't usually patrol the road, but we do check the forest along the road often, at least enough to notice if it was unpatrolled or that there were a fair number of bandits."

"There aren't any Rangers. Not anymore," the woman said.

"What?"

"It's true," the old man said. "About a month ago, shortly after the baron locked himself into the keep, there was some kind of confrontation between Ranulf Stanfield, the cleric and the chief of all of the baron's advisors, and the Chief Ranger."

"Grange?" Rowan asked.

"Yes. No one knows what happened, but word was that he was arrested for treason. Whatever happened, the rest of the Rangers scattered after that. The guard says they are the bandits who've been plaguing the countryside."

"I can't believe that," Rowan said. "And Caros would never commit treason."

"Most of us don't believe it either, but the guard has labeled many of them as outlaws and put bounties on their heads. It's why I decided to leave and take my daughter-in-law and grandchildren with us. We thought it might be safe enough for us to get to Farvale, hoping things would be better there."

"It should be," Osric said. "We were there a month or so ago. In Farvale, seek out Captain Sable Lockwood, tell her you met us and we asked you to talk to her. Tell her about what's happening in Wolfridge."

"Will she help?" the woman asked.

"She's honorable and just," Osric said. "If anyone can offer protection and get word to the king in Celestia, it's her."

The old man nodded, but he seemed exhausted, barely able to keep himself awake. Their journey must have been exhausting, having their lives ripped out from under them and then chased the entire time they tried to run south.

The kids had passed out almost as soon as they finished eating. Not even the promise of hearing from the adventurers could keep them awake.

"You should get some rest. We have to head north, and it's still a good distance to Farvale. It's best if you move as fast as possible. The Farvale Guard patrols a day outside of the city, so you only have to make it, at most, two or three more days. They were active a month ago and I cannot think of any reason why Lockwood would have changed that stance."

"I hope you're right," the old man said, giving a weak smile.

Osric patted the man on the shoulder and walked to the other side of the fire where his bedroll was, next to Rowan's. Jasper and Talia were taking the first watch. She'd learned some kind of magic that would use threads of the Veil as early warning systems, sending a feedback of magic she could feel if it was penetrated.

Rowan was just staring at the fire with a faraway look as Osric sat down, Cinder stretching out between their bedrolls.

"I'm sorry about the Rangers," Osric said softly.

"Grange is a good man," he said without looking at Osric. "Every Ranger looked up to him. Admired him. I just ... how he could have possibly been arrested for treason or the Rangers disbanded. I could never have imagined something like this happening. I know our mission is important, but ... I need to help my people."

"I know. I mean, I don't know about the Rangers like you do, but living in the forest my entire life, I've admired the Rangers. Even met a few of you. We could go to Wolfridge, help you clear their name."

"No." Rowan said, looking at Osric intently. "What we're doing here, protecting the Veil and stopping the Brethren, it's bigger than the Rangers. It's bigger than me. The Rangers guard the Great Forest, but we're trying to save all of reality. I can't put my personal concerns first."

Rowan stood up, picking up his bow and putting it around his back.

"Rowan ..." Osric started.

"I'm going to check the perimeter," Rowan said, cutting him off and walking into the darkness, between the trees.

Osric watched him go, worry gnawing at his chest. Movement caught his attention, and he turned to see Grace kneeling next to the man's daughter-in-law.

Their voices were too low to make out the words, but he saw Grace press something into the woman's hands, a blood-stained coin purse. The woman's eyes widened, and she tried to refuse, but Grace simply walked away, leaving the woman clutching the money.

A small smile tugged at Osric's lips, but he kept quiet. Grace would only deny it if he mentioned her kindness. Talia kept asking him why he kept the thief around, with her brazen and combative attitude and apparent lack of feeling for what they were trying to do.

He wanted her with them because he knew that was her real armor, protecting her from the judgment of everyone around her. Armor built from a life of hardships on the streets. But he could see past that armor. She was a good person, even if she couldn't admit it herself.

As he did most nights after a fight, Osric was slow to fall asleep, the excitement and fear taking time to diminish. When he did fall asleep, it was restless.

Usually, he would fall asleep and wake with memories of a dream, or sometimes nothing at all. This night was different. He could feel the beginnings of a dream. He was asleep, he knew that, but at the same time, he was aware that he was asleep and dreaming.

The vision began in silence, the scene painting itself with muted hues. A man and a woman walked down a narrow woodland path, looking worried. A small child, a little girl no more than six years old with thick, curly red hair walked between them, though she lagged behind, her small legs struggling to keep pace.

The scene changed, and the couple with their daughter was at the door of a small cottage. It was in a village, Osric could tell that much, but everything outside of the doorway of the cottage was blurry, lost in a mist. The door opened and a woman wearing a shawl was there, although he could only see her body, the hood obscured her face.

Although he didn't know how, he knew the person in the shawl was a woman. They spoke for a moment and then the man put his hand on the woman's arm. A signal of some kind. She nodded and knelt, whispering to the child, silently enough that Osric could not make out the woman's words. She kissed the girl's forehead, who was trembling, tears rolling down her cheeks.

The little girl gripped her tightly but with the help of the woman in the shawl, they managed to extract her. The man, her father most likely, reached down and stroked the little girl's red curls and the couple left, the woman looking back at the little girl, tears running down her own cheeks.

With the couple gone, the woman in the cottage turned to lead the little girl inside. As she did, her shawl slipped back, revealing an elderly woman's face.

One that Osric recognized.

Younger than he'd ever remembered her, although still very old, Elder Miriam held the red-headed little girl's hand as she shut the door on the outside world.

The little girl had to be Talia. Of that much, Osric was certain.

55

The dream twisted and the cottage fell away, replaced by a cavernous chamber with a monstrous platform dominated by one of the stone circles, like they'd seen, sitting in the middle of the chamber, waves of magic pulsing off of it. In front of it stood the man and the woman that Osric believed to be Talia's parents, a little older than when they left her with Elder Miriam.

Osric still didn't understand magic well, even with all his interactions with it over the last several months. Still, somehow, he knew this magic felt wrong. It was angry, violent, and unnatural. The couple raised their hands toward the device, waving them in intricate patterns, and everything exploded into blinding light.

Osric jerked awake, his shirt clinging to his sweat-soaked skin. The camp lay quiet around him, his companions' steady breathing punctuated by the soft crackle of their dying fire. Cinder lifted his head from where he lay next to Osric, looking at him with concern.

"I'm fine, boy," Osric whispered, running a shaking hand across the wolf's head, between its ears.

But he wasn't fine. The dream had left him unsettled. He'd experienced visions from the gods before, which had always come with a sense of purpose, an intent behind it. This had been different. The images felt more hostile, like a memory seen through rage.

Osric's eyes adjusted to the darkness as he sat up. The camp lay still around him, most of his companions and the travelers still asleep, including Rowan, who'd returned from his patrol and was on his bedroll, facing away from everyone else. Just outside the circle, Jasper sat cross-legged, eyes closed in meditation.

Like Talia, Jasper relied more on his abilities to perform the watch rather than patrolling, although instead of a weave of magic dropped around the camp to alert them, the gods granted Jasper some type of awareness of their surroundings.

Or that's how he explained it.

If Jasper was still up, then it was still first watch, which meant Talia was still up, but for a moment, Osric couldn't find her. When he did, he saw she was perched against a tree trunk at the camp's edge. Osric rose and picked his way through the sleeping forms to join her.

"Everything alright?" he asked, settling beside her.

She shrugged one shoulder but remained silent, her expression distant. He didn't push her. He knew Talia. She'd speak when she had her thoughts worked through, and the best thing he could do was stay silent and give her the room to do just that. The silence stretched between them until she finally spoke.

"What if we're wrong about all of this?"

"About what?"

"The Blackstar. The tower. Everything." She pulled her knees to her chest. "Everyone acts like once we find this artifact, we'll just … use it. But they mean I'll use it. And I don't know if I can."

"Of course you can. You've learned so much already …"

"For a novice, sure," she said, cutting him off with a bitter laugh. "But the people who made the Blackstar were masters. They understood magic, understood the Veil enough to make it and the stone rings that let them cross the entire continent in a moment and throw rings through time. Even with all that knowledge, they still lost control. They destroyed everything, the artifact, their tower, almost all of our reality, from what the Sage told us about their history. They turned the plains into a dead swamp. How can someone like me hope to succeed where they failed? I've never even seen the Conclave, let alone studied in it."

"Jasper will help …"

"Jasper understands theory, but he's not a mage. He's never felt what I feel when I touch magic. He doesn't know what it's like to reach into the Veil and pull that power through. The gods push magic into him. It's different."

"But his knowledge can help you. Besides, it doesn't matter. Elder Miriam chose you to train. She wouldn't have done that if she didn't see something special in you. Hells, you've shown that she was right throughout this entire journey. The things you've been able to do. It's miraculous."

"Maybe she was wrong."

"It's not just her. The druids recognized your talent too. The Sage recognized it. You're the smartest person I know, Talia. We'll figure this out."

She placed her hand on his knee, the touch sending warmth through him despite the cool night air.

"Thank you," she whispered.

Osric remained quiet, letting Talia sit in silence again. He knew she was struggling, and he didn't know how to help her with that, other than to remind her that he believed in her and to stay by her side.

Her hand lingered on his knee for a few moments longer before she drew it back, wrapping her arms around her legs again. She seemed to retreat inward. Osric wanted more than anything to put his arm around her and hold her close. Comfort her, but he'd come over to her for a reason and couldn't keep it to himself.

"So, I actually came over to tell you something. I had a dream. A difficult one."

"Difficult as in unsettling? Or difficult as in … visions?"

"The second one," he admitted. "At least, I think it was. It felt similar to the other times the gods communicated with me. I don't know how to explain it exactly. There's a sense to it. Like it's not from me. It's almost … it has a taste to it."

"Actually, I think I know what you mean. Magic can feel like that. Like you're touching something that isn't yours, something from somewhere else."

"Yes, like that. But … this dream was also different from the other ones I've had. It felt different. Talia, I saw your parents."

She stiffened. "What?"

"I saw a man and a woman with a little girl. Red hair, thick curls. They brought her to a cottage, although not one I recognized. They handed her over to an old woman wearing a shawl, clearly upset they were leaving her behind. At first, I didn't recognize the old woman, but when her hood fell back …" He met Talia's gaze. "It was Elder Miriam."

"I … I remember bits of that day. The path through the trees. My mother crying. But you could know that from me telling you about it."

"Maybe, but there was more." Osric hesitated. "After the scene at the cottage, it changed. I saw the same couple in a huge chamber. It had one of those Calaphium stone circles we saw in the ruins. There was magic everywhere, wild and out of control. They were weaving something, intricate patterns with their hands, and then there was this … explosion of light. The power coming off of them was incredible, but wrong somehow. Violent."

Talia shook her head. "That can't be. My parents were farmers. They went to Eldamar to help a friend of theirs, and they never came back. They weren't mages. They didn't know magic."

"I'm just telling you what I saw. It was them. The same people I saw leaving you with Elder Miriam. And it felt real. More real than any dream I've ever had."

"It doesn't make sense. None of it. Farmers don't ..." She stopped herself, shaking her head again. "It can't be true. My father grew wheat and raised sheep. My mother made cheese and wove blankets. They weren't from the Conclave, and they didn't know magic. You're wrong."

Osric rested a hand on her arm, giving her a reassuring squeeze. "I'm not saying it is. Maybe there's another explanation. Maybe the gods were showing me something symbolic, not literal. Either way, I thought you should know."

She looked off again into the darkness, and Osric didn't press her. She'd never talked about her parents, although he knew she'd always held a little anger toward them for not coming back for her.

Still, it seemed very possible that they knew magic. They knew Elder Miriam, and she had taught Talia magic. Would she have done that if Talia's parents hadn't also practiced the arts? It seemed likely that was even how they knew Miriam.

More concerning, at the moment, was why the gods decided to show him that vision, and why it felt the way that it did. Was this going to be important to their mission to find the Blackstar? Was it a warning?

Osric just wished things were simple, like they were with forging. Gods and magic and ancient civilizations were just too far outside of his understanding to be able to comprehend fully.

It's why he needed Talia. He just hoped she'd be able to come to terms with what he'd seen so she could help him analyze it and figure out what it meant.

The Bounty

After leaving the travelers to make their way south as best they could, they turned back north. Thankfully, the days had been uneventful, although the road was indeed nearly empty, as the travelers had described. The small section he'd seen in Farvale had been a near-constant flow of people, and Osric had been picturing at least half as much as he'd seen there.

Instead, in three days of travel, they had only passed one other group, also travelers who'd been nervous to pass a heavily armed group. Osric felt bad leaving them behind to travel south on their own, but if they started escorting every group of travelers they encountered, they'd never complete the rest of their mission.

As they neared the very end of their time on the road, before continuing north as the road curved away northeast toward Wolfridge, Osric thought they might get off the road without any further issues.

They'd seen signs of bandits along the way, but it seemed like they'd decided to avoid well-armed travelers and look for easier targets instead. While Osric would have been happy to rid the world of their kind, he was also happy not to have to deal with it.

His hopes for an uneventful remainder of the trip were dashed when Rowan, traveling a bit ahead of the group, held up a hand. They didn't pull their weapons, except for Rowan who had his bow held loosely, but they put hands to hilts as they moved to fan out behind him.

A group of seven men on horseback appeared wearing worn but well-made armor, to Osric's eye. While they weren't brandishing weapons either, they also had hands on hilts.

Which was fair. It was a dangerous road these days and everyone was nervous when encountering others there.

The riders drew their horses to a halt a dozen yards away.

"Ho there, travelers," Rowan called out, holding up a hand.

"Move aside and let us pass," one of the men said.

"Gladly. Be careful on the road. Bandits are thick, and the Rangers are spread thin of late."

The leader of the mounted group tilted his head, studying him.

"Rangers? Your kind don't exist anymore."

"As long as I'm standing, the Rangers still exist," Rowan replied, more calmly than Osric would have expected.

They started to step to the side of the road to let the men pass when one said, just loud enough for the group to hear, "Weren't the boy and girl supposed to have others with them? An old man, a wolf …"

"They didn't say anything about no ranger," his companion replied.

Osric's hand tightened on his sword hilt. "What are you talking about?"

"Seems there's a good-sized bounty out for a young man and a girl traveling together. Word is, they came from somewhere near Farvale. You lot wouldn't happen to have an old ring on you, would you?"

"We want no quarrel with you," Rowan said.

"Then leave the boy and girl. They're the only ones listed on the bounty." The leader shrugged. "Or step aside and let us search them. If we don't find a ring, you can all go on your way."

"We're not going anywhere," Jasper said.

"That's fine by me," the scarred leader said, drawing his sword. "The bounty says 'dead or alive.' We can check their corpses for the ring just as easily."

When the leader drew his sword, and the rest followed his lead, pulling their weapons. Osric cursed himself for relaxing when they weren't instantly hostile. They'd split themselves to make room for the riders, and now half his people were on the other side of the road, too far away from him to support.

It could have been worse. At least Talia was with him. Jasper was on the other side, but he had Rowan with him, who was more than capable of defending himself and the others.

Grace was her own story. As soon as the leader started to pull his sword, she took two large steps backward and disappeared into the forest. A month ago, Osric would have been worried that she was abandoning them, running to safety. After what he'd seen over the last few weeks, she'd shown that there was more to her. That she did care about others, regardless of what she said.

Her disappearing was part of a plan. Something these men would regret.

Surprisingly, Talia was also already in motion, her hands drawing symbols in the air, moving in an intricate pattern. She hadn't let herself relax, even if only to wait to see what the men would do.

She never took her eyes off the men as she pressed her palms together, rotated them apart while drawing her left hand down as her right moved up, fingers spread wide.

As she brought her right hand sweeping across her body, a roiling ball of fire leaped out of thin air, pushing away from her outstretched hands and speeding toward the group, which had just started their horses charging forward.

Her aim wasn't perfect; the ball exploded behind the group instead of in the midst of them, spreading out in a roar of flame and heat. Horses screamed and reared and the three men furthest back joined them, ripping burning cloth from their skin, which was blackened and charred.

Surprisingly, they managed to regain control of their mounts, which must have been well-trained indeed to not run at the first hint of pain.

The leader spurred his mount forward, charging straight for Osric. His blade came down in a vicious arc that Osric barely managed to deflect. Osric let the impact push him back, rolling away from the warhorse, its hooves slamming into the cobblestone where Osric had stood a moment before.

On the other side of the road, Rowan surprised Osric by shooting an arrow not at one of the men, but burying the shaft into one of the animal's rump. The animal, already scared from the burns it had received, had reached its breaking point, instincts taking over as it reared up, spilling the man on its back onto the roadside.

Osric popped back to his feet and lunged forward at the scarred leader, the tip of his blade sliding under the thigh plate of his armor, drawing first blood. The leader grunted in pain but kept his seat, wheeling the animal just out of Osric's reach, turning it to put his blade in a position to attack again.

"Heathus protect him!" Jasper called out, loud enough for his voice to be heard over the shouts and clashing steel.

Osric felt the familiar warmth of the gods coursing through him again, filling him with purpose and strength.

A scream from the trees drew everyone's attention as Grace suddenly emerged from the forest, leaping out of a tree and onto the back of one of the mounted men. Her arm locked around his throat as she buried her short sword into a gap in his armor.

Rowan took advantage of the momentary distraction to send two more arrows flying, again into the rump of a horse. Not a fatal blow for the animal, but enough to send it rearing up, its hooves pawing the air as it threw its rider to the ground.

That was enough to jolt everyone back into action, with the leader pressing his attack on Osric, who, feeling the surge of energy from Jasper's blessing, moved just in time to deflect the blow.

"Give us the boy, and the rest of you can live," the leader yelled.

None of Osric's friends bothered to reply. They'd already made their decision. Talia, in response, sent a wave of golden light rippling across the field of combat from her outstretched hands, washing over Osric, Grace, Rowan, and Cinder. Osric had felt the energies when the gods had healed him and when Jasper had blessed him but this was something ... else. Something more raw.

He felt incredibly fast. Impossibly fast.

Osric's blade recovered from the deflection a moment before and moved lightning fast, striking under the leader's parry and cutting into his thigh, drawing both blood and a scream.

"Kill the girl first! She's the dangerous one!" he yelled through gritted teeth.

One of the men spurred his mount toward Talia, but his wild swing went wide as she ducked behind Osric.

On the other side of the road, the fighter Grace had been clinging to finally stopped his struggling and slumped forward as she continued to press the sword deeper and deeper. She pulled her sword free but kept him pinned to the animal, using his dead weight as an anchor to help her fight from.

"One down!" she yelled triumphantly.

Osric grimaced. Even in battle, she took nothing seriously. Rowan, for his part, continued to retreat as fighters closed on him, putting more arrows into another horse, just as one of the men started to make a charge at Jasper. Rowan was smart. The attackers had come into the fight with a clear advantage, and he'd made it his mission to bring them to the ground, take their advantage from them.

The attacker fell from his horse, which bucked as the animal reacted to the pain, ending his attack before it started.

Osric stepped back himself, pushing Talia almost into the trees. It created more space between himself and his friends, but with the new rider and the leader, he was feeling pressed from two sides.

The leader may not have been possessed with speed granted by arcane magic, but he was still fast. Osric managed to parry his first strike against his sword's crossguard. Osric was distracted as, at almost the same instant, the man who rode for Talia took another slash, thankfully directing his ire at Osric and not Talia.

His distraction caught up with him.

Osric managed to dodge to the side, still locked against the leader's blade, and avoided the slash, but that left an opening for the leader to counter his stroke, the blade drawing a line across Osric's arm, where the metal chest piece he'd acquired could not protect him.

The stroke had been imprecise, a counter against a target moving sideways, so it didn't take his arm clean off, but Osric still grunted from the pain of the slash.

"Duck," Talia yelled as her hands moved quickly in front of her, manipulating the energies only she could see.

Osric didn't need to be told twice and ducked enough to give her room. He couldn't see what she did with her hands, but three of the diamond-shaped bolts of energy flew past him, slamming into the new attacker's chest, burning holes clean through the leather armor he wore and burying themselves deep into him.

The man's eyes rolled back in his head as he toppled from his horse, dead before he hit the ground.

Across the way, one of the men thrown from his horse earlier pushed himself off the ground where he had fallen from his animal and began to run at a retreating Rowan, clearly angry for the attack that caused him to be thrown from the saddle.

Jasper clearly didn't want the same thing to happen twice, and he reared back with the mace he'd been carrying but had hardly used since their adventure began. It was a powerful, vigorous blow, if ill-aimed. The man had been helpless against the attack, but Jasper's blow only hit his shoulder. It clearly hurt, but a prime moment to take a fighter out of the battle with a blow to the head while he could not defend himself was wasted.

The man screamed but rolled away from Jasper and pushed himself to his feet. He was forced to take another step back as a gray streak leaped past him, almost crashing against him, and grabbed onto one of the few remaining mounted men. Cinder's fangs tore into the man's leg as the wolf pulled him from his saddle, shaking his head violently, causing his sharp teeth to dig even further into the man's skin.

Grace, seeing Jasper in combat, pushed away from the dead man on the horse and landed beside the cleric with a fluid twist, her blade already in motion as she hit the ground. The short sword whipped out with deadly precision, slashing through the hip where the leather chest piece was tied together, cutting the bindings and biting into flesh. The man's quick backpedal caused the blade to only open a long gaping wound, instead of piercing through into his organs.

On his side of the road, the leader was poised to strike at Osric again. Osric prepared himself, his arm still burning from the earlier hit, when suddenly, three bolts of pure force whipped past him, streaking unerringly toward the leader. They struck the man in rapid succession, each impact drawing a grunt of pain.

"Your bounty's not worth dying for," Talia called out, not that like this was the type of man to run from a fight.

A few steps from Grace, Rowan shifted his bow to his left hand while drawing his short sword and slashing out as one of the men got close to him. It drew blood and caused the man's own attack to become clumsy and wild, allowing Rowan to step aside easily, the desperate attack cutting through nothing but air.

The leader, bleeding from multiple wounds and his chest still smoking, seemed to be undeterred from his attack. His blade came down with crushing force toward Osric's already injured arm. Osric tried to dodge, but he had limited space to maneuver if he wanted to continue to protect Talia, which allowed the edge of the man's sword to bite deep.

Pain flared through Osric's arm, but he refused to give ground. Behind him, he heard Talia moving, preparing another spell. Allowing her time to work was the smart move.

Osric gathered his remaining strength, ignoring the burning in his arm and, with both hands gripping his longsword, drove the blade forward with all his might. The leader's eyes went wide as Osric's sword punched through his armor and into his chest. For a moment, time seemed to stop as their eyes met.

Then the leader's grip on his weapon loosened, the sword falling from nerveless fingers as he toppled from his saddle. He hit the ground with a dull thud, blood pooling beneath him.

With their leader gone, the fight seemed to go out of some of the remaining combatants.

One of the men, who'd been unhorsed earlier, saw the battle going against them and turned to run, sprinting away from the conflict as fast as he could go. The movement drew Cinder's attention. The animal abandoned his previous victim, releasing the man's leg, and took off after the fleeing target. It was not difficult for the wolf to catch him, his jaws clamping down on the man's leg with devastating force. The mercenary screamed as Cinder's teeth tore through leather and flesh, falling to the ground as his forward momentum was suddenly halted.

"Please! I yield!" the man cried out, trying desperately to crawl away while fumbling for his dagger.

Not all of them could run. The wounded fighter near Grace and Jasper was trapped between them, with nowhere to flee, instead swinging his blade in a clumsy arc, trying to create space to escape. Grace ducked under the attack with casual grace.

"Really? That's the best you can do?" she taunted.

Jasper seized his opportunity as Grace kept their opponent distracted. His mace came down in a powerful overhead strike, connecting with the man's shoulder. Bone cracked beneath the impact, sending him to his knees.

That left one man standing, and he, too, had seen enough. He took one look at his fallen companions and turned to flee into the forest.

Grace reversed her grip on her weapon, moving in to finish the man off. Osric wasn't sure how much different this was from cold-blooded murder, but considering what these men had planned for him, he wasn't seriously worried about the morality of it either. The mercenary weakly tried to block the blow, barely able to hold himself up, but it did no good. She kicked his blade away and drove her sword through his back, impaling him. He collapsed, the last of his life leaving his body.

"And stay down," she muttered, already seeking her next target.

Through the trees, the last mercenary was running with almost no care about the noise he was making, crashing through the undergrowth. Talia's hands were already in motion, and she twisted, so that instead of pointing to where the leader once was, she instead pointed to the running man. Osric was amazed when, as her hand cut a diagonal line and then both hands thrust forward, a brilliant bolt of lightning erupted from her outstretched fingers, accompanied by a deafening crack. The sheer power of it was terrifying. The electric blast struck the fleeing man square in the back, lifting him off his feet and sending him flying forward, rebounding off a tree. He convulsed once in the dirt, wisps of smoke rising from his scorched armor, and then stopped moving altogether.

Osric had no idea she was capable of such incredible magic.

Near the tree line, Rowan faced off against the fighter still on his feet, the man desperately trying to fight his way free to try to flee as well. The ranger showed how skilled a fighter he was as he shifted his weight, feinting left before darting right. His opponent took the bait, committing to block the false attack. Rowan's actual strike came in low, his short sword finding flesh beneath the mercenary's guard, ending his life.

Osric looked around the now-littered battlefield. A dozen paces down the road, Cinder looked up from the body of the man he had caught and now mauled. That was all of them.

The battle was finished. Now came figuring out exactly what had just happened.

Osric wiped his blade clean on a fallen mercenary leader's cloak, then knelt beside his body checking him for any clues. It didn't require a thorough search. A leather scroll case hung from his belt, a rolled scroll inside with a seal that he did not recognize.

"Everyone all right?" he asked, glancing at his companions.

Talia nodded, though she looked weak. Osric imagined it took a lot to channel such powerful magic. Grace, of course, was already rifling through the dead men's belongings.

"Let me see that wound," Jasper said, coming to him.

"Answers first. Do you recognize this seal?"

When the cleric shook his head no, Osric broke it and unrolled the parchment. It was a bounty, which wasn't surprising after what the leader had said. Nor were the rest of the contents. Descriptions of himself, Talia, and the ancient ring he'd discovered what felt like a lifetime ago. More unexpected, however, was that it mentioned Jasper and Cinder.

"Well?" Talia peered over his shoulder. "What does it say?"

"A lot, and none of it good. Whoever put out this bounty knew about us. You, me, the ring. Even Jasper and Cinder."

"The Brethren?" She asked as he passed her the document.

"It's what makes sense. If it was just us, perhaps it would be something else, but I have not been showing the ring around. Who else would even know about it to describe it so closely."

"Look at the horses," Grace called, interrupting them as she led one of the less-skittish mounts toward them. "Well-bred, well-trained. These weren't common sellswords."

Rowan lowered his bow slightly. "Why doesn't it mention Grace or myself?"

"What do you mean?" Osric asked.

"It mentions Jasper, which means wherever they got their information, it was after we returned to Farvale, well after we killed Godfrey. We hadn't found Jasper at that point. Yet whoever wrote this doesn't mention Grace or myself, who were also there when we returned."

"That doesn't make sense. No one survived that fight, and Captain Lockwood covered for us afterward," Talia said.

"Unless ..." Jasper's voice was heavy. "Unless they knew about me separately. They knew about the three of you and your wolf, from before Rowan joined you and before you found me and Grace. The only answer is that they took that information and put it together with my name, independent of the fight in Farvale."

"But how?" Osric asked.

"They knew I had knowledge of the document's other half. That I was one of the few who even knew it existed. After I left the Brethren, they kept tabs on me. Checked occasionally to ensure I wasn't causing trouble. But they considered me harmless, just a mad old man in a hut."

"Until you vanished," Grace said, understanding dawning on her face.

Jasper nodded. "When their people at the sunken temple were killed and the document taken, they must have connected the pieces."

"That's all speculation," Osric said, but the theory made sense. "What matters is they haven't given up. And now they're using bounty hunters."

"Makes things more complicated," Rowan agreed. "We'll need to be more careful in towns. Avoid main roads when we can."

Grace finished securing the horse's reins. "At least we got some decent mounts out of it. Better than walking."

"I'll help you gather up the others," Rowan said, leaving with Grace to catch the horses that had run off during the fight.

"And supplies," Talia added, examining the saddlebag.

Jasper stepped closer to Osric. "Now, about that wound."

Osric had almost forgotten the slash on his arm. The pain returned as Jasper examined it. "How bad?"

"Clean cut. Nothing vital." Jasper closed his eyes in prayer. Warmth spread through Osric's arm as the wound sealed under the cleric's touch. "But we should move soon. That fight wasn't quiet."

"Agreed." Osric rolled his shoulder, testing the healed muscle. "We need to get off this road before more bounty hunters show up. Or worse."

They spent the next few minutes gathering useful supplies and distributing them while Rowan and Grace brought back four more horses. The others seemed to have started running and never stopped, but it was enough. There were five of them, not counting Cinder, and five horses.

Rowan quickly patched up the animals that had been injured and showed amazing ability to soothe them, calming their nerves. Within twenty minutes of the end of the battle, they were ready to travel again.

"Let's keep going. With horses, it won't be long before we reach the Claws," Osric said, pulling himself up into the saddle.

Far From Home

Osric crouched near a spot of level ground just out of sight of the road, clearing enough rocks and brush to make a good space for his friends to camp.

It had been a difficult day, at least the latter part of it. It seemed like, except for their time in Avendell, his life was destined to be one life-or-death fight after another. He wasn't the only one who felt this way.

Talia entered the small clearing as he rose, dusting off his hands. She wore a frown that had lingered ever since they finished that tense skirmish. She was on edge. And rightfully so. Now, they weren't just looking out for the Brethren's own people which, according to Jasper, were not overly numerous. They also had to worry about hired mercenaries trying to track them down and dispose of them.

Of those, there was not a limited amount.

"This should be enough room for all of us," he said, trying to distract her with mundane things.

It didn't work. "After everything, I'd prefer to keep everyone in sight."

He did not like this version of her. Gone was the feisty girl he'd known all his life. Well, maybe not gone, but suppressed, weighed down by fear and worry.

Osric nodded in silent agreement. He caught sight of Jasper, pulling two of their purloined horses into the clearing. He, too, looked worn, although Osric thought maybe that was from the journey and the exertion of the fight. He wasn't sure how old Jasper was, but the man was notably older than the rest of them and had spent years living by himself in a cabin.

This quest was a lot to ask of him.

As Osric got a fire going, Grace and Rowan joined them, bringing the entire group together. Of all of them, those two seemed the least affected. Rowan had made it his mission to deal with poachers, bandits, and thieves, so maybe for him, this was old hat.

And nothing seemed to bother Grace.

"No, we still need to get all this off and brush them down," Rowan was saying as they tied the horses up. "They'll have picked up rocks and burrs under the saddles, and it isn't good to leave the bits in their mouths overnight. It can cause wearing and sores. We should also check the wounds of those who were injured in the battle. I know Jasper healed them some, but I want to make sure they aren't suffering."

"Sure," Grace said, unusually helpful, starting to disconnect buckles and straps for the removal of saddles. "These beauties deserve better than those thugs, anyway."

'An odd pairing, those two,' Osric thought.

He was happy to see them getting along so well, however. More surprising was, after they finished tending to horses, she made her way over to where Jasper sat near the fire while Rowan went to collect his bow.

"We'll need food for tonight," he said.

Cinder rose and padded over to stand next to him.

"I believe he wants to go with you," Osric pointed out.

"I believe you're right," the ranger said, and the pair disappeared into the quickly darkening forest.

"Why not just ask your gods to make it all better?" Grace asked as Jasper checked a small wound on her arm.

"It is not a small thing to ask the gods for help. In battle, fighting in their name, yes, Heathus held protection over me. Helping a mother birth a child or the infirm battle sickness. These are worthy of bothering the gods for assistance. Small cuts like this, that would be ... rude. Besides, keeping in practice on basic medical skills never hurts," he said, wrapping a bandage over the wound to keep the poultice he put on it in place.

"What do they care, lounging up there, wherever they are? I'm sure they're bored, and looking for entertainment."

"They aren't 'up there.' I believe, as the veil separates us from other realities, there are levels to the veil. They exist between our veil and another world's veil. Part of our world, but apart from it."

"How can you be part of something and not part of something?" Grace asked, turning to Talia. "Is that how it works? Like, layers of bedding or something?"

"I have no idea," Talia said. "Until this all started, I'd never heard of the veil, let alone knew anything about it."

"But you read all those books the Sage had," Osric said.

"I did, but I'm not sure how much the Sage or the other druids know about it either. They may be descendants of the ancients, the Calaphium, but it does not seem a lot of their knowledge came with them. Bits and pieces, yes, but that's just it. A scattering. Enough to know the veil exists and even how it is damaged, but not enough to actually understand it."

"Do you think there might be more information in the tower?" Osric asked. "I mean, if it was such a central part of their power, for repairing the veil, wouldn't they have had all kinds of books there?"

"Do you remember seeing much in the way of books in the temple we went to?" Jasper asked.

"I mean, I remember the document," Osric said.

"A document protected by powerful magic, so that even the Brethren could not destroy it, only hide it. Beyond that, there were no scrolls, tombs, or archives. Trust the word of an old man who spent his life collecting knowledge from books; they are not meant to last. A few hundred years, and books begin to fall apart, brittle to the touch. Another few hundred, and they are little more than dust. The Calaphium ended over three thousand years ago. I doubt very many of their books, if any, have survived."

Talia looked even sadder with that thought. It hadn't occurred to Osric that she may have been hoping to do just what Grace suggested, find new works to expand her knowledge. As much as Grace craved coin, Talia craved magic.

Another way this quest had let her down.

They busied themselves getting the camp ready before dark fully fell, setting out bedrolls, brushing the horses, and repairing clothes and armor as best they could after the fight on the road.

After about an hour, Rowan and Cinder returned, the ranger carrying three plump rabbits.

"This wolf of yours," he said, settling down to clean his catch. "He's something else. Knew exactly how to drive the rabbits toward my position. Even waited for my signal before moving in."

"The gods touched him somehow," Osric said, watching Cinder settle near the fire. "Regular wolves are clever, but the Sage said that Cinder was different. Given intelligence beyond his species."

The wolf's amber eyes met his, seeming to acknowledge the conversation about him.

"Well, he is very smart. I wish I had someone like him with me all these years, watching my back," he said.

Osric was just glad they had the ranger. He knew more about this kind of life than any of the rest of them. Osric had been a village boy, and a tradesman at that. Or training to be a tradesman. He knew little about hunting or preparing game. Master Ironhand would purchase meat and vegetables from the farmers and hunters around the village, saving them the trouble of skinning their own game.

It had been a privileged life, and one that had ill-prepared him for the one he lived in now.

Before long, the ranger had the rabbits skinned and on a makeshift spit, cooking over the fire.

"Watch these, yeah?" He said to Talia. "I'll take first watch and want to do a good check of the area. Save some of that for me and, if you could, don't have that warding spell or whatever you put down burn me to a crisp if I come back in late."

"You'll be fine," Talia said, but she laughed seemingly in spite of herself, a little of that darkness fading.

As they ate, the group got quiet, each lost in their own thoughts. Jasper and Grace both turned in shortly after they finished eating, both falling asleep quickly after such a long day. For a while, Osric just sat, staring into the fire, thinking.

Finally, he said, "This has been hard on you. I never wanted you to face situations like today."

"We've been through this," Talia said.

"I know, and I'm not saying I don't want you here. I'm saying I'm sorry for it being necessary. The more this goes on, the sadder you seem to get. I don't like that I've been the cause of your pain."

"You haven't," she said, turning to him, her green eyes reflecting the firelight. "It's … I'm more bothered by me than by what we've had to do."

"By you?"

"Yes. I know you think the killing is weighing on me, and I won't say I'm apathetic to the death I've caused. I'm not like Grace, or even Rowan. I do wish we could find a way to not be the cause of pain, but I don't feel bad about it. And that's what bothers me. I think I should feel worse about the killing, and I don't."

"Maybe it's because you understand what we're fighting for. The stakes we are fighting for."

"Perhaps," she said, pulling her knees to her chest. "But don't get me wrong. I wouldn't want to change what has happened to us, even if it means I've had to kill. Being here, learning real magic in Avendell, it's more than I ever dreamed possible. I'm not the same girl who left Eldham. That simple little village girl."

"You were never a simple little village girl, Talia. Everyone knew how special you were. Elder Miriam saw it. She took you in; no one else ever earned that honor."

"Maybe so." She looked around their camp, where Grace and Jasper were sleeping. "It's not just what I've learned though, it's … this. I would never have thought I would meet people like this and yet, we've become something more than just strangers thrown together by circumstance."

"I think I know what you mean. Since Avendell, things have changed for all of us. We're not just racing to stop the Brethren anymore. We've become …"

"A family, of sorts," Talia finished, standing up and brushing off her dress. "And that's what I wouldn't give up, if I had to choose again, some things are worth the price."

She turned and walked to her bedroll, leaving Osric to contemplate her words in the growing dark.

The horses picked their way carefully over the uneven ground as the group crested what Rowan had promised would be the last rise before they got to the base of the Claws. The darkened, jagged peaks had been in the distance since the day after they left the Great Road and the forest on a small dirty road heading north.

That had been four days ago, and after each day of riding from sunup to sundown, it never seemed closer, and Osric had started to wonder if they'd ever reach it, or if it was just a mirage, always on the horizon but never reachable.

Seeing the path leading from the gently rolling plains begin what looked to be a treacherous ascent up the mountain, he almost wished he'd been right.

Osric had not seen mountains before, but he hadn't imagined that they would look like this. Steep cliffs seemed to appear from nothing, as if they had ripped out of the plains into existence.

Although, based on what Jasper had told them, that might be true. Craning his neck up, Osric looked where the tops of the peaks seemed to pierce the sky, their sharp angles and unnatural formations like some monstrous hand clawing its way out of the earth.

It was easy to see where the place got its name.

A little snow dotted the tops of the highest peaks, but the rest were almost blackened to an unnatural color.

"By the gods," Grace muttered, the sight halting even her unrelenting pessimistic optimism. "It looks like something out of a nightmare."

"It feels wrong," Talia said. "I can feel the energies rolling off that place."

"How does it feel wrong?" Jasper pressed.

To Osric, the cleric sounded almost excited, as if this were an academic exercise and not a place they would soon be risking their lives to enter.

"It's hard to explain. It feels … twisted. Chaotic. I can feel it pressing in, like a physical weight."

Osric thought maybe he could feel that, too, and wondered if the magic was so strong that even those who could not wield it could be affected by it.

It would explain the sparseness of the area. They hadn't seen a cultivated field or a farmhouse in almost a day, shortly before the dirt road had given way to a barely discernible track. Even the wildlife seemed to have abandoned this cursed place. The only sign of life was the occasional twisted tree, their branches gnarled and contorted into grotesque shapes, or the scattered boulders that littered the foothills, like the remnants of some ancient, cataclysmic battle.

Movement caught Osric's eye, way in the distance, near one of the far peaks. Osric squinted, trying to make out what it was. Something wheeled about in the air around the peaks, but their size seemed much too big.

"Are those …birds?" he asked, squinting, "They'd have to be monstrously huge to be seen so far away."

"If those are birds," Jasper said. "Expect them to be unlike any you have ever seen. This place … it warps everything. Once we venture into it, don't expect anything to be what it seems, even if it looks familiar on the surface. Trust nothing."

The humans weren't the only beings that were troubled. Their new mounts stamped the ground and shook their heads. The animals were restless. Even Cinder, who stared at the path that disappeared into the cliff face, had his hackles raised.

"If this tower is where your vision indicated, I expect it to be two, maybe three days' ride into the mountains, at the center of the range. It would be closer on more even terrain, but here … it will probably be more."

"Should we take the horses in there? If the ground is precarious?" Talia asked. "They don't seem happy with the idea."

"I imagine not," Rowan said. "No, it might be best to leave them. I can see about arranging a temporary corral for them."

"That will have to work," Osric said. "The last thing we need is them getting spooked and injuring one of us. We need to decide if we're making camp here or pushing on. Neither option feels particularly appealing."

"Those things up there," Grace nodded toward the distant shapes, "they're going to be harder to spot in the dark. We're already going to have to spend several nights in that place; no reason to add to that."

"There's an outcropping over there," Rowan said, pointing to an area far to their left. "It would give us some cover, at least on one side. Better than staying exposed here."

Osric didn't know how Rowan's eyes had spotted it, but after a moment, he found what the ranger was pointing out.

"Works for me. Let's go. The sooner we're under some kind of cover, the better."

As they turned toward their temporary shelter, a distant sound came from the far distance, inside the Claws. Not exactly a howl, but not a scream either. It was something strange and otherworldly that sent a chill down Osric's spine.

Into the Claws

The night spent in the shadow of the Claws had been an uneasy one, and Osric wasn't sure anyone got enough rest. It was made worse by sounds, ranging from howls to strange clicking, that went on throughout the night.

At least it made it easy for everyone to be up and get an early start. They already knew they were going to have to spend one night on the way in and one night coming back out actually in the region of the Claws. Osric wanted to avoid having to add to that, so after putting the horses in the temporary corral Rowan had set up, they were on their way.

It was strange, crossing onto the dark, rocky ground that made up the Claws. It was like a line separated it from the land around it, as if magic had dropped it in their world.

Which was essentially what had happened.

The landscape before him bore little resemblance to the world he knew. Jagged spires of rock thrust upward at improbable angles, their surfaces pitted and scarred as if charred by a roaring fire. What little vegetation clung to life here was twisted and malformed, leaves curled inward as if recoiling from the very air.

A gust of wind brought an eerie chorus of sounds; a high-pitched scraping intermingled with more of the strange clicks that set Osric's teeth on edge. His friends looked as uneasy as he felt as they slowly ascended the narrow and winding path.

"This place," Talia said. "It makes my stomach hurt. It's worse than that creature in the lake. It doesn't belong here."

"The veil is thin here, just like at the pond in Avendell," Jasper said. "But unlike there, it doesn't lead to a realm of benevolent gods. It leads to something much more twisted and dark. We must be careful."

As if in response to his words, a tremor rippled through the ground beneath their feet. Osric stumbled, catching himself on a nearby boulder. The stone felt oddly warm to the touch.

"Watch your step," Rowan cautioned. "Even without the tremors, the rock here is brittle. One wrong move and you could find yourself tumbling down the mountainside."

Grace snorted. "Charming. Any other delightful features we should know about?"

Before Rowan could answer, a stronger tremor shook the earth. A cascade of rocks clattered down a nearby slope, kicking up clouds of dust. Cinder growled low in his throat, his hackles raised.

"We are going to get crushed if we stay on this path," Talia said.

"This is the only way through. We need to keep going. It can't be like this the entire way to the tower."

"Now who's being naive," Grace said, lacking much of her normal joviality.

The fact that the constant rumbling was enough to dampen even her spirits was telling. And it wasn't just the rumbling. Osric might not be able to feel the magic that Talia could feel, but this place still felt wrong. It felt like eyes were watching him, tracking his progress.

As they passed a particularly narrow part of the trail, where they could only walk single file through two tall, narrow rocks that resembled pillars more than a mountain face, Osric saw that the rock faces were scored with deep gouges, as if some massive beast had clawed its way through.

The others may not have seen it yet, but when Osric unsheathed his sword, they followed suit. Thankfully, the path opened up much wider on the other side. It was still steep and they could still feel the tremors, but if something happened, they at least had a chance to dodge.

"We should spread ..." Osric started, before Rowan held up a hand.

"Listen," he whispered.

Osric strained his ears, at first hearing nothing but the whisper of wind through the rocks. Then, faintly, he caught it. The rhythmic scraping sound again, like metal on stone, but much closer than it was before, and definitely ahead of them.

"What is that?" Talia breathed, her voice barely audible.

"Nothing good," Rowan said.

They continued forward, slowing here or there to pass through a narrow spot or a particularly bad tremor, for over an hour, as they ascended higher and higher on the path, which twisted along the mountainside, curving in toward the center of the Claws.

The direction of the path put any view of the green plains they had left behind out of sight, making the trip feel all that much more cut off and isolating.

Even with that, they sped up, making good time, although mostly because none of them wanted to remain there any longer than necessary. Several times, Rowan had to warn them to slow down, but most of the group wanted to keep moving as quickly as possible.

Rowan looked as if he was about to offer another warning when the ground beneath their feet shook. It felt as if the entire mountain had begun to tremble violently. The vibrations intensified rapidly, causing loose rocks to clatter down the steep slope, showering them with jagged pieces of stone.

"Look out!" Rowan shouted.

Osric looked where the ranger was pointing, and felt his blood run cold. A massive section of the rock face was breaking away, sending a deadly avalanche of boulders and debris hurtling toward them.

"Run!" Osric yelled, his instincts kicking in.

He grabbed Talia's arm and pulled her with him as he dove to the side. They hit the ground hard, Osric shielding her body with his own as rocks rained down around them.

The world became a chaos of noise and dust. Osric could hear the others shouting, but their voices were drowned out by the thunderous crash of falling stone. He held Talia tightly, praying that the others had found safety.

As the dust began to settle, Osric cautiously lifted his head and rolled off of her.

"Talia, are you alright?" he asked, his voice hoarse from the dust.

She nodded, coughing as she pushed herself up. "I'm fine. The others?"

Osric looked around frantically, relief washing over him as he saw Rowan and Grace emerging from behind an overhang where the ranger had pulled them. Cinder at their side had apparently gone with them, still half under the rock face, perhaps for protection.

But his relief was short-lived as he realized someone was missing.

"Jasper? Jasper, where are you?"

A weak groan answered him. It took a moment for Osric to find him, and when he did, his heart sank. The cleric was pinned beneath a pile of rocks, his face was contorted in pain, blood trickling from a gash on his forehead.

"By the gods," Osric breathed, rushing to Jasper's side, the others close behind him.

Jasper coughed weakly and, in a raspy voice, said, "Leave me, you have to ... keep going. The mission ..."

"Be quiet," Osric snapped as he turned to Talia. "Can you do something? Anything?"

Talia looked over Jasper and the rocks pinning him to the ground and nodded, her expression becoming determined. She closed her eyes, her hands moving in intricate patterns as she began to weave her magic. After a moment, some of the smaller rocks, and even one or two of the medium-sized ones, lifted off Jasper's body, hovering in the air for a moment before clattering to the ground a few steps away.

The largest of the boulders, however, barely budged, trembling slightly before settling back into place. Jasper cried out in agony as the boulder shifted.

"I'm sorry," Talia said, as she lowered her arms, sweat beading on her forehead. "It's too heavy. I don't know a spell powerful enough to move that much weight."

Jasper's eyes fluttered open, his eyes unfocused. "Please. Leave me. Do what you came to do."

"I told you to be quiet," Osric growled.

He wasn't going to leave Jasper behind, not like this. Taking a deep breath, Osric moved to the large boulder pinning Jasper down. He planted his feet firmly on the unstable ground, bending his knees as he gripped the rough edges along the bottom of the rock.

"Osric, what are you doing?" Grace asked.

"What needs to be done," Osric grunted, his muscles straining as he began to lift.

For a heart-stopping moment, nothing happened. The boulder seemed immovable, mocking his efforts. But Osric refused to give up, channeling every ounce of strength he possessed into this singular task. Rowan, Talia, and Grace ran over to join him, trying to help lift the boulder.

Slowly, agonizingly, the rock began to shift as they put their entire bodies to the task. Osric's arms trembled with the effort, sweat pouring down his face as he fought against the crushing weight. Inch by excruciating inch, they lifted the boulder off Jasper's battered body.

"Pull him out!" Osric said through gritted teeth as he braced himself to be able to hold up the rock as one of them let go, his vision blurring from the strain.

Grace moved first, carefully pulling Jasper's limp form from beneath the raised boulder. As soon as Jasper was clear, Osric let the rock drop, stumbling backward and gasping for air.

Jasper lay on the ground, his breathing shallow and labored. His face was deathly pale, and Osric could see the unnatural angles of broken bones beneath his torn clothing.

Kneeling beside his injured friend, Osric closed his eyes, reaching out to the Veilguard with every fiber of his being.

"Please," he whispered, his voice barely audible. "Help me save him."

As he placed his hands on Jasper's battered body, Osric felt a warmth spread through him. A soft, golden light began to emanate from his touch, enveloping Jasper in its gentle glow. After a short time the cleric's breathing eased, and some color returned to his ashen face.

Jasper's eyes fluttered open, relief replacing the pain that had clouded them moments before.

"Thank you," he murmured, his voice weak but much steadier than it had been.

Osric helped Jasper to his feet, supporting him as the cleric regained his balance. The others gathered around, their faces a mix of relief and lingering concern.

"Are you okay?" Osric asked.

The cleric felt along his legs, which had been clearly broken just moments before. His pants were cut and torn, but the skin underneath was whole again. Unblemished and unmarred.

"I am, thanks to you and the gods."

"We need to keep moving," Rowan warned. "That was too close and this whole cliffside could come down at any moment."

Talia moved closer to Osric, her hand brushing his arm.

"Are you alright?" she asked softly. "That was ... incredible, what you did."

Osric managed a weak smile, still catching his breath. "I'm fine. I'm just glad we didn't lose anyone."

Before they could collect themselves and start forward again, a new sound cut through the air. At first, Osric feared it was the rockslide Rowan had warned about, but the sound was wrong. This was a rhythmic thumping, growing louder with each passing second.

Whomp ... whomp ... whomp ...

The rhythmic thumping grew to a thunderous crescendo as dark shapes swooped over the cliffs to the west. Eight massive creatures that almost looked like moths descended upon them, their wings stretching wider than a man's height, with blazing red eyes and snapping razor-sharp mandibles.

"Spread out," Osric shouted, raising his sword.

The first moth darted toward Rowan at a terrifying speed. The ranger tried to bring his bow up, but the creature struck before he could nock an arrow. Its mandibles tore into his shoulder.

Talia must have been adjusting well to their new, exciting life because her hands started moving as soon as the creatures appeared, waving in front of her.

"Get back!" she yelled.

A small bead of orange fire shot from her fingertips, streaking between her companions before erupting into a massive fireball. The explosion engulfed all eight moths in searing flames. Their inhuman shrieks pierced the air as fire scorched their wings and bodies.

The creatures proved resilient, though. They emerged from the flames, their grey bodies blackened and still on fire in some places, but still airborne. One of the creatures dove at Grace. The thief tried to dodge, but they were incredibly fast for their size, and the creature's teeth tore into her arm.

"Damned oversized bugs!" Grace snarled.

She whipped an arrow from her quiver and loosed it point-blank into the moth's thorax as it swooped back toward the sky. The shaft buried deep, dark ichor oozing from the wound. Rowan followed suit, steadying himself on a boulder enough to let an arrow follow after Grace's, hitting another moth that was about to dive at Jasper.

The arrow didn't kill the creature, but it did divert it.

Talia wasn't as lucky; the talons of one of the creatures slashed across her back, leaving a trail of blood.

Fighting them was difficult. The narrow mountain path left little room to maneuver, and the ground still trembled from aftershocks of the earlier rockslide, making their footing even more treacherous.

Worse, the creatures kept swooping down out of the sky and then back above them in long arcs, making it difficult for Grace and Rowan to hit them with their arrows.

As if to prove the point, Grace fired again, hitting another of the hairy-winged creatures with an arrow. The celebration was short-lived as Talia was again cut by one of the beasts. Osric moved to defend her better, but with the creatures above him it was impossible to block them from reaching her as he had done with previous dangers.

Another beast swooped low, aiming to get revenge for being burned earlier. Osric swung wildly overhead, trying to catch it before it got to her. Thankfully, even with his wild swing, he managed to hit it, his blade slicing across the creature's body, opening its thorax and spilling its insides, sending it plummeting to the ground.

Talia's face was pale from blood loss, but she wasn't giving up. Her hands moved again in the way she used them to make her magic. He almost expected another ball of fire to come streaking out, but instead, a powerful gust of wind erupted from her out-stretched hands, slamming into five of the moths. The creatures, caught off guard, were thrown into the opposite cliff, smashing into it and then falling onto the ground. Not dead, but out of the sky for a moment.

She staggered from the effort and the cuts. Osric was about to go and help her when Jasper appeared at her side. He gripped her tightly and called upon Heathus's healing power. The god, as it had many times before, heard his call, and her wounds stopped bleeding and closed, relief washing over her face as the pain ebbed.

"Thank you," Talia gasped, her color returning.

But there was no time for conversation as the remaining crea-tures swept down at them.

Grace managed to dodge to the side as one of the beasts tried to clamp down on her, rolling and coming back to her feet.

"Blasted bugs!" she snarled, steadying herself against a jutting rock. "Can't we just squash them and be done with it?"

"These aren't ordinary insects," Jasper called back, his voice tight with pain from his own wounds. "They're creatures of chaos, born from the twisted magic of this place."

As if to emphasize Jasper's point, two of the moths unleashed a spray of corrosive spit. The acidic substance hissed as it struck the rocks around them, eating away at the stone.

"Watch out for their spit! It'll burn right through you!" Osric said, narrowly avoiding a glob of the caustic substance and swing-ing at the creature as it flew past.

The blade caught the creature's wing, tearing through the mem-branous tissue and sending it crashing to the ground, its severed wing rendering it earthbound.

Another moth took to the sky, climbing higher to prepare for another diving attack. Talia moved next to him, throwing her hands forward, sending a jet of flame out of her fingers in a wide spray, engulfing it before it could reach them. The creature's shriek cut off as it plummeted from the sky, its body reduced to ash.

Jasper, who had used limited magic or divine favor, or whatever it was, to only heal them, surprised Osric.

Pointing at one of the creatures, he called out, "Heathus, bind this foul beast."

It seemed to cause the beast to suddenly freeze mid-flight, its wings locking in place as if it was frozen, and it dropped to the ground like a stone.

"Strike now!" Jasper commanded. "The spell won't hold it long!"

Osric didn't have to be told twice; he stabbed down with his sword, piercing through the eye of the creature and into its brain.

"Ground them if you can," Osric yelled. "We can handle them on the ground."

Grace was starting to slow down from multiple cuts and bites, her arrow hitting a creature's leg instead of its body, with minimal effect. Rowan did somewhat better, striking one of the creatures in the wing joint. It still flew, but its pattern was more erratic and it had lost much of its maneuverability with the shaft of the arrow embedded as it was, keeping it from flapping its wing fully.

"They're slower when wounded!" Rowan called out.

Not that it was out of the fight. In fact, it seemed rage had taken over, as it abandoned all attempts at self-preservation and dove right at Rowan, latching onto him and trying to lift the ranger, who weighed much more than it, into the air, all but immobilizing the creature.

Osric stabbed up as hard as he could, his sword sinking deep into the creature's abdomen as it tried unsuccessfully to lift Rowan. It was difficult to dislodge it even when it was dead, as its jaws seemed locked in place, but at least it was no longer a threat.

Osric tried to pull his sword free quickly as another creature came swooping in, when suddenly a struggling moth came hurtling sideways, against any known mechanics of winged flight, smashing into the attacking moth with a satisfying crunch before both creatures dropped onto the narrow path.

Talia had a look of intense concentration on her face, dropping her hands as the creatures fell. Although Osric had no idea how she'd done that, he knew she had.

"Now that's more like it," Grace said as she rolled out of the way of an attack. "Though I wouldn't mind if you did that to the rest of them."

"Working on it," Talia said through gritted teeth.

The spell had clearly taken its toll. Osric knew that magic took a lot out of her, and she looked drained and tired already.

The last three moths circled overhead, all injured to different degrees and flying unsteadily, but still dangerous as they swooped in to attack once more.

Osric readied himself as one came diving at him when a gray blur shot past him, bouncing off a rock almost as a springboard and twisting over in mid-air. The wolf's powerful jaws snapped shut on the injured moth's thorax, putting his weight on the creature's back. Both animals crashed to the ground, although Cinder managed to use the moth's body to cushion his own fall. The moth thrashed wildly, but Cinder's teeth clamped down again, crushing through its exoskeleton, and shaking hard, sending a spray of dark ichor against the rocks next to him.

Meanwhile, Talia reached out toward one of the still-flying creatures, her fingers pinched together before drawing a clawing motion with her other hand. She touched her pinched fingers to the clawing hand and thrust forward. As she did, a greenish arrowhead materialized from her fingertips, slashing through the air and striking one of the remaining moths. The creature let out a shriek as the magical acid splashed over its body, causing it to smoke.

The beast tried to fly higher, maybe to escape what was causing it pain, but it only flapped a few times before the acid did its job. The moth's wings slowed and then stopped altogether before it spiraled downward, crashing into the rocks below.

"Only one left," Grace said, nocking another arrow.

The final moth dove toward them, spraying acid in a wide arc. Osric dove to the side, tackling Talia and throwing her behind a boulder. The foul liquid just missed her, splashing against the stone.

The last moth wheeled around for another attack but found only empty air as arrows from Grace and Rowan forced it to veer off course. It climbed higher, preparing for one final assault.

"We need to end this quickly," Rowan said, drawing another arrow. "The tremors are starting again."

He was right. The ground beneath them had begun to shutter again and small stones skittered down the mountainside, a warning of what might follow.

"Let's not give it the chance," Osric said, raising his sword. But there was no need.

The moth suddenly plummeted from the sky, as one of Rowan's arrows found its spot, impaling its wing against the moth's body. The creature spiraled widely, landing hard but on its claws as it tried to pull its wing free.

Osric didn't give it the chance, lunging forward and driving his blade through the moth's head. The creature gave one final spasm before going still.

Osric's chest heaved as he caught his breath, the adrenaline from the battle slowly ebbing away. He surveyed his companions. They were all injured but still standing.

"Is everyone alright?" he asked, his voice hoarse from exertion.

"I'll live. That was … intense," Talia said.

"Understatement of the year," Grace muttered, wincing as she prodded a nasty gash on her arm.

Jasper held his hands over the group and prayed. "Heathus be praised; we survived that onslaught. Help us and prepare us to continue to fight in your name."

While it wasn't as complete as the magic he'd used on Talia earlier, and the gashes had not disappeared entirely, it was clear that everyone felt somewhat better after his prayer.

Osric wondered why there was a difference, and if maybe helping them took something out of the gods, since they could clearly do more than this, when they wanted to.

Or maybe their favor was mercurial. They felt they had granted enough favors for today and would do no more.

"We should move. There's no telling if …" Rowan started to say, when they all heard a sound that was now much too familiar.

The rhythmic beating of wings, but amplified tenfold. Osric's blood ran cold as he looked up to see a swarm of moths coming over the top of the mountain, easily two dozen strong, descending upon them.

They could not survive this.

"Run!" Rowan shouted, already sprinting down the path.

Osric didn't need to be told twice. He grabbed Talia's hand and bolted after the ranger, the others followed close behind. The narrow trail made their escape treacherous, loose stones skittering beneath their feet with each step, but none of them dared slow down.

Osric dared a glance back, only to push himself harder as he saw the swarm gaining on them.

"We can't outrun them!" Grace yelled.

Talia paused, her hands flying through the air and pushing out hard, sending a wave of solid blue into the path of the massive insects. Several of them crashed into it and rebounded off, but it only held for a moment before the blue shimmering field shattered. Thankfully, the moths were not intelligent creatures and they tested the air, flying around in a swarm instead of after them, yet to realize their path was clear again.

Osric pulled Talia hard, getting them back up to speed. They'd figure it out soon. The path ahead began to narrow, squeezing between two towering cliffs and Osric hoped it would slow the creatures down too.

As they burst through the narrow passage, the landscape before them shifted dramatically. The jagged, blackened rocks gave way to smoother, almost tannish stone, with a little more vegetation present.

The change in the landscape, however, wasn't what drew Osric's surprise.

The swarm hovered at the edge of the passage they'd just exited, their wings beating furiously. One spit a glob of green acid-like substance at them, but they were too far away and it fell short. The moths chittered and scraped at the stone, some even biting at one another in their frenzy, but they didn't advance. It was as if an invisible wall separated them from their prey.

"What in the name of all the gods?" Grace breathed.

As they watched, more moths arrived, joining the swarm. Soon, there were easily fifty of the monstrous insects along the imperceptible boundary.

"It's as if they're afraid to cross. Even up there," Talia said, pointing to the top of the stone where some of the insects had come over the two large pillars of stone that had fallen together, instead of trying to go through.

Even those, however, would not come to the other side.

"Whatever's magic is keeping them at bay," Osric said, "I'm grateful for it. We wouldn't have lasted much longer against that many."

"I'm not sure it's magic," Jasper mused.

"See, it's saying things like that that make people not want to talk to you," Grace said.

"Either way, we can't go back and we still have a job to do. Let's go."

The Hermit

Osric breathed a sigh of relief as he and his companions finally moved out of sight of the moths. They might not be able to cross whatever invisible line had stopped them, but the very sight of them unnerved him, along with the scraping, clicking sound they made with their awful-looking maws.

As they ventured deeper into a small collection of mountains, it was impossible not to notice the stark contrast to their previous surroundings. The jagged, blackened peaks with their loose rocks and masses of chipped stone had given way to smoother, tarnished stone formations. It was also less barren, with vegetation, though seemingly dead or dying, clinging to small fissures and cracks all along the rock face.

He wouldn't call it lush, but it didn't look quite as scoured as before, either.

"This is … different," Talia said as they climbed even higher.

Grace snorted. "Different, but no less creepy if you ask me."

As they pressed on, Osric noticed the strange flying shapes he'd seen in the distance before they began to climb, although he couldn't tell if they were closer than before or not. Unlike the aggressive moths, these beings seemed content to observe from afar, never approaching the group. They remained far enough away that it was difficult to even tell what they were other than that they were large. Often, they seemed to blend into the landscape in a way that made Osric's eyes hurt if he tried to focus on them for too long.

At least their progress was markedly easier now. The ground beneath their feet was more stable and the tremors that had plagued them earlier had all but ceased. Even though it was safer, at least from the constant threat of rockslides, it was all but impossible for anything here to feel normal.

As they crested a slight rise in the terrain, Osric looked back and noticed Rowan, who was bringing up the rear, slowing. He lingered further and further behind the group, continually looking toward the distant abominations. It was impossible to miss his uneasy expression.

After ten minutes of continually looking to his friend, who seemed unusually oblivious to being observed, Osric stepped off the main path, allowing the others to continue ahead while he fell back, matching Rowan's pace and walking beside him. Their eyes met briefly, but for a while, neither said anything.

"Something on your mind?" Osric asked finally.

At first, he thought the ranger hadn't heard him, but then his shoulders sagged ever so slightly, like he had a weight bearing down on him. "I can't shake this feeling. These creatures, this place ... it's all wrong."

"I know what you mean. It is a strange place."

"No. It's more than that. These abominations, they're an affront to nature. To everything Wyndra stands for. How can she allow such things to exist?"

Osric had learned over the last few months how devout Rowan really was to the god of the wilderness. It made sense, and he was pretty sure most rangers worshiped the Queen of the Forests. She was, after all, the god that oversaw the wild places of the world. The forests, rivers, and animals.

He could also see how a place like this would put her most devoted followers ill at ease.

"Did you know," Rowan said after they walked a while longer in silence. "I can't feel her anymore. In my prayers, I've felt nothing but silence. No guidance, no reassurance. It's as if ..."

Rowan trailed off, looking out again at the flying shapes.

"As if what?" Osric prompted gently.

"As if she has abandoned us. Or worse."

"Worse?"

"What if she hasn't abandoned us? What if this is on purpose and this is some sort of test? A cruel game?"

Osric frowned, considering Rowan's words carefully. "I don't think it's that simple, Rowan. The gods ... they can't directly intervene in our world. It's why we had to go to such lengths to even find out what the Veilguard wanted us to do. If they could interact directly, they wouldn't need to send us on this quest. They'd handle it themselves."

"Or they just didn't want to do it and handed it off to the first people foolish enough to sign up. Or maybe ... What if Wyndra is deliberately allowing this corruption? What if she's complicit in some way?"

He was spiraling, that much was clear. Concern that something was amiss, that Osric could understand, but Rowan was now jumping to conclusions way past that. He was afraid. And angry. A bad combination.

"Why would she do that? This place, it's from beyond our world, yet it was allowed to come here. They allowed it to come through into our world. They have this power ... you've seen what Jasper has been able to do. And that is just a fraction of their power granted to one believer. Maybe ... maybe this is some form of selection, cruel as it may be, to see who is strong enough to live and weed out the rest."

Osric didn't reply right away. What could he say?

"I've dedicated my life to following Wyndra's teachings," Rowan continued. "But now, I'm questioning everything. Do I even want to follow a being capable of allowing such horrors? What if it isn't deliberate? What if this place is beyond Wyndra's reach? Or worse, what if she simply doesn't care? The thought that such might be the case terrifies me more than any creature we've encountered."

Osric felt a pang of sympathy for his friend and placed a comforting hand on Rowan's shoulder. "I understand, Rowan. Truly, I do. Questioning the gods, questioning your faith ... it's not easy. I question what I'm doing every day we've been on this quest."

Rowan looked at him, surprise momentarily replacing the fear in his eyes. "You do?"

Osric nodded. "After everything we've been through, how could I not? But from what I've learned, especially from my interactions with the Veilguard, the gods aren't all-powerful or all-knowing, at least not in the way most people believe. It's clear a lot of this has caught them off guard. I think they want to see the right thing done, but like I said, they can't act directly. It's why they need us, why they guide and inspire rather than intervene. This place, these creatures ... I don't think it's something Wyndra would allow if she had the power to stop it directly."

"I hear what you're saying, and it makes sense, intellectually, but ... I don't know," he said with a sigh.

"I get it. Faith isn't always easy, especially in places like this. Maybe you should talk to Jasper about this. He might have more insight. I mean, I'm just a blacksmith's apprentice. What do I know, really?"

"Don't sell yourself short. You may be a blacksmith's apprentice, but you were chosen by the gods. In some ways, you've had more direct contact with them than any cleric in this world."

"Maybe," Osric conceded. "But I think he still might have more insight than I do. I'm just making this up as I go."

"You and me both. Thanks for listening, for understanding."

Osric smiled, giving Rowan's shoulder a squeeze before letting his hand fall away. "That's what friends are for. Now, shall we catch up with the others? I'm sure they're wondering where we've gotten to."

Rowan gave one last look to the figures in the distance and picked up his pace. Osric was pretty sure his crisis of conscience wasn't over, not with everything he'd seen since he joined them.

Osric just hoped he wouldn't let those concerns overwhelm him.

They spent the bulk of the day traveling up and then back down the first peak. Osric had no idea how many miles they'd gone, but he was exhausted. As hard as the climb up the pass between the two peaks had been, the path down had almost been harder.

The jagged, weaving path they followed narrowed, its crumbling ledges that were brittle to begin with and had been chipped away by time and the elements. Several times, parts would crumble when they stepped near the weakened edge, once nearly sending one of them tumbling down the mountainside.

Reaching the bottom wasn't the end of their journey; another set of towering peaks rose up in front of them. They were making good time, though.

In spite of their concern over why the moths had stopped following them, they hadn't run into any other creatures, which was the thing they'd thought would slow them down the most.

Not that it made them feel any better. While they didn't see any living creatures, they saw a lot of dead ones. No bodies of moths, reinforcing they couldn't go past a certain point, but all kinds of other creatures lay scattered across their path. Twisted, malformed wolves with extra limbs jutting at odd angles from their bodies. Strange, elongated deer with too many eyes dotting their flanks, their antlers grown into impossible spirals. Most disturbing were the humanoid shapes, things that might have once been people, but were now warped beyond recognition. The sight made Osric's stomach churn.

They hadn't died peacefully either. They were hacked apart, gutted, and stabbed. The way their bodies were bloated, Rowan said it had maybe been a week since they were killed, although that was a guess since even the well-traveled ranger had never seen or heard of creatures like this. What had done it, though, was impossible to tell. Unless they did it to themselves, there was no sign of any bodies of the people, or maybe things, that had done the murdering.

"The light's fading fast," Rowan said as they got about a quarter of the way up the next mountain face. "We need to find shelter before night sets in. There's a chance whatever has been killing everything along this path is nocturnal."

That was all Osric needed to hear to agree with him. The problem was that a safe place to camp seemed in short supply. There was very little vegetation and what plants were scattered around them were twisted, without much in the way of leaves or cover.

Anywhere they slept, they would be out in the open and uncovered.

"Is that a cave?" Talia said, looking up the cliff face and a little to the east.

It wasn't on the path they were taking and some of the terrain between them and it was very rough, but it did, indeed, look like the mouth of a cave.

"Let's check it out. Even if it's shallow, it'll offer us some protection," Rowan said.

It was even slower going once they left the path, having to watch every step as they crossed the side of the mountain, careful not to start a rockslide.

The entrance to the cave was narrow and low, forcing them to duck as they went inside. The air had a thick mildew smell to it, along with a hint of something even worse that assaulted Osric's nose. A kind of sickly-sweet rotting smell.

It wasn't until they were all the way in, descending down, that Osric caught a whiff of another smell, one that was much more alarming.

Smoke.

Looking back at Rowan, the ranger nodded. He smelled it, too. Osric switched the torch he'd lit at the entrance of the cave to his other hand and pulled his sword. After checking that everyone was ready, he started down the sloping path again, careful to watch his step.

As they rounded a slight bend and the ground started to level out, he saw the glow of the fire before he saw the actual flames. What was surprising, however, wasn't the fire, but the small figure hunched over it.

It was a man wrapped in tattered rags with strands of matted white hair that framed his gaunt face. He was filthy, with longish dirt-caked nails that looked almost like claws and he was holding a stick over the fire with some kind of meat skewered on it.

Even with the torch Osric was carrying and the sounds they were making, the man didn't seem to notice them right away. He was mumbling to himself, almost like he was having an argument, but softly enough that Osric couldn't really make it out.

They stood there, frozen for a minute, unsure of what to do as the man continued to mutter, staring into his fire, completely oblivious to their presence.

Suddenly the man froze in place, cocking his head to the side like he was hearing something. He nodded once, then twice, before looking directly at them.

Osric stiffened, ready for anything, but instead of screaming or laughing at them, the man's face broke into a wide grin, revealing rotting teeth.

"Friends. What a surprise! Yes. Yes, please come in. Sit. Sit," he said, gesturing at spots around the fire. "Join me for supper. It's rude to not feed guests. Come. Eat. Eat."

Osric looked at his friends, who all looked as surprised and confused as he was.

"Come. Come," the man said again, waving more emphatically.

"That's a rat. You're eating a rat," Grace said.

"And why not? Feathered beast, crawling beast, what does it matter? All bellies grumble the same."

"Who are you? Why are you here? How are you here?" Osric asked, unable to contain his curiosity any longer.

"Here? Yes, yes. Here I am. Because I was called. The song, the stone—it sings, it hums, but not for me, never for me. The doors closed behind me. Always closed. Always locked."

"Called by what?" Talia asked.

"Called here! Called here!" he said before his words trailed off and his grin faltered as he took in Talia, as if seeing her for the first time. "A daughter of the lost. So sad. So sad."

Talia froze. "What did you say?"

"No, no. Too late, too late," he said, and then turned quickly to the fire, as if reacting to something, squatting down and shaking his finger at it. "Stop listening when you shouldn't!"

"So this guy's just crazy," Grace stated flatly.

"Don't judge him too quickly. He's managed to survive in this place all by himself for who knows how long," Osric said to her before asking. "We're looking for a tower, in the center of these mountains. Do you know of it?"

The man began to rock back and forth on his heels, agitated as soon as Osric mentioned the tower. "Tower, yes, tower holds the shadow. Shadow that eats the light, whisper that steals the mind. Things move in cracks between. They come, they go, they take. Shouldn't go. Never go."

"What things? What moves in the cracks?"

"Metal men. Men of iron and steel. Oh yes, yes, they broke the quiet. They woke the little ones. The little ones listen, always listening, always hungry. Can't say, can't say!"

Rowan frowned. "Metal men?"

"They clanked and rattled, they shouted and bled. They woke the little ones. The little ones do not like being woken."

"Men in armor?" Osric asked Jasper.

"Who knows? His mind is obviously wild and off balance. It could mean anything. Or nothing."

"But someone came, right? He said they came and left. And we saw all those bodies. Maybe they killed the creatures when they passed through," Osric said before turning back to the strange man. "How many men were there?"

The hermit rubbed his fingers together, as if counting something, but he kept switching fingers out and getting lost in it.

"Many. More than fingers, more than toes. They marched, they climbed, they screamed. Some left. Most stayed. Didn't want to go."

"Have you ever gone to the tower?"

The old man jerked his head violently. "Never near. Never near. Stay out of its home. Screams. Screams."

Grace snorted. "So that's a no then."

It was clear to Osric they wouldn't be getting an answer from him. He wasn't even sure if the guy understood them.

"Do you mind if we camp here tonight?" Osric asked.

"Friends, friends! Yes, yes, stay! The fire is warm, the cave does not listen. Stay, stay, stay ..."

Both Talia and Grace looked at him like he was crazy, but Osric did not like the idea of spending the evening outside in this place.

"He's right," Rowan said softly to the others. "Better here than out there. One of us will keep watch. Besides, look at him, he can barely stand on his own."

Talia and Grace looked like they didn't buy it but grudgingly agreed.

"Okay, let's get settled," Osric said, dropping his things.

Jaspers Secret

The night was an uneasy one. Even with someone on guard, no one slept well. The crazy old man wasn't the problem; he curled up and slept the sleep of someone completely unbothered by his surroundings. The rest of them couldn't help but listen to the noises outside the cave.

It was like the night before when they entered the Claws, but worse, because any noise could be a sign that the creatures out there followed them into the cave. That their safe haven for the night wasn't safe after all.

And yet, none came. They passed the night completely unbothered by whatever lived out there.

The old man barely roused as they packed the next morning and prepared to leave. It was only when they were fully ready, having eaten a small breakfast, that he finally woke, looking confused and a little wild, mumbling to himself and the rocks around him.

Osric still felt a little bad for the wild old man.

"You could come with us," he said as they started to leave. "We can help you get back to the world beyond these mountains."

"No, no, no," he muttered, rocking back and forth. "Can't leave. Never leave."

Grace rolled her eyes, slinging her pack over her shoulder. "This is going to be hard enough without bringing crazy with us."

"Have some compassion," Jasper chided her. "We don't know what horrors this man has endured."

She shrugged and moved to head out of the cave. Osric was prepared to ignore what she had said. Grace might have been crass, but she wasn't wrong. The man's mind was pretty far gone. The old man, though, for some reason, had locked on to Jasper, staring at him with intensity.

As they turned to leave, the old man said to Jasper, "The girl, the blonde girl, she screamed for you, holy man. She screamed your name. She asked why you didn't come. Why you didn't protect her like you promised."

Jasper froze, his face draining of color. Osric looked to the others, all of whom looked as perplexed as he was, with the exception of Grace, who glared at the cleric for a moment before turning and storming out of the cave.

Rowan hurried to follow, knowing how dangerous it was for any of them to be out there alone.

"Jasper," Osric said gently as the cleric stared back at the old man. "We don't want to get left behind."

Jasper seemed to shake himself enough to follow the others, who'd paused to wait outside the cave for them.

For a little while, they trudged up the hill in silence, but Osric couldn't stop thinking about what the old man had said. Yes, he'd said a lot of crazy things since they found him, but this last comment had hit home. He'd mentioned a blond girl, and, given Grace's reaction, he couldn't help but wonder if maybe the girl was Grace.

Osric had always felt there was more between the two of them than either let on, although he had no idea it was this serious. After thirty minutes of walking, it seemed that Grace couldn't take it anymore.

"You lied to me," she shouted, seething and pointing a finger at Jasper's chest. "You said none of it was true."

Rowan and Osric both looked around, worried her shouting might draw creatures they'd been lucky enough to avoid so far.

"What are you talking about?" Talia asked. "What isn't true?"

"I first heard of Jasper from others near Farhaven. They said he wasn't to be trusted, that he'd done something. Some people thought he'd killed someone. Not just someone, an innocent. When he … found me borrowing things from him, I asked him about it. He denied it, and I believed him. But that old man, he might be crazy, but he knew stuff. So tell me again that it's a lie. Say it to my face!"

"You, of all people, have no right to lecture me about lying," Jasper said, a lot more harshly than Osric had ever heard him speak to anyone.

But she might have a point.

"Grace isn't wrong, though," he said softly. "He said it was nothing to me, too."

The thief's head snapped toward Osric. "You know about this too? And you kept it from us?"

The hurt in her voice was palpable. Osric was surprised by that. He and Grace got along well enough, but they'd only known each other for a few months, and she was usually fairly snarky with him.

He hadn't imagined that his withholding information would bother her so much. She clearly held back what she knew about Jasper, too, after all.

But he'd only stayed silent because he'd trusted Jasper. Because he saw him as a man of integrity. If Grace was right ... then Osric had made a mistake staying silent.

"When I went into the pool, the gods actually showed me two visions. They showed me not just the tower, but a vision of Jasper with a young girl. A young blonde girl. Something felt off about it, but the vision didn't give me any more information. I spoke to him about it afterward, before we left Avendell. He said he didn't want to discuss it, that it was nothing. I ... I believed him and respected his privacy."

"Well, I want to know," Grace demanded, crossing her arms.

Rowan nodded in agreement. "If the gods themselves are showing visions of this, it's something we should all be aware of."

Talia nodded, agreeing with both of them. Jasper was outnumbered.

Jasper's shoulders sagged, the fight draining out of him. He looked older suddenly, weary beyond his years.

"It's why I left the Brethren. There was a girl, her name was Nora. She was no more than twelve or thirteen. I was told she posed a danger to magic itself. They told me it was my job to stop her. I asked them to explain, explain why she had to die, but they refused. I begged them, but they kept insisting it wasn't something that someone of my status needed to understand. That it was my duty to accept their judgment on faith alone."

He paused but refused to look up at any of them. Osric could hear the pain in his voice. It was raw. Visceral.

"When I met her, I found only an innocent child. She was so excited when she found out I was a cleric and that I'd come to visit her. She said she heard voices that told her someone was coming to help her. She said it was the gods, and they were preparing her for some great mission to help the world. She said a lot of other things, most of which made little sense, like our friend in there. I thought perhaps she was ... touched. I felt sorry for her. I couldn't understand how this sweet, confused girl could be a threat to magic itself. I also thought, maybe these voices were something else, something corrupting her."

He finally looked up, his eyes almost imploring them to believe him. "The thought of harming her was repugnant. I thought, if someone was manipulating her, I could help her. Get her to resist whatever it was. That way, she wouldn't have to die. But ... I had to get her away from the Brethren first. I tried to help her escape. I was woefully unprepared. The others found us easily enough. They put me in chains while another member, a man I thought was my friend, carried out the execution I had refused to perform. I begged him to stop, but he didn't even acknowledge me."

"If they had you in chains, how did you live to say anything? Why would they let you live after disobeying them?" Talia asked.

"They claimed that, while it needed to be done, it had been given to me as a test. A test of loyalty, of my willingness to do what needed to be done to protect magic and the world from the evils trying to end it. They said most recruits failed the first time, that it was hard to become the type of person who could do what was needed. They welcomed me back with open arms. They said I could try again. But I couldn't. I started questioning everything about them, about their methods and their goals."

"But you told us you were a minor member of the Brethren," Osric said. "Why would they give a minor member a job like that, or tell you that you were being tested?"

"I was. One of the lowliest of the low. That's likely why they gave me that task. For the early ranks of the Brethren, I think it's not about protecting anything. I think it's about breaking you down. Telling you you're special and capable of helping save the world.

They make you feel like you are part of something, all so that when they ask you to do something unforgivable, you'll do it. That's what it's about, to get you far enough in so that you'll make that one choice you can't unmake. Once someone does something like that ... the guilt, the shame, it binds you to them forever. You become malleable because fighting back means accepting that you're a monster. So you have to believe it was the right thing to do, and that they're right. It wasn't a test. It was a trap."

The cleric reached out and grabbed Osric's hand between both of his, squeezing it hard. "It's why I was so willing to believe in you, Osric. To follow you. I know now that she was actually talking to the gods, gifted with visions, and so were you. You were both chosen. I saw in you a second chance, an opportunity to truly do their will. To be forgiven for failing."

"Then you weren't the first they did that to. How did you stay with them for so long? What made you believe in them?" Talia asked.

"I was lost, looking for answers, and they are masterful at indoctrination. It wasn't just blind faith or fear that kept me there. They showed us concrete evidence of magical disasters they'd prevented. Extensive historical records of catastrophes they'd stopped. They wrapped their lies in truths, making it very convincing. And very hard to ignore."

"But surely you must have questioned some of their methods?" Rowan asked. "They're obviously ready to murder people at the drop of a hat, so they've done it before."

Jasper nodded slowly. "I did question them, at times. But they mixed genuine threats with their more questionable actions. It made it ... difficult to separate truth from manipulation. But it was more than that. They made us feel chosen. Special. Every mission was framed as part of a noble legacy of protecting the world. Doubt was weakness. Questioning orders was seen as dangerous not just to us, but to everything."

"But you're not some simpleton. How could you not see through their lies?" Grace said.

"They isolated us from outside perspectives. Gradually conditioning us. It became nearly impossible to maintain independent judgment. I couldn't see it, or what they truly were, until I was away from them."

"If it was so powerful, how did you manage to stop being indoctrinated?" Talia asked.

Jasper's gaze fell to the ground. "I didn't, not really. Not until Nora. Yes, I questioned them a lot, and though it got me in trouble, they always smoothed things over. The incident with her ... it forced me to confront the reality of what they were asking me to do. It shattered their web of control."

"I'm as shocked by this as all of you," Osric said. "But we can't afford this right now. Look where we are. This isn't exactly the place to fall apart."

Grace's eyes narrowed. "So we just ignore what he's done?"

"I'm not saying we forget this. But the fact is, we'd all be dead already if it wasn't for Jasper. We wouldn't even be here at all if it wasn't for him. He's been critical to our mission from the start. And we have a job to do. A job that could mean the difference between saving the world and watching it tear itself apart. We need to focus on that for now."

Rowan nodded slowly. "Osric's right."

Talia sighed, her earlier anger seeming to deflate. "I don't like it, but ... you have a point."

Osric looked to each of the others, who slowly nodded. Grace was last. The look she gave Jasper was still more wounded than angry, like he'd let her down. But then she, too, finally agreed. Osric knew this wouldn't be the last of this, but it was enough, for now.

"Alright then. Let's move out."

The rest of the walk up the mountain was as grueling as it had been the previous day, but a weight had settled over all of them since the confrontation. By midday, when they finally made it up the side of the mountain and crested it, none of them had spoken a word. Osric stopped short as the mountain path, although calling it that was being charitable, opened onto a broad cliff face, finally giving them a view of what lay on the other side.

Below the mountains stretched a wide valley going a few miles in either direction before more mountains pushed up, creating an almost egg-shaped flattish region that Osric thought might be the center of the Claws.

In fact, he was certain it was because there, sitting in the center of the valley, was the tower from his vision. Its wide base sprawled outward like the roots of some ancient tree, while the central spire thrust up, high above the base. It was in a sad state, with holes and chunks missing where sections had crumbled away over the years. Large pieces of masonry littered the ground around the base.

The centuries had not been kind to what must have been an impressive sight in its day.

"What a wreck," Grace said, coming up behind him.

As if to emphasize what she said, a massive shape wheeled through the air near the tower's peak, dark wings spread wide against the gray sky. The creature banked sharply before vanishing either behind the structure or into some fallen-away opening near its crown.

"This is it," Osric said, his hand instinctively moving to his sword hilt. "This is what I saw in my vision, although it was much newer then. They kept the Blackstar there, in that section near the top."

They all stopped for a moment to look down at its impressive shape before starting down the mountainside toward it. As with every other piece of mountain they'd covered, it was slow going, with the very ground constantly threatening to slide out from under their feet.

They were all happy to be on flat ground again once they reached the valley itself. The walk from across it to the tower wasn't long and held signs of what this region must have looked like before the ground lifted it up high above the rest of the plains and surrounded it with mountain peaks.

Jasper still hung back, far behind the rest of them, but seeing the tower and realizing they had reached their goal had finally broken the cloud that had settled over them.

They started seeing hints of a crumbling road, its ancient stones still visible in patches, becoming almost recognizable for what it once was the closer they got to the tower itself.

A reminder that this used to be connected to a larger world, built by a society that no longer existed.

As they approached the tower's entrance, its true scale became apparent. The doorway loomed nearly twenty feet high, though the massive doors that once sealed it hung askew on rusted hinges.

"This reminds me of that keep where we found the first document," Talia said. "Although maybe it's because both are old and falling apart."

"Maybe, although this is so much bigger," Osric replied, walking up to the door and running his hand along it, feeling the deep gouges in the ancient wood. "Someone's been here recently. These marks are new."

Rowan crouched near the threshold, examining the debris. "Axe marks. Whoever came through here had to break their way in."

"Think it was those 'metal men' our crazy friend mentioned?" Grace asked.

"Probably," Osric said. "These doors might be old, but they are really thick. Those guys must have wanted inside pretty badly."

"Which means we're not the first ones here," Rowan said. "They may have already ..."

A low whine from Cinder cut him off. The wolf had broken away from the group and stood near a dense thicket of thorny bushes that had taken root in the tower's shadow. His hackles rose as he sniffed the ground.

"What is it, boy?" Rowan asked, already drawing his bow.

Cinder turned to look at them and then back at the bush, standing stock still, as if pointing at it.

Osric took several careful steps toward the thorny bush, trying to see what had caught Cinder's attention. Reaching down carefully, so he wouldn't be caught by a thorn, Osric pushed the thick branches aside and stopped as a powerful stench of death struck him.

"It's a body!"

The body was in a full set of plate armor, an expensive piece of equipment that few could afford. It was hard to make out the details of the armor through the thick branches and the leaves of the bush.

"Help me pull him out," Osric said.

With Rowan and Osric both grabbing a foot and the others pushing the branches back, they managed to pull the man's body out from under the shrubbery. What they saw when they did was ghastly.

The body was bloated, barely contained by its armor shell, and the smell was overpowering. The blood that had spilled on the armor had long since dried. The man's helm had been knocked away to who knew where, and most of his face was gone, probably ravaged by scavengers.

One thing that wasn't hard to see was the crest in the center of the breastplate. Osric hadn't seen it in person before, but Master Ironhand had described it to him several times.

It was the arms of House Blackthorn, the family that ruled Greenwood.

"What is a House Blackthorn knight doing here?" Osric asked.

"I don't know," Rowan said, kneeling beside the corpse. "But he died violently. Look at the side of the armor. Something tried very hard to rip him out of it. The gouges look like they are from claws. And they cut very deep into the metal. Something's also been feeding on him. Probably scavengers."

Grace, who had circled the clump of bushes, said, "Maybe this was one of the scavengers?"

Osric stepped away from the knight and went around to stand next to her, with the rest following to see what she had found. The thing was almost clear of the thorns, but what it was, he had no idea. It had been ripped into, and what looked like a big chunk was torn out of it, as if a larger creature had taken a bite.

"What is it?" he asked, unable to hide the disgust in his voice.

For a moment, no one said anything, they just stared at it. Osric looked to Jasper, who usually had something to say in a moment like this, but the cleric still hadn't spoken since that morning.

"Jasper?" Osric prodded.

"I've never seen anything like it," Jasper said softly. "But given the other things we've seen in these mountains and how much weaker the veil is here, there's a chance it's not even something from our reality. Like that creature in the lake or the one in the temple."

"Do you think it's one of the 'little ones' the crazy old man was talking about?" Grace asked.

"Maybe," Osric said. "There would have had to be a lot of them to take down an armored knight."

"I don't think this was what killed him," Rowan countered. "For one, the claws are too small. Also, it looks a lot fresher. Some of the wounds are still soft. If I had to guess, it was killed within the last day. The knight, though … he's been here for several days at least. He's already started to bloat," Rowan said, standing and brushing dirt from his knees. "I think this confirms what the old man told us, though. The 'metal men' he mentioned must have been Baron Blackthorn's knights. Although why he'd send them here is a mystery. Everyone knows it's a death sentence."

"More importantly, why did he send them here, to this specific tower? How does he know this is here? No one has been in the Claws in living memory, so how did they know about it?"

"It's too much of a coincidence," Rowan said. "Wolfridge is much closer to here than we were. If they were only a few days to a week ahead of us, they would have learned about our destination not long after we did."

"Maybe someone knew we were coming," Osric suggested. "Wanted to get here first."

"Who? The Brethren are the obvious choice, but how would they know we were coming here?" Rowan asked, looking at Jasper.

For a moment, Osric thought he might not answer. The cleric looked away, still a little ashamed, but then seemed to shake himself and look Rowan in the eyes.

"They shouldn't," Jasper said. "Also, I know of no connection between the baron and the Brethren. That doesn't mean they're not involved, of course. They, or an agent of theirs, could have convinced the baron to send his men."

"Do you think they were after the Blackstar too?" Osric asked. "If they knew we were coming, they might have tried to beat us to it."

"And succeeded, by the looks of it," Grace muttered. "The old man said they left, remember? If they came for the Blackstar and already got it, we've wasted our time."

A heavy silence fell over the group. All that work, and what did it get them?

"We can't give up now," Osric said firmly. "Even if the Blackstar is gone, there might be other clues in there. Information about what it is, how it works. We need to know everything we can if we're going to have a chance at repairing the veil. And if they did take it, we know where they are, right? So first, let's find out what this place has to tell us."

"What about ... whatever did this?" Talia asked, gesturing to the body. "It could still be in there."

"Then we'll deal with it," Rowan said. "We've faced worse on this journey."

Each of his friends looked to Osric, to decide what they'd do next. It was clear none of them were thrilled about the idea of going into a tower that, if the old man was right, killed dozens of armed knights, but still, they looked to him.

Osric didn't know when he, who was younger than all of them save Talia, became the deciding factor. Or if he was ready for that kind of responsibility.

But he wasn't going to let them down.

"We've come this far," he said, drawing his sword. "We aren't stopping now."

The Tower

Osric pushed against the massive doors, straining hard to get them to move enough to let them in. The entire thing strained against its ancient hinges. Osric wondered that if the baron's men did hack at the door to get it open and passed through it into the tower, how did the door close?

It seemed unlikely they pulled it closed as they left, so what closed it?

As the door yielded, a gust of stale air rushed past them, carrying the scent of decay and mold. A harsh, moist smell. They ignored it and continued in, their eyes taking a moment to adjust to the gloom inside the tower.

When they did, what they saw was awe-inspiring, even in its crumbling state. The vast entrance hall stretched before them, its grandeur barely diminished by neglect. Particles of dust drifted through shafts of light that pierced the gloom from gaps in the stone high above.

"Look at this place," Talia said. "The power they must have wielded to build something like this would be immense."

Osric couldn't agree more. It was impressive. Walking into the room, head swirling around, taking in the sight, he couldn't help but notice the thick layer of dust on the floor, small puffs of which kicked up with each step. It filled the air and got in his mouth, causing him to cough to clear it.

Around them, crumbling pillars rose into the darkness, their bases littered with fallen stone. A massive chunk of stone, probably one of the ones that fell off the tower and littered the ground around it, had partially crashed through the ceiling at some point, wedged at an angle half in and half out of the room, casting strange shadows across the floor.

Jasper was as awed as any of them, the reserved nature he'd had since that morning's argument replaced by the academic in him. Specifically, he was taking in the faded and chipped murals that covered every wall, illuminated by thin shafts of light coming through the ceiling.

"Talia, would you mind?" he asked.

A few gestures later, several small spheres of light jumped out of her hands and danced above them, spreading light across the room, causing more shadows to dance about them.

Jasper traced his fingers over a section where the paint had clung stubbornly to the stone. Figures, barely discernible, stood in a circle, hands raised in what looked like a ritualistic gesture.

"This must have been part of a depiction of the tower's creation. I wish more of it was still intelligible, to give us some kind of idea how they managed this. Imagine the power they wielded, raising this edifice, especially considering what was housed at the top. A building capable of controlling and harnessing that kind of power ... extraordinary."

"There are tracks here," Rowan said, kneeling off to the side and running his hand over what Osric guessed, but couldn't tell, were footprints. "The knights came through here. Several sets of boot prints. Pretty recent ones."

"We knew they were here," Osric pointed out.

"Not just here. The prints are a chaotic jumble, overlapping each other. They were moving around, frantic, not just marching in a straight line. Some are also much deeper than the others, like they were carrying a heavy load."

"That's not the only thing left behind," Grace said near one of the pillars.

When Osric walked over to her, she nudged something half-buried in debris, pushing a half-melted blade out from under a piece of stone, a broken gauntlet still gripped around the hilt of the weapon.

"Hand's still in there," Grace muttered.

Osric realized she was right. He could see the bone, and a little more, although that looked picked at by animals just like the body outside, sticking out of the bottom of the ripped metal.

"Where's the rest of him?"

"Maybe he didn't die. Just lost his hand and kept going," she offered.

A gruesome thought.

A chill swept through the chamber, although if it came through the broken ceiling or still-ajar door, Osric didn't know. Either way, it stirred up the dust, creating small eddies of choking substance before it whipped further down the hall, out of sight.

The momentary movement in the long-dead ruin sent a fresh wave of unease through all of them.

Osric turned back toward the darkness in front of them. The walls, the stone, the very air made the place feel like something lost to time. Very much like how he'd felt in the keep or the Calaphium temple where he found the two pieces of the document. Remnants of a world long forgotten, both because of time and on purpose.

"They kept going that way," Rowan said, standing up and pointing down toward the end of the hall, where another set of doors stood.

"Then so will we," Osric said.

They followed the boot prints through the door and deeper into the tower, past crumbling stone archways into what appeared to be ancient guard chambers.

"They just continue on through this room into the next," Rowan said, kneeling briefly to look at the footprints. "Not one of them stepped off the straight line to investigate anything in here."

"All knights, maybe," Osric said. "They had a mission and they were going to stick to it. They weren't here to learn anything."

"Maybe," Rowan said.

Neither Talia nor Jasper agreed with the knights' approach however, and started looking over every inch of the room, examining everything. Both were so alike in a way, drawn to the history of this place, their excitement at learning almost coming before the actual mission.

Although, if the knights did take the piece of the Blackstar at the top of the tower, then the whole point of being here was learning, so maybe they were doing the right thing.

Osric was content to just stand in the middle of the room and wait for them, at least until something caught his attention.

Cocking his head to the side, Osric walked to a breastplate that had been discarded on one side.

Or at least, he thought it was discarded until he nudged it and part of some bone fell out of it, which confused Osric even more. The armor had the same symbol as he had on his ring, so it wasn't from the knights. This was old armor.

Very old.

And yet, it didn't look old.

"This armor should have corroded to nothing by now. How is it still intact?"

Jasper joined him and ran his fingers along the breastplate's surface. "Many Calaphium artifacts were imbued with protective magic that preserved them against normal wear and tear. This was the same place the document was from, we think, and remember the condition that was in. The enchantments appear to have outlasted their creators."

"That's some serious staying power," Grace said, nudging a twisted sword with her boot. "Though clearly, not everything got the special treatment."

"Their magic wasn't infinite," Jasper explained. "They had to choose what to preserve."

As interesting as this find was, it didn't impact their mission. Beyond the guard chambers, they entered a vast circular room that Osric had actually been expecting, although he'd thought it would be further in than this.

Stone circles as tall as two men lined the walls, each mounted on ornate pedestals. Every Calaphium place they'd visited had had these. The portals they used to travel about.

Although these weren't quite identical to the others. Dark, unfamiliar metal sealed many of the circles, while others lay in pieces on the floor.

Talia moved closer to study the nearest intact portal, her fingers tracing worn engravings. "These match the patterns we saw in the temple and the keep, although in a different order. It looks as though someone deliberately damaged or removed many of the markings."

"Maybe to stop the magic, so that it couldn't be used," Jasper suggested.

"Why seal them instead of destroying them completely?" Grace asked, peering at the strange metal blocking one portal. "Seems like a lot of work when a sledgehammer would do the job."

"The magic binding these portals together was incredibly potent," Jasper said. "Breaking them completely may have been impossible. Whatever inspired such drastic measures must have been truly terrifying."

"Or they were keeping something in," Grace pointed out. "Making sure nothing could escape."

That hit all of them hard, causing each to look back at the portals. They had some hint, from the records and Osric's vision, of what had happened here. The man who'd sent the document through time, looking for help, had been desperate. Perhaps he had been desperate enough to keep his people here, instead of letting word of this place escape.

Osric shook himself and said, "Let's keep moving. We still need to find any sign of the Blackstar."

They followed the boot prints, which again showed no sign of stopping to look at the portals, deeper into the tower, toward the center of the complex. The next part of the passage opened into a warren of smaller chambers. A quick examination of the closest room proved it to be some kind of living chamber.

"The knights' footprints move past these and keep going," Rowan said.

"We should look into them," Jasper said. "We are looking for some clue as to the power and history of the Blackstar, for when we find it. This seems like a reasonable place to do that."

Osric wasn't sure Jasper believed that or just wanted to see what was here and what he could learn. But, he also wasn't wrong.

"A quick once through and then we keep moving," Osric said.

They spread out, not exactly separating, but each looking in different rooms, seeing what was there. Some rooms had collapsed entirely, while others remained eerily pristine beneath thick layers of dust. Broken furniture and moldering tapestries filled many spaces, yet other chambers appeared untouched by time's decay.

"Osric's right. The preservation magic seems awfully ... selective," Rowan observed, pointing to a perfectly intact wooden table next to a pile of rotted debris.

"Their reasoning died with them," Jasper said. "We can only guess at their priorities."

Osric discovered torn papers and damaged books scattered throughout several rooms. "They didn't bother preserving their written records?"

"No," Jasper said as he examined some of the books. "These look deliberately destroyed."

"Why?"

"Again, I'm not sure we'll ever know."

For an expedition to learn more about the Blackstar, they certainly weren't learning very much.

In one of the better-preserved chambers, Jasper's eyes locked onto something half-hidden beneath fallen stonework. He carefully extracted a leather-bound book, its cover showing remarkably little wear despite the centuries that had passed.

"Wait!" Grace said. "It could be a trap."

"The Calaphium weren't prone to curse-traps or magical wards," Jasper assured her. "Their magic focused on practical applications, not malicious tricks. This appears to be simply a preserved text."

Jasper carefully opened the front cover, his fingers moving with reverence across the weathered pages.

"This is remarkable. It's written in Low Calaphium."

"The what? There are different kinds?" Grace asked, peering over his shoulder.

"Yes. Most preserved texts that have been found, and there are not many since they're considered evil and are destroyed immediately, are written in High Calaphium, the formal language of nobility and ceremony. It's what the document we found was written in. Low Calaphium was rarely on preserved paper, and so hardly ever survived. It was used by soldiers, merchants, and common folk. It's much more straightforward."

"Can you read it?" Talia asked, moving closer.

"Yes. The grammar structure is similar to High Calaphium, but there is a lot less of it and it's less contextual, so it's much easier to read. It appears to be a guard's journal."

"If it's so rare to find because they didn't get the magically protected paper, how does this guard have it?"

"Hard to say. This was a place of intense magic usage, so maybe they were more free with it here. Or maybe he took something he shouldn't have and kept it for himself. Not something completely unbelievable."

It made sense, Osric thought, looking over his shoulder. "What does it say?"

Jasper began to read, translating as he went: "'*Another quiet watch. The abbot remains sealed in his chambers with orders not to be disturbed. Dalst fell asleep on watch again, and I think the commander might have him strung up for real this time.*'"

"Thrilling," Grace muttered.

"Looks to be a journal of some kind. Maybe ..." Jasper said and fell silent as he started flipping through the pages, looking for something. "Here. '*It's all gone, and everything's changed. I was on watch in the portal room two days ago when a man fell through the spire portal, bleeding and burned. He was barely comprehensible. Before he died, he warned they were under attack and the council had fallen. The abbot ordered all portals sealed immediately, although the commander isn't sure how to really do that yet.*'"

"The spire?" Osric asked.

"I'm not sure, but I've seen that referenced in a few other works. I think it might have been the seat of their power, but it's unclear. It was important, whatever it was."

"Keep reading," Talia urged.

"'*We're now surrounded by mountains. They weren't there yesterday. It's like they ripped through the very ground,*'" Jasper continued. "'*We were woken by screams. We thought we had the portals sealed. We were wrong. Things came through, things I can't even start to describe. They ripped through the men on guard. Dalst won't ever fall asleep on duty again. We managed to push them back, but I lost half my squad doing it. They were ... I don't even know what. Twisted shapes of flame. I could see through one of the portals, before the abbot did whatever he did, and burned off the runes. It didn't go to the south like it should have. On the other side, it was only fire and molten stone. The commander says we're cut off now. There are ... things outside the tower and we've sealed the doors. No way to know if anyone else survived.*'"

Jasper flipped past a few very short passages, although Osric didn't know if it was because they were unimportant or he couldn't translate them.

"'*It's been fourteen days. Food stores are running low and the third scouting party failed to return. Creatures keep attacking the doors, but the spells are still holding. We haven't seen the abbot in five days and the men are getting restless. Some are talking about breaking in and forcing him to reopen the portal and send us home. Two others tried to sneak out. The commander caught them and had them executed. He says we need to keep protecting the tower and following our orders, but orders from whom? Is there anything left out there, and for how long? I don't want to starve.'*"

"Poor bastards," Rowan said softly.

Jasper waved him off and kept reading.

"'*The abbot still hasn't come down from the tower. The commander tried to get him to tell us what to do, but he wouldn't answer. We hear strange sounds at night, chanting, sometimes screaming. It's making the men even more nervous. Jens says he's working on something big up there to fix this. The Blackstar is up there and we think it has the power to fix all of this, but no one tells us anything.'*"

"That has to be the Blackstar, right?" Talia asked.

Jasper nodded and kept reading: "'*Four weeks and we're down to quarter rations. The commander has finally agreed that we need help and is organizing a special scouting party. We're going to travel light and bring only our best men to hopefully give us a chance where the other three parties failed. I've been chosen to go. I don't know if anyone's left out there, if anyone even knows we're trapped here, but we have to try. I can't take this with me, so I'm going to hide it. This may be my final entry. I hope the gods have mercy on us.'*"

Jasper flipped through the rest of the book, but the pages were blank. Osric tried to imagine the guard's final days, trapped in this tower as the world literally fell apart around them with no idea of what was happening outside their doors.

Terrifying.

"Your vision said the Blackstar exploded. He didn't mention an explosion," Talia said.

"Maybe it hadn't happened yet," Osric said. "Or maybe it happened but they couldn't hear it. He said they didn't know if the abbot was alive or not.

"The knights' tracks still lead that way," Rowan cut in, gesturing toward the corridor ahead. "Whatever happened here, standing around won't give us answers. We need to get to the center and find out what happened in the upper chambers."

Osric cast one last look at the journal in Jasper's hands. So many had died in this tower, Calaphium guards, whatever horrors emerged from the portals, and now Blackthorn knights.

This wasn't a place he wanted to stay in.

Automatons

Other than the journal, which gave context for what was happening in the tower when the Calaphium fell, there wasn't much else in the living area to give them information on the Blackstar. They headed back to the central corridor and followed the footprints to a large, spiral staircase in the center of the tower.

"The knights went straight up. They ignored everything beyond this point," Rowan said, kneeling to study the floor and pointing past the stairs to another corridor that continued beyond the stairs through an archway, presumably to the other half of the lower floor.

"I assume we check that out before continuing?" Grace asked.

"It's worked so far," Osric said.

They moved through the archway into another hallway flanked by rooms, similar to the living area, except instead of side hallways and a series of small rooms, these led into long, wide chamber-like rooms.

They were also much more bare and practical than what they'd seen in the living area. Wooden workbenches lined the walls, their surfaces scarred and stained from centuries of use.

"A workshop," Talia said. "Like the keep but bigger. Look at all these tools."

Scattered across the surfaces were strange implements, delicate metal instruments, crystalline containers, and devices whose purpose Osric couldn't begin to guess. Everything was covered in a thick layer of dust.

"Lot of fancy equipment. Probably worth a fortune to the right buyer," Grace said.

"Don't touch anything," Rowan warned. "After what we've seen in these mountains, who knows what these tools were used for."

"Remember what the journal said. They were here before the mountains appeared. This predates the mountains," Talia said.

"And yet, something they did caused the veil to tear as badly as it did, and they had ways of working with the veil we'll never understand," Jasper said. "So maybe it's best to leave it alone."

They passed through an archway into a second workshop chamber. This one contained what appeared to be a forge, though unlike any Osric had seen during his apprenticeship. The hearth was small and precisely shaped, with channels carved into the stone.

"This is where they crafted their instruments," Talia said, examining the setup with clear fascination. "See how the workspace is arranged? Everything flows toward the forge. They were channeling power through their creations."

"Like the Blackstar?" Osric asked.

"I don't think so. This all seems too small compared to what you described. I'd guess it was for smaller works," Talia said.

She moved to a nearby shelf, where rows of tiny tools were arranged with mathematical precision.

"Look at this," Jasper called from across the room.

He stood before a series of diagrams on one of the benches. Together, they seemed to form some kind of complex geometric pattern.

Osric joined him, studying the diagrams by looking over his shoulder. "Can you read any of it?"

"Not exactly. But these patterns remind me of things I've seen before. Similar principles, at least."

"It makes sense. They wouldn't just start with giant magical constructs. They would have started with smaller things first," Rowan said.

"Can't control something if you don't know what makes it tick," Grace added.

Talia had moved to another workbench, this one covered in smaller instruments. She lifted something that resembled a tuning fork, though crafted from some dark metal Osric didn't recognize. The object seemed to absorb the light from her staff rather than reflect it.

"Jasper just said to be careful touching anything," Osric said.

"It's fine. This is a measurement tool, I think. For detecting magical resonance."

"How can you tell?" Grace asked.

"The shape, the material ... it's similar to instruments Elder Miriam showed me, though they weren't exactly like this. I wonder ..."

Before anyone could stop her, she gently tapped the fork against the edge of the workbench. A soft note rang out, barely audible but somehow reaching deep into Osric's bones. The sound seemed to ripple through the air.

For a moment, nothing else happened. Then, the fork began to vibrate, giving off a faint purple glow as the note grew slightly louder and more complex.

"Talia ..." Osric started, taking a step toward her.

The fork's vibration intensified. Tiny cracks appeared in its surface, spreading like frost across a window. The purple glow flickered, then faded as the ancient instrument suddenly crumbled into fine powder that slipped through Talia's fingers.

"Well," Grace said. "That was dramatic."

Talia stared at the dust coating her palm.

"It wasn't meant to last this long. Maybe the enchantments were too delicate and unbalanced after all these years," she said, brushing her hands clean. "At least we know their tools still hold power."

"And that we should probably avoid testing any more of them," Rowan added pointedly.

"Agreed," Jasper said. "Though this does confirm we're on the right track. The Calaphium clearly used this space to study and manipulate magical energies, which is essentially what it sounds like the Blackstar did."

Osric moved to the next archway, peering into yet another chamber beyond. "There's more. How many of these workshops did they need?"

"Knowledge requires experimentation," Talia said. "And experimentation requires space. Especially when you're dealing with forces that could tear reality apart if handled wrong."

"Comforting thought," Grace muttered.

Osric walked into the next chamber, which was much like the one they'd just left, except on one side of the wall was a series of metal stands that held twisted fragments of metal that might have once been something but now were unrecognizable. Talia touched one, her fingers tracing the strange patterns etched into its surface.

"The markings resemble those used in binding rituals, but are far more complex than anything I've seen before," Jasper said, looking them over.

"Binding what?" Grace asked.

"There's no way to know."

"But there's nothing here now," she pointed out.

"No. They could have disappeared, or perhaps just escaped their binding."

"I was afraid you were going to say that."

They walked around the room, looking at different parts on the work tables, broken pieces, and leftover experiments. None of it seemed familiar outside of the other runes from the time of the Calaphium they'd found. Remnants of a long-ago time whose use had long passed out of memory.

Not even Jasper or Talia could tell what most of this was used for.

In one corner, Osric found a metal box roughly the size of a travel chest. Heavy clasps, eaten through with rust, lined its edges. When he tried the lid, it creaked open with surprising ease.

"Found something?" Rowan asked, moving closer.

"Empty," Osric said, showing him the interior. Black marks scored the metal walls inside. "But something was in here at some point."

Talia joined them, running her fingers along the scorch marks.

"These are like the other markings. I think Jasper's right, they used some kind of binding, similar to what I draw for my alarm spell, but drawn in reality instead of with threads of the veil. Whatever was in here, they went to great lengths to keep it stable."

"Or to keep it from getting out," Rowan said.

Grace wandered past them to investigate a shelf lined with metal containers.

"More empty boxes. Lots of empty boxes," Grace said, investigating a shelf lined with metal containers before picking up a small cylinder, rattling it. "Though this one still has something inside it."

"Put it down," Jasper warned.

"It's sealed shut. But there's definitely something rattling around in there."

"Let's leave it that way," Osric said, taking it from her and putting it back in place.

They continued through the workshops, passing tables strewn with shattered glass and rusted implements. The remnants of countless experiments lay scattered about, perhaps failed attempts to understand the forces they sought to control.

"Look at this," Rowan called from the edge of the room.

He stood in a doorway leading to a chamber different from the others they'd been through. Instead of workbenches and tools, this room held rows of bookshelves surrounding a massive desk. Some of the books were pristine, as if they had just been put on the shelf, without a trace of dust, while others were half disintegrated, with the books in pristine condition transitioning into frayed and torn edges where the remainder of the book should be. In other spots, there were only metal clasps on a pile of dust and decayed leather.

"Finally," Grace said. "Something worth taking."

Jasper joined her, picking up one of the pristine books and flipping it open. "This is in High Calaphium, the same as the writing in the document.

"Even better. Rare books are valuable books."

"They're also dangerous," Jasper said. "The Calaphium weren't just recording history or poetry. Remember what people think of the Calaphium, what you thought before we started this journey. It might not do for you to be carrying around a book written by monsters that nearly caused the destruction of the world at the beginning of time.

Talia had already pulled a volume from the shelf. When she opened it, half the pages crumbled to powder. "The preservation spells are failing. Whatever magic kept these intact is breaking down."

"Good riddance," Rowan muttered.

"No, you don't understand." Talia carefully turned what remained of the pages. "This could be centuries of knowledge about the veil itself. About how magic really works."

"We might know from the Sage's history that they were trying to protect the veil and only controlled magic to keep it from tearing our reality apart, but we don't know the lessons they learned to be able to control it and get to this place. We also don't know exactly how they lost control of that power and how it almost destroyed the world," Jasper pointed out. "Better to leave it to history. Besides, it would take years to translate even one of these books."

"But think what we could learn ..." Talia started.

"He's right," Osric cut in. "We're here for the Blackstar. That's all."

Grace moved along the shelves, examining bindings, finally selecting a particularly well-preserved volume and slipping it into her pack.

"Grace." Osric fixed her with a stern look.

She shrugged. "What? Maybe it's a cookbook. Or poetry. Won't know until someone translates it. Besides, I was promised loot, and so far, all we've found is a bunch of dusty tools. I'm not a guardian of forbidden knowledge, that's your department. If I can sell this, I will."

Before Osric could argue, Grace pulled her bag back onto her back and walked out of the room, heading toward the next one. Osric sighed. She might be more than she let on, but the years of stealing to survive were still there, alive and well.

"Come on, we should stick together," Rowan said, following Grace out.

The rest followed them, although Jasper and Talia seemed particularly reluctant to leave behind the wealth of knowledge contained in those ancient tomes.

She had headed through the archway in the back of the hall that led to what seemed, to Osric, to be the furthest edge of the base of the tower. On the other side was a vast chamber that dwarfed anything they'd seen so far. At its center stood a massive furnace that was larger than any furnace Osric had ever heard of. It was as if they knew the small forges in the other workshops were inadequate, and built their exact opposite here.

He couldn't imagine what kinds of things such a massive furnace was required for.

"What is this place?" Talia asked.

Before anyone could answer, Cinder let out a low growl, staring at something beyond the furnace, deep in the shadows of the room, his hackles ruffled back.

A distinct warning.

Osric pulled his sword, an action copied by the rest preparing their weapons, as they stared into the dark, trying to see what the wolf saw.

The answer came in the form of heavy, metallic footsteps. Three hulking figures emerged from the darkness , each easily twice the size of a man. Their bodies were a complex network of gears, pistons, and metal plates, adorned with glowing symbols. Each had a strange face, as if the smoothest helm that had ever been made was attached where a head should be, with an eerie yellow glow coming from where there should have been eyes.

"What in the abyss is that?" Rowan said, pulling his bowstring back.

Not that there was time for an answer. The machines had clearly reacted to their presence, and were advancing menacingly enough that none of the group had to guess at their intentions.

Talia reacted first, her hands weaving through the air and snapping forward, sending a barrage of the small glowing diamonds of energy streaming toward the machines. Osric had seen her do this several times, usually with great effect, but this time was different. When the bolts reached one of the creatures, it lifted a hand that seemed to draw in and absorb the magical energies, causing them to come apart and vanish.

"What?" Talia gasped.

The automatons didn't let her attack even slow them down. Each had one arm that ended in what looked like some kind of precision tool rather than a weapon, although still sharp enough to be deadly, and the one that charged at Osric raised it above its head, bringing it down in an arc aimed at taking his head off. Osric brought his longsword up, barely able to parry the blow, the strength and weight of the machine felt like a mountain, the weight pressing down on him as he parried the blow.

The force of the impact sent shockwaves up Osric's arm, nearly numbing it. He gritted his teeth and pushed sideways, using the beast's own weight to send it staggering to one side, creating space between them. With a quick step and a twist of his body, Osric brought his sword around in a half circle, coming back across with a powerful slash aimed at the construct's midsection. His blade was on target, but instead of the satisfying bite of metal cleaving metal, Osric felt as if he'd struck a wall. The automaton staggered back slightly, but the damage was far less than it should have been.

Scratches in the metal, and that was it.

Talia, who'd scrambled back a few steps when they charged, was forced to dive out of the way as another of the automatons lifted its other hand, which was like a half of a hand but with a wide circular shape in the center of it, out of which came a line of deep blue energy, the color of a river during a bad storm. She managed to just avoid it, the line of energy striking a nearby table, reducing it to splinters.

In response, Rowan sent an arrow flying at the machine. As always, his aim was true, but the arrow only bounced harmlessly off its metal exterior.

The third construct advanced on Grace, who had drawn her short sword and was circling, trying to stay out of its grip. Cinder leaped at the automaton as it reached for her, his jaws clamped down on its arm, but the wolf's teeth couldn't penetrate it. With a casual swipe, the automaton sent Cinder flying across the room, smashing into a far wall with a yelp, and then crumpling to the floor.

"Cinder!" Osric shouted, starting toward the fallen animal when the machine next to him took another swipe, sending him scrambling back for safety.

The machine continued to press, pushing him away from his friends, circling around as he parried and dodged, until his back was almost to the dormant furnace. His sword connected again and again, but each blow seemed to do less damage than the last.

Talia, after diving for cover, scrambled back to her feet and quickly began to weave another spell. This time, a green triangle, dripping and sickly looking, shot out of her hands toward the creature coming at her.

Once again, the creature waved it away, dissipating it before it could make contact.

"It's no use!" Talia cried, ducking behind a workbench as another blast sailed over her head. "They're disrupting my magic somehow!"

"Try something else, something less direct," Osric yelled, parrying another blow.

Grace, almost caught between two of the hulks, rolled between them to avoid being surrounded. As she came up, her short sword flashed, seeking the joints and seams in one of the metal bodies. She managed to briefly wedge her blade into a gap, eliciting a shower of sparks, which caused the beast to stagger slightly.

Their first sign of success.

Rowan, backed almost out of the doorway, must have seen her success, because his next arrows flew toward the shoulder of one of the automatons. Two bounced harmlessly off its metal shell, but the third lodged in the joint as the creature was lifting its arm, causing something to start leaking out of it.

"The joints!" Rowan called out. "Aim for the gaps in their armor!"

Osric, who'd been facing them and had seen both successes, feinted low, then brought his sword up in a swift arc, targeting the area where the automaton's arm connected to its body. The blade bit deeper this time, and a spray of sparks rewarded his effort.

Still, they were small victories, and the automatons continued to press their attacks. One pinned down the still-whimpering Cinder, while another drove Osric further back, keeping him from helping his friend, and the third was pushing Talia back, further and further into the corner.

She raised her hands, weaving until a translucent shimmering light blue circle flickered into existence before her, but the automaton's fist smashed through it as if it were made of spun sugar.

"Talia!" Grace shouted, pulling a dagger from her side and hurling it toward the automaton threatening her friend.

The blade spun through the air and struck the neck of the construct, causing it to take a step back, swinging erratically, clearly affected by the strike.

Their victories, however, were being outdone by their losses as the automaton turned and charged at her. She started to scramble away, but was too slow. Rowan tried to interpose himself between the two, but the monster slammed a heavy arm into the Ranger's chest with bone-crushing force, sending him sailing across the room, his bow sliding across the floor away from him.

Jasper ran toward the ranger, sliding to his knees next to him, praying fervently to the gods for aid.

Osric, seeing Cinder still pinned and struggling, made a desperate move. He dove around his opponent, using its slower turning speed to his advantage, and crashed into the one holding Cinder down. It felt like smashing into a wall, but it was enough, causing the automaton to stumble back, freeing the wolf.

"Cinder, go!" Osric commanded, scrambling to regain his footing.

Talia waved her hands, bringing them down in the direction of the automaton that had just hit Rowan, as if she was setting something invisible on it. As she did, a sphere of pure blackness engulfed its head, causing it to stop its charge as its vision was obscured.

To Talia's dismay, the automaton swiped a hand at the darkness surrounding it, causing it to begin to dissipate, as if being eaten away.

Osric was distracted for a second, watching Talia's spell fail, and had lost track of the hulk he'd escaped until his manipulator arm clapped down on his shoulder from behind. The pressure was immense, crushing his gauntlet and forcing him to drop his weapon with a cry of pain.

He struggled against the iron grip, but it was like trying to bend a mountain with his bare hands. Panic began to set in as he realized how helpless he was.

Grace must have seen the trouble he was in. She was moving to get behind the automaton that had been shrouded in darkness, the one that had charged at her, when she changed her trajectory as Osric was grabbed. She jumped up on a workbench in the corner, kicked off a wall and landed on the back of the creature that was holding him.

Pulling out two more daggers, she began stabbing at the exposed point in its neck, where its metal plating opened up, showing its inner workings. Again and again she brought the daggers slashing down, ripping into the monster, sending sparks and strange liquid flying.

The automaton released Osric as it began flailing around wildly, allowing Osric to wrench himself free and stumble away. His arm throbbed, and he knew without looking that it was badly bruised, if not broken.

From across the room, Jasper pointed at Osric and called down Heathus to protect him. A moment later, a shimmering aura enveloped Osric, almost as if he had additional armor protecting him.

With the beast distracted and out of control, Osric slashed at the back of its knee where the armor plate opened. The creature, still being cut apart by Grace, began to stagger, going down to one knee as its leg gave way.

Talia was rescued from the attack of the automaton that burst through her shield as Rowan, who was now back on his feet, put two arrows into the back of its neck, both sinking deep and forcing it to take a step back, looking around for what caused it damage.

She took that chance to run out of the way while waving her hands. Instead of some big display of magic, however, this time, pieces from the ground, chunks of ceiling and concrete, partially decayed tools, and parts of the destroyed bench began flying at the creature, smashing into the joints of the monster wherever they were open like a tidal wave of clutter.

Each piece alone might not have been enough to cause any real problems, but the sheer volume caused more and more of the pieces to lodge in its joints, getting stuck in gears and cogs, causing them to lock up and slowing its movements to almost a crawl.

The automaton that had been crushing Cinder raised a hand and fired one of the beams of light at Grace, catching her in the side and sending her sailing off, crashing into a pile of discarded equipment.

They needed to end this. Osric charged in with a roar, his sword in front of him, stabbing it as hard as he could, driving up through a gap in the automaton's chest plates and piercing deep into its core mechanisms. For a moment, the construct stood motionless. Then, with a whine from its failing systems, it collapsed to the ground, inert and lifeless.

Jasper, on the way to check on Grace, whispered a prayer over his mace, causing the weapon to glow with a yellow light as he brought it into the center of another of the automaton's chests, hitting the glowing, pulsing symbol. As soon as the blessed mace connected, there was a bright flash of blinding light that caused a wave of blue energy to crackle over the body of the beast. As the energy cascaded over it, its limbs locked in a form of rigor, and then it toppled over.

Jasper barely paused as the automaton fell, leaping over it and running to check on Grace.

The final automaton was struggling from the damage already done to it, standing almost still, making it a perfect target as Rowan sent another arrow directly into the eye slit, causing a similar cascade of energy before it joined its fellows on the floor.

The battle had been so fast, and they'd been off balance the whole time, that all of them looked almost stunned when it was over. For a moment, no one moved, as if afraid that any action might bring the automatons back to life. Then, with a collective exhale, the tension broke.

Jasper immediately moved to tend to the wounded. He knelt beside Cinder, channeling healing energy into the injured wolf. Osric limped over, cradling his injured arm, relief washing over him as he saw Cinder's tail begin to wag weakly.

"He'll be alright," Jasper assured him, before turning his attention to Osric's arm.

The warm glow of divine magic soothed the pain, knitting together bruised flesh and mending hairline fractures in the bone.

"What were these things?" Talia asked, nudging one of the beasts as Jasper moved on to help Grace.

"Guards?" Osric suggested.

"More likely they were to help with the projects here," Jasper offered while he knelt next to Grace. "Look at their hands. I think they were some kind of construct to do dangerous work on magical tools."

"This thing is much larger than the others we've seen here," Osric said, pointing at the furnace. "Could this be where the Blackstar was made?"

"It's possible," Jasper said. "But it's been dormant for a long time. I'm not sure anything's left if it was."

"It's still worth checking," he said, helping Grace up off the ground.

For the next twenty minutes, they checked every inch of the room. Osric mostly focused on the forge, which was not so different from the one in Master Ironhand's smithy, except for its size and some strange channels built into the side.

It was interesting, but ultimately told them nothing about the creation of the Blackstar, or even if it had been made there. Likewise, nothing else in the room revealed much that gave them useful information.

The only ones who seemed to be learning anything were Jasper and Talia, who went over every inch of the automatons.

"Anything?" Osric asked.

"Something, perhaps. The way it seemed to dissipate magical energy sounds a lot like how you described the Blackstar. I think they might operate on the same principle."

"Okay, but can you figure out how they did it? Maybe how to build something similar if we don't find the Blackstar?"

"No," Talia said. "It's going to take a lot of study, and even then, that might be beyond us."

"Still," Jasper said with a grunt, managing to wedge the manipulator hand off the creature. "I'm taking this with us. I'll keep working on it and see what I can find."

"Okay," Osric said. "Then let's get going. Although, we should keep an eye out. No telling what other kinds of things they left turned on when they all disappeared."

A Caged Rift

After looking over the automatons one last time, Osric led the way as the group retraced their steps to the central chamber and the large spiral staircase. For a moment, they all just paused there. Osric didn't know about the rest of them, but after the things in the workshop area, he wasn't sure he wanted to know what was up these stairs.

Especially since it had taken the lives of so many trained knights, at least according to the old man.

"Well, no time like the present," Grace quipped, although Osric could hear the nervousness she was trying to hide.

With one last look at each other, Osric led the way, his sword out in his hand. They ascended cautiously, ready for anything to suddenly jump out at them. They reached a level where the landing extended outward, with a damaged door partially opened leading to whatever was on this floor. Rowan put a hand on Osric's shoulder and held up his other hand, stopping them.

"Look," he said, pointing to faint smears on the floor. "Blood trails. Dried but probably only a week or so old."

"Of course it leads in there," Grace said, gesturing toward the partially open door.

Osric nodded grimly. "Stay ready."

As soon as they pushed open the door, Osric lifted his sword as if to strike, then froze in place. There were maybe a dozen furry-looking beetle things about half the size of Cinder scattered around the room. They were mostly lying on their backs or split open, showing a greenish dried ickiness around the openings that might have once been some type of blood. Whatever it was, they were clearly dead. As were the two knights that lay sprawled in the center of the room, their armor rent and bloodied.

"By the gods," Jasper breathed, his face pale. "What are those things?"

"I've never seen anything like it," Rowan said, nudging one of the beetle bodies. "There must have been a lot more of these things, if they managed to kill these guys."

"Well, there were some that didn't get killed, I think," Grace said, wrinkling her nose and pointing to one of the bodies. "This one's been nibbled on. Something's been having a snack."

"You don't think there could be … creatures in here with us?" Jasper asked.

"We should remain vigilant," Osric warned.

The cleric nodded and moved closer to examine the wounds on the knights' bodies. His expression grew troubled as he studied the injuries.

"That one was mauled pretty badly, but this one. These wounds … they're superficial and I don't see anywhere that they got through his armor."

"What are you saying?" Talia asked.

Jasper straightened, his face grim. "I believe they may have succumbed to some form of poison or venom."

Osric felt a little sick at that thought, but kept himself focused. He'd noticed something on one of the men's armor and bent closer to look at it. His fingers brushed against the insignia stamped into the armor.

"What's this?"

"A commander's insignia," Rowan said. "I've seen this in Wolfridge. These weren't just any knights. They were Baron Blackthorn's personal guard. These were his very best knights."

"Look at this," Grace said.

The room wasn't terribly large and wrapped around the stairwell partway before ending in a curved wall with a half-broken-down door in the center of it that she was pointing at.

Osric walked over to see what it was she pointed at and picked up a broken longsword and a dagger, both dropped near the door, far away from the dead knights, who still had weapons on them.

"Whoever owned those went through there, I think," Talia said.

"Probably," Osric replied, and pushed on the door, which swung open loosely on its last remaining hinge.

Behind the partially destroyed door, they discovered three more knights and another dozen of the furry beetle creatures. These had clearly died fighting, their weapons still clutched in lifeless hands. Nearby, the shards of a broken vessel lay scattered across the floor. It had been large, although not so large that it would have held all these beetles.

At least, not without magic, Osric thought.

Other than their bodies, the men provided no further clues than the ones in the front room had. Dead men who'd tried, and failed, to defend themselves.

They pushed deeper into this level, which looked to have been used for more research, with workbenches much like the ones they'd seen down below. It wrapped all the way around the stairwell, one lab space after another, until they reached a final chamber. The door had been wedged shut well on this one, although holes along the bottom suggested whoever closed it didn't keep the beetles out.

"Should I?" Osric asked, looking at his friends, then the door.

"If there are more of these things in there, they can come out through the holes, and I'd prefer not to leave them behind us," Rowan said.

Osric couldn't find any flaw in that reasoning and everyone else seemed to agree, so with two solid kicks, he broke the door open, sending it flying back on now-broken hinges.

There weren't any beetles in there. At least not any live ones. What was in here must have been some kind of last stand. Furniture had been piled against the door in a futile attempt at a barricade. Four more knights lay dead, their bodies positioned back-to-back.

Rowan crouched beside them, looking over their scarred bodies.

"These bite marks are bigger than those things' mandibles and look to have had rows of teeth. Whatever ate on these guys, it wasn't the beetles."

Before anyone could respond, a skittering sound came from the floor above. The group froze, eyes darting to the ceiling.

"What was that?" Grace hissed.

Osric raised his sword, "I don't know, but I don't want to get trapped back here like these guys. We need to keep moving. Up to the next level."

Their nervousness was a little premature.

As they climbed past what Osric was pretty sure was the twentieth floor, it felt like his chest and legs were on fire. While he was happy to have his breastplate and heavy sword for protection, he was starting to consider whether he needed either as he lugged them up another set of steps.

His companions, especially Jasper, seemed to be doing no better, gasping and struggling as they continued upward. Floor after floor, they hadn't found any sign of more dead knights or beetles or whatever had made that clicking sound they heard earlier. It was mostly just room after room of what must have been more workshops or research areas, although half didn't have remnants of that any longer. It seemed the higher they went, the less and less objects retained the magic that kept them from decaying. The last ten floors were completely bare.

"Let's take a break," Rowan asked, looking at Jasper who nodded weakly, leaning against the wall.

"What's wrong, old man?" Grace said, walking past him. "Need a walking stick?"

Her anger from that morning was all but gone, distracted by everything they'd seen in the tower, and her words had no heat to them.

"Not here," Osric said, taking Jasper's arm to bear some of his weight. "We're too exposed. Let's get to the next level first."

The stairwell opened onto another floor, stone walls, high ceilings, and that was it aside from broken glass and a few pieces of metal.

"More of the same," Grace muttered, kicking a twisted piece of metal.

"Something must be up here though, to strip the magic from these things. Downstairs, nearly every room had something in it," Talia said. "It's like …"

Whatever else she was going to say was cut off by a sharp, crackling sound, as if lightning had just struck the tower.

"What was that?" Osric asked, looking around, trying to place where the noise originated.

"It's fine outside," Grace said, looking out a small window.

"I think it's coming from above us," Rowan pointed to the ceiling.

Everyone looked up just as the air cracked again. If he hadn't been standing next to Grace by the window, he would have thought the whole building had been struck by lightning, as loud as the crack had sounded. The air felt charged, the hairs on his arm standing on end.

"We're going to have to check on that, aren't we?" Grace asked.

"Yeah," Osric said. "We don't know what's up there, and it doesn't sound good. If it's building to something …"

As if to punctuate what Osric was saying, a third crack of electricity sounded, if anything, louder than the first two.

Everyone pulled their weapons and got their game faces on as they went back to the center of the tower and up the stairs, the sound of electricity crackling getting louder as they walked. Strands of Talia's hair even began to lift up, an invisible hand pulling her red curls slightly up off her shoulders.

Arriving at the next level, Osric reached out to open the door, his hand pausing as strings of blue energy reached out, like the door itself was trying to connect to him.

He looked back at Jasper, who gave a nod.

Osric took a second before reaching the rest of the way. Thankfully, nothing shocked him as he pushed down on the handle and pushed the door open.

What lay beyond stole his breath. Unlike most of the rooms they'd looked into since starting up the stairs, this one was not empty. It also wasn't full of equipment or workbenches either.

In the center of the room was a large tear in the Veil.

Unlike the other tears they'd seen, this one didn't hang by itself. It was suspended in a massive metal sphere that looked like a grate with gaps between each strip of metal, allowing them to see exactly what was in it.

Atop the grated, metal sphere was a huge, winged creature the likes of which Osric had never seen. It resembled a monstrous manta ray with a wingspan twice Osric's height. Slate-blue hide covered its body, marked with patterns that pulsed with the same unnatural light as the rift. It had eyes on almost triangular extensions coming out the sides of its wide head. The weirdest part, however, was a sucker-like mouth in the center of its belly surrounded by whip-like appendages, the ends of which were wrapped through the grated metal, holding the creature in place.

Its mouth was pressed against the grate, pulling strings from the edges of the Veil to it, like it was sucking it in.

A waft of air from a massive hole in the tower wall carried a scent not unlike that just before a heavy rain.

On the floor around the sphere, being ignored by the winged creature, were six of the fury beetle-like creatures they'd seen with the bodies of the knights, although somehow more disturbing as they shifted through the droppings left by the flying creature.

Osric didn't know if he made a sound, or if they just realized the door had opened, but suddenly the beetles all lifted their bulbous heads toward him, staring at them.

For a moment, everyone was frozen in place, just staring, and then one of the beetles opened its mandibles wide and let out a horrible screeching sound.

As if it were a sign, the flying creature detached from the globe, tentacles withdrawing as it twisted to face the intruders, flapping its massive wings to hang in place.

And then all hell broke loose.

Osric did not hesitate, charging toward the nearest beetle, his blade held high. The creature reared up on its hind legs as he approached, letting out a chittering, screeching sound. Osric brought his sword down hard, striking against the edge of its shell. He put every ounce of strength into the blow, but did not pierce its hard outer layer. The best he had managed was a spiderweb of thin cracks beneath the hair protruding between the plates.

In return, his arm almost felt numb from the force of the impact.

Rowan tried and fared no better, sending three arrows in rapid succession into another one of the beetles. Each bounced off, just as Osric's sword had, barely disturbing the rust-colored fur.

"The shells are too tough!" Rowan called out, already nocking another arrow.

Jasper raised his mace, his lips moving in prayer to Heathus, then he froze, his face falling in surprise.

"Something's wrong," he called out. "Heathus blesses me, but her energies slip through my fingers like water!"

Next to him, Talia had a similar expression. She had been weaving her hands in a now familiar pattern, sending three diamonds of energy streaking toward one of the beetles just as Rowan released his arrows.

But her magic, too, had failed.

Before the projectiles could strike the creature, they turned like iron drawn toward a lodestone, curving into the mouth-like protrusion on the belly of the wyrm-like creature. Instead of puncturing or harming it, however, the creature seemed to absorb the shards. Feeding off of them.

"It absorbs the …" she began to say when one of the beetles rushed at her, causing her to stumble backward.

Just before it reached her, a gray blur flashed past, smashing into the beast. Cinder's jaws clamped onto one of its rear legs, wrenching the creature sideways, causing it to topple over, its spindly legs thrashing in the air. Cinder lunged in again, ripping the leg clean off. The creature thrashed wildly, green-black ichor spraying across the floor. It snapped at him but was unable to right itself, and the wolf was able to dart away from the smashing jaws.

The beetle Osric had struck launched at him, snapping at his extended sword arm. He sidestepped, but the creature moved faster than its bulky frame suggested was possible. It clamped a mandible around his forearm, the serrated edges piercing through his leather bracer and into the flesh beneath it.

The entire limb burned with a hot, searing pain. He gritted his teeth, refusing to cry out as the creature's grip tightened, threatening to crush the bone. He tried to wrench free, but the beetle held fast.

"Osric!" Talia screamed.

She weaved her hands and then thrust them forward, palms out. Maybe the wyrm was still digesting the shards from her prior attempt, or maybe it couldn't eat fire, but this time, the magic worked.

A cone of searing flame erupted from her fingertips, washing over two beetles in its path. The rust-colored fur covering their carapaces caught fire immediately, the creatures emitting high-pitched screeches as they thrashed in agony.

The distraction gave Osric the moment he needed. He twisted his body with all his might, feeling skin tear as he wrenched his arm from the beetle's grasp. Blood flowed freely down his forearm, but at least he was free.

The beetles were all charging now that the initial surprise had worn off. One ran straight at Rowan, but the agile ranger dropped to the floor as it leaped at him, rolling beneath it. As it started to land, its front half pointing to the ground while its rear trailed behind, still in the air, he came up on one knee with his bow in hand, an arrow already nocked. He released the arrow, sending it sinking into the beetle's soft, unprotected underbelly at nearly point-blank range.

The beetle twisted as it hit the floor, landing on its side, its legs buckling as ichor leaked from the wound.

Grace was less lucky. She had just leaped at one of the beetles, her daggers extended, apparently prepared to sink them into the creatures' clustered eyes, when the wyrm's tail lashed out, whipping across her back and sending her smashing into the stone floor.

The impact was hard enough that her daggers flew out of her hands, skittering away, with one sliding dangerously close to the edge of a massive hole in the outer wall.

Jasper made to move toward her, but a beetle intercepted him. Before he could bring his mace to bear, the creature's mandibles clamped onto his arm. The cleric cried out, his mace clattering to the floor. He managed to pull himself free, but his face was filled with horror as his arm still hung numb at his side, fingers barely moving.

"They have some kind of paralytic!" he warned, grabbing the dangling limb.

Osric had been bitten, too, but felt nothing like that even as blood continued to flow from the wound on his arm. Not that there was time to consider it for more than a moment, as the beetle he had shaken loose from was coming for him again. He struck his

126

sword at the creature again, aiming for the same spot he had hit earlier, which was visibly cracked. With both hands gripping the hilt of his sword, he drove it downward, putting all of his strength and weight behind the blow.

This time, the blade did pierce the creature, separating the cracks in the shell and driving through its carapace and into its body, pinning it in place. Its legs scrabbled frantically for a moment before it stiffened and stopped moving.

Osric yanked his sword free and turned to find which of his friends needed help.

They all did.

The large wyrm had tucked its wings and was plummeting toward Talia, tentacles extended like grotesque fingers.

"Talia! Move!" Osric shouted.

The warning came too late. Rowan tried to help, releasing a trio of arrows in rapid succession. Two managed to pierce the thinner membrane at the edges of its wings, seemingly causing the beast no problem. The third hit closer to its body, but simply bounced off its slate-blue hide, barely marking it.

On the other side of the room, Grace was also in danger as she pushed herself across the floor, barely managing to grab one of her two dropped daggers, to avoid another beetle's jaws from snapping across her midsection.

Thankfully, Cinder saw her and dropped the beetle he had just killed. Racing across the chamber, he slammed into the side of the beetle pursuing her, his weight sufficient to knock the creature off its intended path, although not enough to turn it over.

Seeing that she was okay, Osric continued toward Talia, but his distraction at checking on Grace had slowed him. The wyrm's tentacles had wrapped themselves around Talia's waist and arm and were lifting her off the floor. As they did, a white light extended from its open mouth to her as the tentacles pulled her toward it. Instead of fighting, though, she screamed and then went almost limp, only able to struggle weakly as it seemed to draw the very essence from her.

Osric reached her just as the tentacles pulled her to the creature's mouth, his sword slashed out and severing the appendage that was wrapped around her midsection. It emitted a high-pitched screech that shook dust from the ceiling but did not drop her entirely. Instead, she hung from her arm held by the remaining tentacles, like some kind of marionette with some of its strings missing.

Two arrows flashed past Osric and into another of the tentacles. It was still moving, but the pain seemed to be enough that it released her. As soon as it let go, Talia dropped toward the floor like a sack of old grain.

Osric lunged forward, but he was too far away to catch her. She struck the floor with a sickening thud, her body rolling limply before coming to rest near a fallen pillar. Her eyes fluttered open briefly, consciousness returning in fragments, but she remained too weak to stand.

Cinder beat him to her, positioned himself protectively over her, snapping at the wyrm every time it flew too close.

The wyrm screeched again, this time in pain and rage. Its remaining tentacles lashed out in all directions as it flew around the room in a blind rage. One of the tentacles caught Rowan across the chest as it flew by, throwing him backward into the wall with a bone-jarring force. His bow clattered to the ground, sliding away across the stone floor.

Jasper was only a few steps away, barely holding his body up, the paralysis seeming to affect every part of him. His face contorted with effort as he fought to remain conscious, his left hand fumbling with the pouch on his belt.

A beetle was coming for him, maybe hoping to finish off its prey, but Grace had seen that he was in trouble and was on her feet now. Unfortunately, she was still not on her own. A beetle launched for her: she vaulted over it, twisting in midair to drive her dagger down between its mandibles. The blade sank to the hilt, finding the vulnerable connection between the head and the thorax, causing it to convulse violently before collapsing.

Her victory was short-lived. The second beetle caught her leg as she landed, mandibles piercing through her pant leg. She cried out as the paralytic venom entered her bloodstream, collapsing as her legs suddenly stopped working.

"Grace!" Jasper called out.

In spite of his own paralysis, he began crawling toward her, dragging his unresponsive right side across the floor through sheer force of will.

Grace saw a beetle coming toward the two of them and reached out, grabbing one of Rowan's deflected arrows, and prepared to use it against the beetle that seemed to want to finish its meal. Just as it was coming in to bite her, she drove the steel point of the arrow into its exposed face, just above its snapping pincers. The creature shuttered once and then collapsed.

Grace, her last gasp used in her desperate defense, joined it, going limp, lying flat against the floor.

The wyrm was still flailing about the room, smashing into the metal cage that encircled the rift hard enough to send shards of it flying across the room like razor-sharp missiles. Osric raised his arm to shield his face, feeling several cuts open across his exposed skin. His breastplate prevented worse damage, but blood still trickled from a dozen minor wounds.

Jasper had managed to reach Grace. Struggling, he pulled some kind of leaf from the pouch at his belt and shakily opened her mouth, pushing it onto her tongue.

"Chew," he ordered weakly, pushing her jaw closed.

She was still conscious enough to give a few weak grinds of her teeth. Osric hoped Jasper knew what he was doing because they both looked very bad.

The wyrm seemed drawn to Talia, continually swooping back toward her. It was obsessed with her, and it took everything Osric and Cinder could do to keep it back. If anything, this thing's hide was tougher than the beetles. Even with his hardest slashes, he barely managed to cause small cuts.

Unless they figured out something different, killing this thing was going to be impossible.

Thankfully, Talia began to stir, regaining consciousness. For a moment, Osric thought she was going to join the fight, hopefully figuring out something clever that would end it. Instead, she looked in the direction of the rift and froze.

She wasn't paralyzed. He could see her eyes blinking and fingers moving occasionally, but she just sat there, staring into the void.

At least Grace and Jasper were doing better. Grace stumbled to her feet, picking up one of her daggers, and limped over, half dragging Jasper, until the group, save Rowan, were all together again, trying to protect Talia from the flying menace.

The last beetle chased them, but Jasper, finding some inner strength and his retrieved mace, swung with all of his might, connecting solidly with the beetle's head. The creature staggered sideways, momentarily stunned by the impact.

It started to come for them again when Rowan suddenly leaped on its back, his body weight pushing it to the floor.

"Grace! Now!"

Grace pivoted on her good leg and drove her dagger deep into the beetle's eye cluster. The creature convulsed once before going still.

That left them only the flying wyrm to deal with. Osric attacked it head-on, drawing its attention with aggressive sword strikes that forced it to defend rather than attack.

"Keep it busy!" Talia said, finally seeming to break from her trance.

They all did their best, although it wasn't easy. The hits they scored against it, seemingly did no damage, its tentacles still whipped around as it dove past them over and over, pummeling them and occasionally sending one of them flying across the room after a solid hit.

They continued to fight it, in spite of the futility, to buy Talia the time to do whatever she'd figured out.

She dragged herself closer to the rift until she was against the metal sphere encasing it. Closing her eyes, she pushed herself up and concentrated, her hands moving in a complex pattern, fingers tracing sigils in the air.

"Whatever you're doing, Talia, do it faster!" Grace called out, ducking beneath a sweeping tentacle.

Talia ignored the distraction, focusing entirely on her task. Wisps of energy began to coalesce around her, coming from both the room around them and directly out of the rift. Osric wasn't sure, but it seemed as if the color of the tendrils of energy were somehow different, although the shifting colors made it hard for him to say exactly how he knew that.

When the wisps of energy got too close, they almost recoiled from each other. It was as if they were alive, fighting against one another as they gathered around her.

The wyrm suddenly stopped its chaotic flying and again attached itself to the sphere. Instead of going back to feeding off the rift inside, however, it was very clearly looking at Talia, seemingly fascinated. After a moment, it released its hold and flew upward, shrieking once before sweeping down toward her and the ball of competing energies that had formed around her.

"Talia!" Osric shouted in warning as the wyrm dodged his swing, completely focused on her.

She didn't move or flinch. The wyrm shrugged off anything they tried to do to stop it, its tentacles extending greedily toward the swirling vortex around her.

When it made contact, the effect was immediate and dramatic. The wyrm's body expanded as it began to draw the energies around her into its open maw. To Osric's eyes, it seemed as if its near indestructible hide began to stretch, with glowing cracks breaking out across its hide. As if it couldn't contain the energy it was absorbing.

The creature's body convulsed violently, its wings beating erratically as it tried to stabilize itself in the air. The cracks appeared to widen, leaking a luminous blue fluid that evaporated upon contact with the air.

It emitted a screech, so piercing that everyone clutched their ears in pain, and began to thrash wildly. Then suddenly, it exploded in a silent burst of light, releasing waves of stored magical and life energy. The wave threw all of them except Talia across the room before suddenly reversing itself and being sucked back toward the metal sphere and the rift inside.

As the energy made contact with the rift, the air split with a deafening crack and the tear snapped closed with a violent force, the edges sealing together as if they had never been separated.

For several moments, no one said anything, all too dazed by what had just happened. The remains of the beetles lay scattered across the floor, but the wyrm was completely gone, apparently completely absorbed into the rift before it closed.

"What did you do?" Osric finally managed to ask.

"I could see into the rift. The other side was … totally different than here. It was like a place completely on fire, rocks melting and reforming constantly. I think this was the rift the Calaphium was worried about. Not just an opening in the Veil, but an opening between two realities, where they melted into each other. The forces in between were so powerful I could see the energy fighting. I thought, if that creature absorbed Veil energy, then if I got it to absorb both, then the conflicting energies would not be able to exist together. The Sages' documents said that if the Veil fell and the worlds collided, they would not be able to coexist. Apparently that was also true for energies inside the creature."

"That's genius," Jasper said.

Osric couldn't disagree. It was incredibly clever, although it occurred to him that if the Calaphium thought it could destroy the world, then she had just taken a big risk, if the effect had been bigger than just what was around the creature.

Not that he was going to say that to her. She'd just saved all of them and had earned her moment.

What mattered was that they were alive. Battered, wounded, and exhausted, but alive.

The Blackstar Room

They took several minutes to collect themselves. It was a shock that no one had died, considering, especially Jasper and Grace. The herbs Jasper had given them had neutralized whatever toxin those beetles had injected in them, but both were still weak. If they had to face more creatures, neither would be at their full ability.

Not that any of them wanted to quit.

They were close to the top now, and their goal, and they had come too far to give up. Jasper said it would take time, and more of the herbs, properly brewed this time, to rid themselves of the toxin. That meant staying in this place a little longer, and who knew what else was lurking around that might come for them?

So Osric and Rowan half carried their two injured friends as they went up the last flight of stairs. At the top, the thick door that had sealed off the room there was shattered.

Not just shattered, hacked apart by axe and sword. Someone had wanted to get into this room very badly.

The chamber beyond stretched across the entire top floor of the tower. The floor had a complex pattern of inlaid metal and stone, forming concentric circles around a central platform that sat empty, and massive windows, that surprisingly still had their glass in them, lined the circular wall, making the room bright and well-lit. Osric could see some of the flying creatures that they'd spotted from further away, before coming into the valley, but it seemed as if they were flying away from this place.

As if whatever drew them here was gone.

None of that, however, was as notable as the one thing that really shouldn't have been there. A body slumped against the far side of the wall. Not one of the knights like they'd seen in the lower levels. This man wore some kind of robe, although a style Osric had never seen before.

And he was breathing, although barely.

He had a dark tear down the front of his robes, and a dark stain was spreading across it.

"He's wounded," Talia said, pushing past Osric.

"By who?" Osric asked, following behind her.

Osric knew a sword wound when he saw one, and this one was clearly fresh. The blood was wet and still spreading. If a creature had gotten him, that would be one thing, and there was no sign of anyone having been there since the baron and his knights, who the old man had said left a week ago.

"This had to have happened within the last few minutes, while we were downstairs," Jasper said, echoing Osric's thoughts as he examined him.

The old man's eyes flickered open as Jasper checked him. When he spoke, it wasn't in the common tongue but a language Osric had never heard before. A harsh, guttural language.

"What language is that?" Rowan asked.

Jasper had gone stock still as the man spoke, his mouth hanging open.

"I would say it sounds like High Calaphium, but ... that's impossible."

"Then it's untranslatable," Talia said, who was already starting to weave what Osric thought was the spell that let her understand creatures and people. "You said those texts we found ..."

"No," Jasper interrupted. "Only that their written language is confusing. The spoken tongue is different, closer to low Calaphium."

Talia frowned, then turned back to the elderly man before her hands resumed their weaving.

When she finished, she asked, "Can you understand me?"

"You came. The Elders sent you," he said, his voice full of relief. "I feared no one would answer my call."

Confusion passed over Talia's face. "No one sent us. We're looking for the Blackstar."

"Then how ... how were you trained to use magic without damaging the Veil?"

Jasper was ignoring them, still focused on the man's injury. Putting his hand on the man, he began to whisper a prayer, asking for the gods' blessing to heal him. The familiar warm glow appeared briefly around his fingers, then guttered out like a candle in a draft.

Jasper sat back, startled. "The wound rejects divine healing."

"Let me try," Osric said, kneeling beside the injured man.

He placed his hands near the wound, willing the strange power granted to him by the Veilguard, waiting for the glow under his hands and the surge of energies that came with it.

Nothing happened.

"I am beyond the help of gods. I used rift energy to keep the wound closed and to sustain me; it won't let their powers work here."

"Rift energy?" Jasper asked. "That shouldn't be possible."

"The nexus," the man gestured weakly toward the floor beneath them. "The caged rift that powered this tower. I protected it during the event. Used it to protect this tower and prevent this wound from killing me. Not much time left now, though."

"Is that how you stayed alive for so long?"

"Not that long. A few weeks is all. Any longer would have caused serious harm. I only used it to seal the tower from those creatures that appeared outside and protect the Blackstar while we attempted to repair the damage done to the Veil."

"Yes, the Blackstar. That's why we're here."

"Yes. It's as I said in my message. The Blackstar is shattered. I managed to keep one piece here, but the others went through the Veil during the rupture. I attempted to contact the other towers, but got no response from any of them. Nor from the men that followed Jaona into the forest."

"The forest? You mean Avendell? That's where we came from."

"Then ... you got my message. I sent my ring along with the details of what I thought was happening, to prove it was real. I had hoped Jaona would put aside his anger long enough to help, for the good of the whole world. You're from there and not the Citadel?"

"This ring?" Osric asked, holding up the treasure he'd still carried around his neck.

The man sagged in relief.

"Then my message got through. I knew Jaona wouldn't let petty infighting keep him from his duty. Do you have contact with the Citadel or anyone in Calaphium? We don't have much time. There's a rift over the Great Citadel. I've been trying to close it from here, but with the Blackstar broken and the portals shut, I can't draw the necessary power."

"What year do you think it is?" Jasper asked.

"We have ... what?"

"The year? What year is it?"

"Eighteen seventy-six."

"What?" Grace blurted out. "He's addled. Thinks he's been here for five hundred years?"

"I think he's been here longer than that," Jasper said, his voice grave. "Much longer. We use the Aelorian calendar, which dates from the first king of Alor. I believe he thinks it's eighteen seventy-six on the Calaphium calendar, which was three thousand years ago. Coincidentally, the same year their empire fell."

"What are you saying?" The man asked.

"That you've been here for millennia. It must be some kind of distortion in time, if you think it's only been weeks. Something about the Veil energies you were drawing from the nexus thing, along with the tears in the Veil around you. You've been using that energy to more than just sustain your body."

"I don't ... it could ... if the frequency was high enough," the man started saying his eyes moving quickly from side to side, the words becoming almost gibberish.

"He's lost his mind," Grace said.

"Or the tears in the Veil took it from him," Talia suggested.

"We must focus," the man said, waving them off. "If Jaona sent you, then we might yet have time. You must understand, if the Wardens obtain the Blackstar pieces, they could cause the Veil to fail entirely."

"Who are the Wardens?" Talia asked.

"The ones I've been warning about. The people the Elders kept telling me were a figment of my imagination, but I know they are behind this. Several came through the portal before we shut the portals down, trying to get to the Blackstar. They want to tear down the protections for the Veil to bring magic to everyone in Peridia. The fools would end the world thinking they are saving it. They are naive, but they have support my colleagues and I never could find. I knew they were looking for the Blackstar, which is why I had the towers built way out here, while I still had enough pull to get things done."

"These Wardens, do they have any connection to a group called the Brethren?" Jasper asked.

The man showed no recognition of the name, only confusion.

Osric steered the conversation back. "The Blackstar pieces, what happened to them? You said you had one."

The man was starting to fade. He'd lost too much blood. Jasper had bandaged him, but a wound like that was fatal, even with herbs and tending. It would have required a priest to heal, under normal circumstances.

"I once knew their locations. Using my piece to locate the others," he said, seeming lucid again. "The fragments naturally draw toward each other. One can be used to find the others."

"How?" Talia asked.

The man opened his mouth, but then closed it, his head lolling to the side. His eyes closed, fluttered open, then closed again.

"I had almost found them. Was so close to understanding how to repair the Veil," he said, pushing through the delirium and the pain. "Then they took the piece I had left."

"They? Do you mean the knights?" Osric asked, since that was the only 'they' that made any sense.

The man's chest rose and fell with struggling breaths. "Yes. Men in armor. Smashed through the door and demanded the piece. I tried to use the nexus to seal it, but something was keeping it from working, pulling the energies from where they needed to go."

The wyrm like creature, Osric thought. Its finding the rift and feeding from it had disrupted the man's ability to protect the shard somehow. If only they'd translated the document sooner, and beat the knights here, they would have the piece.

"Their leader wouldn't listen," the man continued. "I tried to explain its importance, but he didn't care."

"What did they want with it?" Talia asked.

"Don't know. They just said they needed to have it. That they had to save someone. He kept saying she was sick, dying. I tried to explain that the Blackstar could not heal anyone. That healing wasn't what the Blackstar was used for, but he still demanded the piece I had. I refused and told him what could happen if the Blackstar wasn't reassembled and used to seal the tears. He didn't care."

"He stabbed you," Osric said, not a question but a statement.

"You said if reassembled, it can close the tears. How? How do we reassemble the Blackstar?"

"The fragments naturally want to come together. But you need Veil energy to forge them. Old texts in the Citadel library, they explain the process."

"I don't have access to those texts. Your Citadel doesn't exist anymore. Does the reassembly need to happen in this tower specifically?"

The old man either ignored or did not hear what she said about the Citadel not being there anymore, focusing on the last question. "Any of the ancient towers will do. They all tap into the Veil directly. The towers were built ... natural weak points in it, where the Veil is thinnest."

"Where are these other towers?" Talia pressed.

"There were four besides this one. The Citadel, Corwen, Merseld and Orlwyth. Any would be able to focus the power."

The Citadel was obviously out, destroyed during the event that ended the Calaphium. Surprisingly, Jasper seemed to recognize the others.

"I know two of those locations. Corwen is what many believe a set of ruins on the northeastern coast of Brackendale was called. Merseld," he paused, his expression troubled. "Is what we believe the spot where the Conclave decided to build their tower was originally called, before the founding of Aeloria."

"The Conclave built on an old Calaphium site?" Talia asked.

"It appears so. Though I doubt they know its true significance."

Osric wasn't so sure. He didn't love the idea of coincidences.

"You must be careful," the man said, although he was getting harder to understand him. His voice was going and he was dropping words from his sentences. "The Blackstar ... terrible ... something to, changes them. The Veil tears ... whispers from ..."

"What does it do to people? Is it dangerous?"

The man's eyes fixed on Osric with sudden clarity.

Grabbing Osric's arm with a weak grip he said, "Get it back. Before it's too late. The Veil can't ... withstand ... another ..."

His voice trailed off. For a moment Osric thought he was just gathering his strength, but the man shuddered once, then went still, his eyes staring sightlessly at the ceiling.

For a moment, no one spoke.

"May Heathus guide your soul home," Jasper said, closing the old man's eyes.

"So Baron Blackthorn has a piece of the Blackstar," Talia said, breaking the silence.

"They must have returned to Wolfridge with it, right?" Osric asked.

"So what, we ride into the capital and demand the baron just hand it over?" Grace said.

"We don't have much choice," Osric replied. "We need the Blackstar to close the Veil. You heard him, it's failing and it can't withstand another rupture. Unless we know of ..."

He stopped mid-sentence as a strange sound filled the chamber. They all turned toward the source of the sound, the body of the ancient man. Before their eyes, his flesh began to shrivel, the skin pulling tight against his bones before crumbling away like sand. In moments, all that remained was dust and the tattered remnants of his robes.

"What ... What happened?" Rowan asked, shocked.

"The Veil energy was probably the only thing keeping him alive. Without it, his body reverted to its true age. He must have been sustained by that energy for thousands of years."

"Is that even possible?" Grace asked.

"Apparently so," Jasper replied.

"So what now?" Rowan asked.

"We head to Wolfridge. As I was saying, unless we know of anything else that can close the Veil, it is our only option, and I'm not sure how much longer we have. Besides, you heard his warning. We don't know what it can do to a person. If we leave it in the baron's hands, who knows what damage he might cause, to himself or someone else."

"So we're really going to confront a baron?" Grace asked. "A man with soldiers and resources at his command. For a magical artifact that we were told is dangerous and to be careful around."

"That's exactly what we're going to do," Osric said.

Getting Out

Osric rolled up his bedding as Rowan woke everyone up. It was barely dawn outside, the sky only turning a slightly lighter shade of black, but if they were going to make it out of this place and back to sanity, they needed a very early start.

Even with that, they were looking at a hike that would go well into the night. A dangerous prospect, but at least this time, they knew where they were going, instead of fumbling around looking for the tower as they had on the way in.

Staying in this gods-forsaken tower hadn't been what any of them wanted to do, but it had been too late to do anything but stay or try to make it back to the hermit's cave before dark, and they were all too banged up and hurting to do that.

So it had been decided the only thing to do was to bar the door and pray they weren't set upon during the night.

Thankfully, although sounds outside and from the lower floors continued all evening, nothing tried to get in and they were able to get some rest.

Each movement made his muscles complain, reminding him of yesterday's desperate battles. Jasper's healing had closed the wounds on his arm, but the skin pulled tight when he flexed.

"How's everyone feeling?" he asked.

Talia sat cross-legged nearby, her red hair pulled back in a simple knot, and dark circles underlined her eyes. "Like I fought a swarm of beetles and got fed on by a giant flying leech. Which, as it happens, is exactly what occurred."

"That about sums it up," Grace muttered.

Jasper went from person to person with his satchel of herbs and bandages, applying last-minute tending before they started out.

Rowan stood by one of the windows, looking over the surrounding valley while he waited for them to be ready to go.

"See anything?" Osric asked as he joined him.

"Nothing. That's what concerns me. No movement at all."

"The rift is gone," Talia said. "Maybe the creatures went with it?"

"Or maybe they're waiting for us," Grace said, tucking a dagger into her boot. "Either way, standing around won't get us out of here."

"Grace is right. We need to move. The longer we stay, the more danger we're in," Osric said. "We know the way out, so we make our way back the way we came, although more directly, no detours, no unnecessary risks."

"And if we encounter more of those moth creatures?" Talia asked.

"We'll deal with that if it happens. Let's get moving."

There was no sign of creatures or anything else as they made their way out of the tower, although the evidence of their battles from the previous day remained. What had taken them hours coming in was now only a short trip out, since they did not have to defend themselves or stop to investigate as they had before.

Outside, it was even quieter. Nothing moved through the bushes or on the rocky slopes in the distance and they saw none of the flying creatures they'd seen circling the tower the day before.

Everything was gone.

"This doesn't feel right," Rowan said.

"When has anything in this place felt right?" Grace countered.

"Where did everything go?" Talia asked.

"No idea, but they're all really gone," Grace said. "Even the small buzzing insects that followed us everywhere before. It's like everything just ... left."

"Or died," Rowan added.

"Probably just wandering further afield," Jasper said. "The rift, that the old man called the nexus, was more than just a tear in the Veil. It was an anchor point, a foundation for reality itself in this place. When we closed it, we must have freed everything that was trapped here."

"Or trapped from coming in here," Talia said. "Remember how those moth creatures couldn't cross into this section because of the invisible barrier? It seems likely that was caused by the rift, and if it's no longer keeping things in, that barrier might be gone as well."

"Which means they could be anywhere," Osric said.

"Or everywhere," Grace muttered.

"Let's keep moving. There's a ridge ahead that should give us a better view of the valley."

They proceeded as quickly as they could through the valley and up the slope, while remaining cautious of being attacked by ... whatever was still out there. Thankfully, they reached the ridge without incident. From their elevated position, they could see across much of the valley floor. It wasn't much different than it had been the previous morning.

"Look there," Rowan said, pointing. "And there."

Dark patches moved slowly across the barren ground. As Osric watched, he realized they were groups of creatures, hundreds of them, migrating across the valley floor.

"Where are they going?" Osric asked.

"They look panicked," Rowan said. "Like startled forest game, running from something they can't see."

"Whatever they're doing, they're moving away from us," Grace said.

"Why would they do that?" Talia asked. "If the nexus was keeping them here, shouldn't they be trying to go back to wherever they came from now that it's gone?"

"I don't think it works like that. For one, there's no open rift for them to go through and if there was, I believe the tears only went one way. Also, they have been here for thousands of years. Perhaps they've adapted to this place, unable to live where they came from."

"We should keep going," Osric said.

The descent proved more challenging than the climb, as it had been going down the other side the day before. The creatures may be acting differently, but the stone was still loose and hard to travel quickly over. They spent several hours retracing their steps from their journey to the tower. It still felt weird, how much quieter it was than before the nexus was closed.

By mid-morning, they approached the cave where they'd met the strange hermit. Osric signaled the others to stop.

"We should at least check on him. He wouldn't go further in, but if we could bring him out, maybe he could have a life again."

"Or maybe he turned to dust like the guy in the tower," Grace pointed out.

A possibility, but they all still turned and headed into the cave. The small fire inside was now cold ashes, as if it hadn't been used in a long time, in spite of there being a fire in it just two days before. The crude sleeping mat lay abandoned in the corner. The hermit was nowhere to be seen.

"See, he's gone. I'm sure he got out safely. Now we should do the same," Grace said.

"We should search for him," Talia said.

"The fire's been cold for a day at least. He could be anywhere, and we have a job to do," Rowan said.

"Besides, he chose to live here, and there are no signs of a fight. He's not our problem," Grace added.

"I hate to say it, but they're right," Osric said. "Best we can do is press on, get clear of this place as quickly as we can."

Every part of Osric hated the decision. The hermit had been strange, perhaps even dangerous in his madness, but he hadn't deserved whatever fate had claimed him. But, for whatever reason, everyone continued to defer to him, so it was his responsibility to do what was right for all of them.

With one look back, they left the cave behind and continued south, toward the pass that led out of this place and to safety. By Osric's best guess, they had enough daylight to make it to where they had faced the moths.

But barely.

They set out at a brisk pace. Rowan took the lead now that they followed their own back trail, pausing occasionally to check landmarks, each of them aware of how dangerous it would be if they had to deal with the creatures in the dark.

The terrain grew more rugged as they progressed, the rock becoming more brittle. The reverse of what had happened on the way in. Twice, they detoured around sections of path that had been reshaped by rockslides, costing them precious time. Hours passed, and the sun sank lower.

It was a hard march out after days of hard fighting. They were all tiring, struggling to keep their energy up.

But finally, they reached the crevice they'd crossed through on the way in, where they'd left the moths behind them.

"Be ready," Osric said, pulling his sword as Rowan slowed the pace.

He couldn't hear the beating of wings that had marked the arrival of the moths the last time, but that didn't mean they weren't out there. They passed through the crevice slowly, ready for the creatures to swarm them from any direction.

"What's that?" Osric asked, looking past Rowan at something shimmering on the ground.

Rowan knelt to examine the scattered remains, "It looks like fragments of wings and maybe some kind of discarded scales. If these were normal animals, I'd suggest they molted, leaving behind parts of their old skin."

"But where did they go?" Grace asked, watching the sky nervously.

"No idea," Rowan said.

"Other things are moving into and through The Claws, no longer locked in by the nexus. Could the moths do the same? They'd tried so hard to get into the interior before."

"Or they went out of The Claws. Released into the wilds."

"So what you're saying is, they could be anywhere," Grace concluded.

"I think it's more likely they went deeper in," Jasper said. "The nexus may be closed, but this whole area remains a wound in this reality. That kind of energy will draw creatures sensitive to it in."

But they all knew he was just being wishful.

"Or they're circling around to ambush us further down the path."

"Always the optimist," Rowan said with a wry smile.

"How do you think I'm still alive?" she retorted.

"Either way, we need to move," Osric decided. "Barrier or no barrier, this was their territory. It's better we not remain here."

The scattered remains of moth scales made the footing treacherous and slippery. Twice, Osric nearly lost his balance, his boots sliding on the slick material. Behind him, Talia cursed as she stumbled.

Despite their fears, no moths appeared. The passage remained empty and clear of anything but their sheddings.

"So far, so good," Osric said as they made it to the other side. "Now we just need to ..."

He stopped cold in his tracks as he saw a giant rockslide blocking their way. It must have been a further collapse after the one that almost killed Jasper, because the path had still been partially passable then.

Now, there was no way across.

"Now what?" Talia asked.

"We can climb it," Rowan said. "It will be difficult, but not impossible."

"Unless another slide comes down while we're exposed on top of this one," Grace pointed out.

"Let's go," Osric said, not waiting for further debate, and starting to climb.

Each time he shifted his weight, the entire pile settled slightly and small stones trickled down. He continued upward, occasionally dislodging larger rocks that might endanger those following him.

Cinder regarded the rockslide dubiously, then bounded forward with surprising agility, finding a path among the stones that Osric hadn't noticed. The wolf reached the top well ahead of Osric.

"Show-off," Osric muttered before turning to call down. "The path is clear on the other side. The slide didn't reach that far."

One by one, they made the ascent.

Descending proved more treacherous than ascending. The loose stones threatened to slide out from under his boots with each step.

Osric braced himself, testing each foothold before committing his weight. The loose stones cascaded beneath him like miniature avalanches with each step.

"Watch that section," he called back to the others, pointing to a particularly unstable area. "The whole side looks ready to give way."

There were some close calls and it took time to get everyone down the side, but they managed it without any serious injuries.

The day had transitioned from twilight into night as they did it, though, and not even the moonlight seemed to pierce the constant clouds that sat above the mountains.

"Talia," Osric said as he helped Jasper down the last few feet. "We need light, please."

Talia nodded, stabilizing herself against a large boulder. She placed her fingertips together in front of her, forming an upward-pointing triangle. As she separated her hands while maintaining the shape with her fingers, a glowing orb materialized between them. The pale blue light swelled to the size of a melon before she released it, allowing it to float upward, illuminating their precarious position.

"That won't last forever," she warned.

Not that they had many choices. They were still hours from being out of The Claws, and everyone was on edge after not finding the moths where they expected them to be.

The further along they went, however, the easier the trek got, and their pace quickened. Cinder was the first one who seemed to realize they had made it out, as his ears perked up and he trotted ahead of the group.

"He smells the horses," Rowan said, a smile breaking through his exhaustion.

They rounded a final bend in the path and saw the first sign of normalcy, a pair of real, uncorrupted trees. Straight branches and leaves standing out, after days of looking at twisted and dead-looking things.

It only took a few minutes until all signs of the scarred landscape they'd been in were gone, and they were back in their own reality.

Surprisingly, in the distance, a group of dark shapes moved against the landscape, behind a makeshift fence put up quickly a few days before.

The horses they'd acquired were still there, heads picking up as they smelled people, apparently for the first time in days as well.

"I can't believe they're still here," Talia said.

"Who would steal them?" Grace asked with a short laugh. "You'd have to be insane to come here voluntarily."

Everyone finally let their guard down, the tension they'd been carrying for days finally being let go as they all laughed at her statement.

"Let's make camp," Osric decided. "I don't think any of us can manage riding tonight, and we haven't had a good night's sleep in days."

No one argued. They moved into the same place they'd made camp before setting out, made a fire and laid out their bedrolls. They were still going to have to do two-man watches, just in case the creatures didn't go further in, but were released into the world now that the nexus was gone.

Talia finished setting her wards, now that they were in a place where magic wasn't liable to go wild. They had agreed to take the first watch, and the others were asleep practically before she finished the task. Osric didn't blame them. They had walked for nearly a full day, the sun having gone down four or five hours ago, and they hadn't gotten much sleep the night before.

Osric wanted nothing more than to lay his head back and sleep. But he wasn't going to leave Talia out here on watch by herself, wards or not.

"I never thought I'd be so happy to see a normal rock," he said, lowering himself onto one next to her.

"Or normal dirt. Or normal stars," she said, looking up at the clear night sky above them. "I missed the stars."

Osric nodded, following her gaze up. For a little while, they just sat there, listening to the crackling of the fire, and looking at the stars.

"Do you ever miss it?" Osric asked suddenly.

"Miss what?"

"Life before all this? The simplicity. Knowing what each day would bring."

"Sometimes. Back in Eldham, the biggest problem I had was Elder Miriam catching me practicing spells I wasn't supposed to know yet. Then I thought I'd love nothing more than to get out and spread my wings, maybe visit the Conclave. Now I've seen more magic, and learned more about magic than I think I ever would have, I can't help but think I'd rather be back there."

"Yeah."

They both fell silent again for a few minutes, just looking up at the sky.

"Remember when you almost burned down the village?" Talia said.

"Gods, do I. I lost control of the portable forge we'd set up for the festival, and it caught the canopy on fire, and started to spread to the other ones nearby. Master Ironhand was furious; had me cleaning windows and fixing stuff around the village for weeks, to pay for what I'd damaged."

"The whole village was furious with you," Talia said, laughing now. "Old Beck threatened to tan your hide if you came near him again. By the time everyone got done talking about it, the story was you'd set the entire village on fire."

He smiled, looking over at her. It was good to hear her laugh again. Her laughter warmed him more than the fire. For a moment, it was like they were still back there, like the three months that felt like three lifetimes had never happened.

"Do you think things are the same back there?" he asked. "In Eldham, I mean."

"I don't know," Talia said, hugging her knees to her chest. "We know the Brethren have been in the village, poking around, and Rowan said there were more wild things in the forest as the Rangers started to get spread more thinly. I miss it though. I miss Elder Miriam. I miss her lessons. I even miss her scolding me when I got something wrong."

"Yeah," Osric said.

Not that it mattered. It wasn't like they could ever go back again to the way things had been.

"Do you think you'll go back, after it's all done? After we find the Blackstar pieces and repair the Veil."

"I haven't thought that far ahead. Stay alive first, plan later."

"Very practical," she said. "If not there, then what will you do?"

"I don't know. Something useful. Something that matters."

"Like saving the world isn't enough?" she teased.

"If we succeed," he reminded her. "We still have to get to Wolfridge, confront a baron, and somehow retrieve the Blackstar piece he's already taken."

"Minor details," Talia said, waving her hand dismissively.

The gesture was so unlike her usual seriousness that Osric laughed.

"When did you become the optimist?"

"Someone has to balance out Grace."

Osric laughed as they dreamed about a future he wasn't sure they'd ever see. She talked about the things she learned. About taking all of her new knowledge to the Conclave and showing them what magic really was, the way the Sage had shown her.

He watched her face as she talked, seeing the far-off look in her eyes and the little smile she got as she imagined the reaction of the men in their high tower to the little village girl bringing them truths.

He realized with sudden clarity how much he enjoyed these moments with her. How important they were to him. How important she was to him.

"What?" she asked, stopping her story as she caught him smiling at her.

"Nothing," he said. "Nothing at all."

Knights

Osric was happy when they finally began to leave the Claws behind. Even being out of its monstrous surroundings, the entire place sent shivers up his spine.

They rode for five days, pushing the pace hard, trying to catch up to the baron and his remaining men, although it wasn't clear how much of a lead those men had on them.

Thankfully, they had the horses they'd claimed from the bounty hunters, or their journey would have been even slower. They pushed into the night each day, but that was offset by the times Rowan had them stop when he saw signs of a larger mounted party passing their way, heading east away from the Claws.

It wasn't guaranteed to be the baron and his men, but few ever ventured toward the Claws, and even fewer returned from there.

On the third day, they emerged from the foothills onto flat grasslands, completely clear of any remnants of the Claws. Half a day later, the Great Road stretched before them.

Although not quite back where they started, it still felt like coming full circle since just over a week ago. Once on the road, they made better time.

By the fifth day, the group had all but recovered from their ordeal in the Claws. Between Jasper's herbs and his prayers to the gods, the injuries they'd sustained were fully healed and even the lingering effects from the beetles' poison had diminished. The road took them back into the first civilization they had seen in some time. Past farmland, fields of harvested wheat, and scattered cottages with columns of smoke rising from chimneys in the distance.

"Half a day's ride to Wolfridge, perhaps less," Rowan announced as they paused atop a gentle rise. The ranger pointed north, where the road disappeared into a bank of trees. "We'll reach the city by nightfall if we maintain this pace."

"We should discuss what happens when we reach Wolfridge," Osric said, slowing his pace. "If the baron truly has the Blackstar piece, we can't simply walk up to the keep and demand it. Until now, we were just trying to catch up, but the baron has to have made it home by now, which will make this much more complicated."

"Perhaps we could request an audience," Jasper suggested. "I could claim to be a visiting cleric from the south, researching artifacts and heard he had acquired something."

Grace snorted. "And you just happened to show up a week or less after he found it, and probably within days of him finding his way home? How would you explain how you heard about it so quickly? Only an idiot would believe that story."

"Although I don't agree with her words, she is, in general, correct. Something more patient and cautious is needed."

"Do we have time for patient and cautious?" Osric asked.

They didn't even know why the baron had gone for it, or how he'd heard about it. It wasn't common knowledge. The Blackstar had sat there for millennia, outside of the knowledge of the world. It took a message from the gods for them to learn about it.

Not only did he learn of it, but he beat them to it.

No, something else was at play, and it bothered Osric he didn't know what that was. It wasn't the Brethren. If they had known about it, they would have definitely either collected it themselves or had someone standing guard over it like they had the two halves of the document.

Osric was convinced it was another player, although the others, Jasper especially, was less sure.

They continued to debate what they could do as they rode closer and closer to the city, but by midday, they were no closer to a workable plan.

At least not one that didn't end up with them in a dungeon or dead.

As they cleared a bend in the road, the whole group pulled up short. Ahead, a group of six riders blocked the path. For a moment, Osric thought it might be another group of brigands, like the ones they encountered on the way to the Claws, but after a moment, he realized they were wearing armor much too nice for the likes of brigands.

What's more, this armor was embossed with the sigil for the Barony of Greenwood. These were the baron's men, which hopefully meant that the baron had finally begun to bring order back to the barony now that he'd returned to Wolfridge.

"Osric, wait," Talia said as Osric signaled for them to stop while spurring his horse on.

Osric waved her off and urged his horse forward, approaching the line of knights at a walk. As he drew nearer, he couldn't help but get the feeling that the men were on edge, hands resting on weapons.

Admittedly, his lot was a strange group and heavily armed. If they were looking for brigands, they might fit the bill.

"Good afternoon," Osric said, raising a hand in greeting, making sure to keep it away from his weapons.

He did his best to sound pleasant and non-threatening, hopefully, to make sure the gentlemen understood his group was not a threat.

"Identify yourselves," one of the men with some kind of emblem on his pauldron singling him out as a commander of some sort.

"I'm Osric, a blacksmith's apprentice from Eldham, a ... small village to the southeast of here. My friends and I are heading to Wolfridge looking for work. We'd heard from some others of bandit problems, and are very glad to see you out here protecting the road."

"We are not here for bandits. We are looking for a group of travelers. A group that matches your description, actually. A young red-haired woman. A young man brown of hair accompanied by a wolf. A scholar or cleric of some kind, a dark-complexioned Greenwood Ranger, and a woman of slight build and blond hair."

Osric felt a cold weight settle in his stomach. Behind him, he heard his companions shuffling nervously. The leader reached into his satchel and withdrew a rolled parchment.

"By order of Baron Calwin Blackthorn, lord of Wolfridge and servant to the Crown of Aeloria, you are hereby commanded to surrender yourselves for the crime of treason against the crown."

"Treason?" Osric replied, unable to keep the shock out of his voice. "There must be some mistake. We're just passing through and have committed no crime against Baron Blackthorn or anyone else."

The man ignored him.

Putting away the scroll, he said, "Surrender your weapons and come peacefully."

Osric dismounted, hoping the gesture might ease tensions. He left his sword belted at his waist and approached on foot, hands open at his sides.

"Sir, please. We have a Greenwood Ranger among our number. A man sworn just as you are to protect the barony. Surely that counts for something?"

"The Rangers have been disbanded. Their leader arrested for sedition against the baron. It only goes to further prove your guilt, although you will get your day in front of the lord's justice, just as any traitor does before the headsman takes him. Last chance, surrender or face the consequences."

Behind him, Osric heard weapons being drawn. In response, several of the knights drew their weapons.

"Wait," Osric said, holding up hands to both groups. "This doesn't need to come to violence."

"It seems your friends disagree," the leader said. "Take them."

The knights spurred their mounts forward, the rest pulling swords from scabbards as they went.

The world exploded into motion.

"Move," Talia yelled before Osric could react.

He looked behind him to see her, somehow steady upon her agitated horse, her knees gripping the animal's sides, as she swept her hands apart. A small bead of orange fire shot from her outstretched fingers, a pinprick of intense light that raced toward the charging knights. Osric started to turn and run back toward them, away from what he knew was coming, but he'd only made it a few steps before the bead struck in the midst of the men and detonated. A sudden gout of fire erupted, a blossoming sphere of incandescent fury that engulfed the space between the riders. Osric felt the heat wash over him from a dozen paces away.

Two of the baron's men, caught directly in the conflagration, screamed as they and their mounts were swallowed by the flames. Their horses, wreathed in fire, reared in agony, throwing their riders clear. The men crashed to the earth, their armor smoking, although they both were still moving, writhing on the ground. A third knight, positioned on the edge of the blast, managed to heave his shield up, the wood and metal blackened instantaneously. His warhorse, though scorched and panicked, stayed on its feet, screaming and bucking but not unseating its rider.

The air was filled with the stench of burnt horsehair and seared flesh.

Unfortunately, Jasper had been further ahead than the rest of the group and, other than Osric, had painted himself as a target, especially since his horse had panicked being so close to the flames. The knight who had shielded himself from the fireball, his armor now soot-stained and his shield splintered, spurred his wounded warhorse forward. The animal, half-mad with pain and fear, charged erratically toward Jasper, who sat startled on his own mount, too much in shock to have reacted yet.

Osric saw the danger and moved, his own horse having bolted at the explosion, taking two quick steps, putting himself between the charging knight and the cleric. As the knight bore down on him, his sword raised for a killing blow, Osric lunged. He swung his longsword not at the rider, but at the charging beast's forelegs. The steel bit deep; the sound was that of a sickening crunch of bone and sinew. The warhorse let out a gurgling cry and its front legs buckled. It stumbled, its charge broken, and pitched forward. The knight, caught by surprise, flew over his mount's collapsing neck, his own momentum carrying him from the saddle. He crashed heavily to the ground, his sword clattering away, his planned attack ending in a cloud of dust and a pained groan.

Almost simultaneously, another of the baron's men thundered past the chaos of the fireball's aftermath on the other side of the knight whose horse Osric had hobbled, putting him out of Osric's range.

He aimed his charge directly at Jasper. Seeing the animal charging, Jasper's horse bolted, but a beat too late, causing the two horses to nearly collide. The knight thrust with his longsword, which punched through Jasper's light mail, piercing his left shoulder. Jasper cried out as the knight continued to thunder past.

Grace reacted, turning her own horse to charge toward Jasper, or more rightfully, toward the knight who just injured him. Her timing was impeccable. As their horses passed, flank to flank, she leaned low in her saddle, flicking out with her dagger. It found the narrow gap between the knight's backplate and the tasset that protected his hip, a vulnerability exposed as he focused on Jasper. Grace pulled her blade free as her horse carried her away.

The man who'd spoken to Osric, probably the leader, focused his attention on Rowan, spurring his warhorse in a tight circle around the ranger. Rowan was not an easy target as the cleric and had his sword out, ready to face the coming threat. The knight pulled up short, maybe recognizing the danger a ranger might be and to keep from running right into his blade. Instead, their mounts faced each other, both riders searching for an opening. The knight swung his blade in a wide horizontal arc, but Rowan yanked his reins sharply. His mount sidestepped the attack, the blade cutting through empty air where they had been moments before.

Cinder, seeing his master's friend in danger, bounded forward with incredible speed. The wolf launched himself at the knight's warhorse, powerful jaws clamping onto the animal's front leg. The horse screamed in pain and reared violently, causing the knight to lose his balance and tumble backward from the saddle, landing hard on the ground as his terrified mount bolted away, shaking Cinder loose.

Before Osric could celebrate this small victory, another knight charged past the fallen rider he'd dismounted earlier. The man's longsword flashed downward in a quick thrust. Osric managed to turn, but just in time, taking the blow on his chest plate. The sword skittered off, but nicked his arm as the knight cleared him, creating a small trail of blood.

Osric ignored the pain and lashed out with his own sword, slicing through the leather straps that held the saddle in place. The saddle shifted under the knight as his horse reared in response to the attack. Both rider and saddle slid sideways, falling to the ground with a heavy thud.

Jasper steadied himself in his saddle, clutching his wounded shoulder with one hand while maintaining a grip on the reins with the other. He closed his eyes briefly, his lips moving in silent prayer, but instead of a glowing light around his hand as the cleric healed himself, as Osric had expected, a shimmering blue barrier appeared around Osric instead.

Near Jasper, Rowan was sizing the advantage over the knight unseated by Cinder's attack. Jumping from his mount, he drove his blade downward at the man, who managed to roll aside just at the last moment, the blade slicing across his collarbone instead of below it.

The rest of the knights were not out of the fight, however. One of the knights who had been thrown by Talia's fireball regained his feet, his armor blackened from the blast. His eyes locked on Grace, who was riding toward them. He delivered a brutal overhand chop at her leg as she guided her mount past him, the longsword connected with her thigh, cleaving through her leather armor and cutting deep.

Grace cried out, blood streaming down her leg.

Despite her wounded leg, Grace managed to tumble backward from her horse, landing directly behind the knight, drawing her sword. The blade sliced across the back of the knight's knee joint, finding the vulnerable gap in his armor. The knight howled in pain as his leg buckled beneath him.

"That's for my thigh, you bastard," Grace said through gritted teeth.

The man struggled to maintain his balance, his injured leg threatening to give way with each movement. He gritted his teeth against the pain and made a wild horizontal slash at Grace's midsection. Despite his compromised stance, the blade found its mark, cutting a shallow but painful gash across her ribs.

Grace stumbled backward, clutching her side.

Nearby, the other knight knocked from his horse was also up, burned but alive. Instead of Grace, he took his anger out on Talia, running toward her, screaming in rage. Talia saw him coming and tried to avoid him by turning her horse, which just put the animal in harm's way. The beast bucked as it was injured, throwing her from the saddle.

She fell hard from her mount, landing on the ground with a painful thud. She looked up to see the knight standing over her.

Cinder came out of nowhere, snarled, and lunged at the knight threatening Talia. The wolf's teeth sank deep into the man's forearm as he attempted to bring his sword down on her. The man cried out in pain as Cinder's powerful jaws punctured the chainmail between his armor plates, but he managed to shake the beast loose after hitting the wolf several times.

Talia used the time the animal bought her, hands moving through the air, again tracing intricate patterns. As she did, her form seemed to shimmer and multiply as four identical copies of her appeared, surrounding her position as she scrambled to her feet. Each illusory duplicate mimicked her movements perfectly, confusing the knight who stood over her.

Across the battlefield, the knight Rowan had injured got back to his feet and was pressing the attack. The ranger feinted with his shortsword, then hooked his blade against the knight's weapon. With a powerful twist, leveraging his forearm against the knight's wrist, he wrenched the longsword free. The weapon spun through the air before landing with a metallic clang several feet away.

The man scrambled toward his fallen longsword, but stopped when Rowan took a step to intercept him, realizing that reaching for it would make him an easy target. Instead, he drew a dagger from his belt.

Rowan struck again with his shortsword, targeting the knight's weapon arm. His blade cut across the forearm, causing blood to seep through the knight's vambrace. The knight's grip on his dagger weakened, but he didn't drop the weapon.

Instead, the wounded knight lunged forward, feinting low, then drove his dagger upward, catching the ranger off-guard. The blade punctured Rowan's leather armor below the ribcage, drawing blood.

Rowan grunted in pain, stumbling back a step.

Osric saw this and wanted to help, but the man whose saddle straps he'd cut had gotten back up to his feet and was still a danger. Seeing an opening, Osric delivered a diagonal slash, trying to come at the man's neck, but the knight was fast and danced back a step, the blade only scraping across his breastplate.

The knight recovered quickly and changed direction abruptly, putting his full weight behind a brutal overhead swing. His longsword crashed down on Osric's shoulder. The force of the blow pushed through the shimmering blue barrier around him and dented Osric's armor, sending waves of pain through his body.

Suddenly, the knight Osric had dismounted at the beginning of the fight but had lost track of, reappeared on foot, coming seemingly out of nowhere, seizing the opportunity while Osric was distracted. The man lunged forward with a thrust aimed at Osric's flank. Osric managed to parry the blow but was now facing opponents on two fronts.

The situation worsened again when a third knight, the one stabbed in the side by Grace, still somehow mounted, spurred his horse forward. As Osric focused on parrying attacks from the ground, the mounted knight drove his longsword down at him from horseback.

Surrounded by three knights, one on horseback, Osric adopted a defensive stance, deflecting the attack by the mounted knight. When another of the knights lunged, Osric parried and countered with a riposte that scored a line across the man's breastplate. He immediately returned to his defensive posture, keeping all three knights in view.

One of the knights attempted to capitalize on Osric's divided attention, thrusting his longsword at his exposed side. Osric was blocking an attack from the other side and was not going to be able to parry both. Thankfully, a shimmer of blue appeared as the blade skimmed across the magical shield Jasper had placed there, visibly rippling where the sword made contact.

"Don't let them surround you!" Talia called.

But Osric couldn't break free. As he focused on parrying one knight's attack, another exploited the opening. The knight swung his longsword in a brutal arc that crashed against Osric's back. Though his armor absorbed some of the impact, the blow sent him staggering forward, breaking his defensive stance.

Talia could see the danger he was in. She, and her duplicates, weaved another spell, in spite of having her own opponent facing her. Pinching her thumb and index finger together on one hand, she reached outward with her other hand in a clawing motion, then touched the pinched fingers to her clawing hand before thrusting forward toward the mounted knight threatening Osric.

A greenish semi-transparent arrowhead shot from her fingertips, striking the knight in his shoulder. His armor sizzled, discolored, and then pitted as the acid ate through it into the man beneath. The knight screamed as smoke rose from his wound as the acid ate into his shoulder.

The knight who had threatened Talia, now free of Cinder, charged toward her prone form with his sword raised high, delivering a powerful overhand strike. His blade passed cleanly through one of Talia's illusory duplicates, which shimmered and disappeared. The knight growled in frustration as he realized he had struck an illusion instead of the real mage.

"Damn witch tricks!" he shouted.

Talia scrambled to her feet, her illusory duplicates copying her movements. She extended one arm with her palm facing down while making chopping motions with her other hand. She curled her fingers into a fist as if grasping wind, then released them in a snapping motion.

A powerful invisible force hit the knight standing over her squarely in the chest, lifting him off his feet. The knight flew backward through the air, landing hard in his clanging armor several feet away.

A dozen feet away, Grace circled the knight with the damaged knee as he continued to swipe at her with his sword. Though he could no longer stand properly, his blade still posed a threat. She dodged one wide swing, then darted around behind him. In one swift motion, she brought her blade to his throat, sliding it between his gorget and helmet. Blood spurted from the wound as the knight collapsed to the ground.

Grace barely waited for him to hit the ground before she moved across the battlefield, tumbling between two warhorses dancing around nervously, toward the knights surrounding Osric. She drew her shortsword and caught Osric's eye, signaling her intention with a quick nod.

Osric understood. As one knight slashed at him, he caught the attacking blade with his own. He locked their blades together and stepped inward toward the knight. The knight's look of triumph turned to shock as Osric pulled him close, their armor plates clanging together. He was a big man and probably thought he would win any contest of strength.

Grace appeared behind the locked-up knight, her blade slid through the gap where backplate meets tasset, driving upward into the knight's vital organs. The knight went rigid, then slumped forward against Osric, who stepped aside as the dead man fell.

Unfortunately, locking up the one opponent made him a target for another, who put his weight behind a thrust aimed at Osric's exposed back, aiming at a gap in his armor. Just before the blade could connect, a translucent blue disc materialized in its path. The longsword struck the barrier with a crack, causing the shield to shatter into fragments of blue light, but the deflected blade passed harmlessly to Osric's side, and the knight stumbled forward carried by his own momentum.

Osric turned to look across the battlefield, where Jasper had his hand outstretched toward him.

Not far from where Grace had killed the first knight, Cinder sprinted to one of the still-mounted knights, targeting his horse. The wolf bit into the warhorse's flank, tearing through muscle. The horse reared in pain, hooves pawing at the air. The knight managed to stay seated by pressing his knees against his mount's sides, turning in his saddle and backhanding Cinder, the metal ridges along his hand cutting across the wolf's muzzle, leaving a bloody gash. Cinder yelped in pain as he was spun away.

Rowan, still in a duel with the dagger-armed knight, turned and saw the wolf go flying. With a grimace, he turned and feigned high, drawing the knight's dagger up in defense, before sweeping out with his leg, catching the knight's foot and pulling it forward. The armored man lost his balance and fell backward, his helmet striking the ground with a metallic thud.

Without hesitation, Rowan drove his blade down into the gap between the fallen knight's helmet and gorget. The knight's body went limp as the life left him.

As soon as the knight was down, Rowan reached into his belt and pulled a dagger, flinging out in one smooth motion. The blade somersaulted through the air, catching the knight now standing over the sprawled-out wolf in the throat. The man looked up in surprise as he clutched the blade, before dropping to his knees, gurgling.

The man Talia had injured struggled to his feet, dazed but not defeated. Unable to reach Talia, he drew his own dagger from his belt and threw it with surprising accuracy. The weapon sailed through the air toward Talia, and then through her, unveiling another of her duplicates. The image dissolved into sparkles as the dagger fell to the ground beyond.

"Get Down!" Talia shouted at Osric.

Osric knew what Talia could do and didn't think twice, simply dropping to his belly, a sword whistling through where he'd been moments before.

Her hands moved in an intricate pattern as she prepared her most devastating spell. She interlocked her fingers, pulled her hands apart sharply, traced a zigzag with her right hand, and thrust both hands forward.

Almost at the same instant, a brilliant blast of electrical energy erupted from her fingertips. The lightning bolt arced through the air, cutting through the man standing over her and striking the knight still facing Osric. The electricity surged through their metal armor, intensifying the damage. Both knights convulsed violently before falling dead on the cobblestone road, smoke rising from their blackened armor.

The battle ended as abruptly as it had begun. Six knights lay dead on the road, their bodies scattered among their frightened or wounded horses. Osric and his companions stood amid the carnage, bloodied but alive.

Jasper immediately moved to tend to the wounded. He started with Grace's leg and side, and only healed himself after the rest were made whole. His hands glowed with divine energy as he channeled healing into their wounds.

"That settles it," Rowan said, wiping blood from his blade. "We can't go to Wolfridge now. Not after this."

"Do we have a choice? The other piece of the Blackstar is in Wolfridge. If we run now, the veil will tear and we'll all still be dead, along with everyone else," Talia said.

"Then what do you suggest?" Grace asked, pausing in her looting of the dead. "The baron has declared us traitors. There will be more knights looking for us, and there will probably be wanted posters up. We aren't exactly an inconspicuous group. You expect us to waltz up into the city and no one will notice?"

"We don't have a choice," Osric said. "We've figured it out this far, we'll have to just keep moving forward. First, we need to get off this road. It'll take longer to get to the city, but as you said, we're conspicuous. After that, we go to Wolfridge and see what we're up against, then we figure it out from there. As Master Ironhand used to say, a blade is just a thousand hammer strikes, each an opportunity to do better. Or something like that. I never paid attention."

"Close enough," Jasper said. "The point still stands. We take each step as it comes and figure it out."

"Or end up dead," Grace muttered as Rowan and Osric went to try and retrieve what mounts they could after the chaos.

Wolfridge

They stayed off the main roads for the rest of the trip, far away from the Great Road. It kept them from any new trouble but added days of travel, giving more time for the baron to do ... gods know what with the Blackstar. The group pulled up short as the forest thinned, the city's walls visible across the open farmland surrounding the city.

"This is as far as you go, boy," Osric said, reaching down and running his hand along Cinder's neck.

"He won't like being left behind," Rowan said.

"Better than getting us all arrested the moment we walk through the gates. Maybe we manage to go unnoticed even with our faces on wanted posters, but no way anyone mistakes a wolf for anything else," Jasper said.

Rowan dismounted and led his horse into a small grove of trees off the road. "We'll need to leave the horses too."

They secured the horses where they'd have access to grass and the small stream that ran through the grove. Cinder settled himself near the horses, ears alert.

"Stay here. Guard them," Osric commanded.

The wolf huffed but remained in place. They approached the city on foot, keeping to the edge of the tree line. The wooden palisade of the Lower Ward came into view first, torches already lit along its length. Beyond it rose the stone walls of the Upper Ward, Wolfridge Keep visible on an unusual rise near the northern edge of the city.

"More guards than I remember," Jasper said quietly.

Rowan moved ahead, disappearing into the crops and tall grass. Ten minutes later, the ranger returned, almost appearing out of nowhere. His face was grim.

"Triple the normal watch on the walls. Main gate has at least eight guards, and they've got wanted posters nailed to the gatehouse."

"Posters of us?" Talia asked.

"Couldn't see details from that distance, but we have to assume, don't we."

Osric watched a wagon roll up to the gate. The guards made the driver climb down while they searched his cargo. Even from here, he could see the driver's nervous gestures.

"So much for walking in the front door," he said.

"I think I might know another way," Grace said.

"You said you hadn't been here in years," Talia said.

"I haven't. But those folks we helped on the road, the ones being chased by the bandits? I had a long conversation with one of them about the city."

"You did?" Osric asked.

"I thought there was a chance we might end up back here, so the more we knew, the better. Or so it seemed. Something he mentioned was that there was a storm last winter that caused some damage to the drainage ditch, causing it to back up and cause some flooding. He said they'd complained to the constable, but the baron's men were too busy arresting people to worry about fixing things.

"Well, let's check it out," Osric said.

Full darkness had fallen by the time they circled around to the eastern wall. No roads approached from this direction, just rough ground that sloped down out of the city, making it a natural place for the city's drainage, since no major river went through the city.

"There," she whispered, where a small opening came out of the wall, a rut leading down toward the tree line.

They moved slowly through the fields behind Rowan, keeping as low as they could, until they reached the drainage culvert that emerged from beneath the palisade, its opening partially blocked by debris. Water trickled out, carving a muddy channel down the slope.

Grace examined the iron grating that covered the opening. Rust had eaten through several bars, and others hung loose.

"Told you they weren't maintaining things."

"We're going through that?" Talia asked.

"Unless you've got a better idea."

Osric looked at the bars, at where the metal was rusted and pitted, seeing how a torrent of water and uncleared debris had pressed against it. Although it seemed unlikely he'd ever finish his training to be a blacksmith in his own right, he hadn't lost his eye for the craft. He could see where the metal was the most damaged and weakest in its fitting along the crosspiece holding the vertical bars in place.

Gripping two of the damaged bars, he braced himself and pulled as hard as he could. Metal groaned as it turned and shifted in its seating. His shoulders burned with the effort, but the bars began to bend outward, the corroded crossbar giving way to the bars as he pulled. He was so focused on pulling that when one of the bars snapped free entirely, clattering against the rocks, he almost went sliding down the muddy culvert, barely holding onto his footing.

Everyone froze. Distant footsteps echoed from above, a patrol walking the palisade. They pressed themselves against the muddy bank until the sound faded.

When it seemed as if the coast was clear, Osric resumed his work. Another bar came free, then a third. Even with the removed pieces, the opening looked barely wide enough for a person to squeeze through.

"That'll have to do," Grace said.

She went first, disappearing into the darkness of the culvert.

"Clear on the other side," her voice came back to them after a moment.

One by one, they followed. The tunnel reeked of stagnant water and decay. Osric's shoulders scraped against the sides as he pulled himself through, barely able to fit through the opening. He emerged into a cramped space between storage buildings, their walls forming narrow alleys filled with refuse.

"Charming," Talia muttered, brushing mud from her robes.

More footsteps approached. Grace leaned out for a moment before ducking back and signaling. A guard patrol.

Osric spotted a stack of crates and gestured to the rest of them. They hurried to squeeze behind them just as two guards rounded the corner, lanterns held high.

"Quiet night," one said.

The other man just grunted in response as the pair stopped near the drainage opening. His lantern light played across the bent bars and disturbed mud.

"Look at this."

"What?"

"The grating's worse than before. Completely ruined now. I swear, every time I walk past here, more of the metal has been pushed loose."

"So?"

"So maybe we should report it."

The first guard laughed.

"Report it to who? You think the baron cares about drainage?" He spat. "Nothing gets fixed anymore. Better to just keep your head down, unless you want to be replaced, too."

"Still, if someone used it to …"

"To what? Sneak in and steal from empty shops? Half the merchants have fled already."

Next to Osric, Jasper shifted as his foot rolled on some kind of loose stone. He reached out, in reflex, catching the crate, his fingers raking a small barrel balanced precariously on a ledge. It toppled, rolling across the ground with a hollow clatter.

Both guards drew swords instantly. "Who's there?"

They advanced on the crates, lanterns raised. Osric's hand found his sword hilt, even though a fight would be sure death. If they were discovered now, the alarm would bring the entire garrison.

Grace thought quicker than the rest of them, picking up a broken piece of wood and hurling it toward the opposite end of the alley. It clattered against a wall thirty feet away.

"There!" The first guard took off running toward the sound.

The second hesitated, then followed his partner.

"Move," Osric whispered as soon as they turned the corner.

They wouldn't be fooled by that for long. They slipped from behind the crates and headed deeper into the Lower Ward. The narrow alleys between buildings provided cover but also trapped them if patrols appeared from both ends.

Thankfully, they didn't encounter any more. Jasper seemed to know the city well, leading them away from the main thoroughfare and into a maze of smaller alleys. They passed workshop after workshop, most with their doors marked with red wax seals. Official notices had been nailed to many, the text too small to read in the darkness.

"What happened to this place?" Rowan asked quietly.

"Fear," Jasper said. "Fear makes people accept things they never would otherwise."

They reached an intersection where the main route to the Upper Ward crossed their path. A checkpoint blocked the way, this one manned by six guards and two knights in Blackthorn colors.

"Can't cross there," Grace said.

"I know another way." Jasper studied the buildings. "Through the service passages. Merchants use them to move goods without clogging the main streets."

He led them through a narrow gap between buildings into a small courtyard. A stone well occupied the center, surrounded by rear entrances to various shops. More passages opened off the courtyard, creating a warren of interconnected spaces.

"How do you know about these?" Talia asked.

"I had contacts here. People who needed healing but couldn't afford the temple prices."

They navigated the maze, passing through private yards and service areas. Twice, they had to duck into doorways as patrols passed through adjacent streets. They finally crossed into the Upper Ward through a series of connected courtyards. The buildings here were older, built of stone rather than wood. More prosperous, though many windows remained dark.

The market sprawled before them set up on either side of the Great Road as it passed through the city, its stalls empty and barren. During the day, this place would bustle with merchants and customers, but they had all gone home with the setting of the sun.

"Baric's shop is in the northernmost quarter," Jasper said.

They kept to the edges of the market, avoiding the open spaces. Osric had heard many stories of the city from Master Ironhand, none of which matched the city he saw now. It felt too quiet. Too barren. It felt as if the whole city was holding its breath.

And everywhere, there were guards.

"Jasper?" A voice croaked from a darkened doorway.

They all froze at the calling of his name, but instead of more guards, a beggar, filthy and bent, emerged from a shadowed corner.

"It is you! Haven't seen you since ..."

Grace moved fast, pressing a coin into the man's palm while her other hand rested on her blade. "You're mistaken, old man."

"No, no, I remember. He helped my daughter when the fever took her. Didn't ask for payment neither."

"What happened here, Willem?" Jasper asked quietly, waving off Grace.

"You haven't heard? Baron's gone mad, they say. Locked himself in the keep. That cleric of his, Ranulf, runs things now. New rules every day. Papers for this, permits for that. The baroness is dead. Funeral was yesterday. They say the baron killed her, although I heard others say he was out of the city when she died."

"We need to reach the northern quarter."

"Won't reach it by the main streets. Not if you're avoiding the guards," the old man said, looking at them still huddled in the shadow of an alleyway, out of sight. "But there's a way through the old Brennan warehouse. Fire gutted it last year, but you can cut through the ruins."

"I know it. Thank you, Willem."

"Don't thank me. Just go. And be careful. The city's not what it was."

They found the burned warehouse, its stone walls still standing but the roof collapsed. Moonlight streamed through the gaps, illuminating charred beams and debris. They picked their way through carefully, emerging on the far side into what Osric assumed was the correct section of the city.

The shop Jasper led them to sat between a weaver's establishment and a dye merchant, unremarkable except for the faint light visible through gaps in the rear shutters. They watched from across the street, checking for patrols.

"Seems quiet," Rowan said.

"Only one way to find out." Jasper looked to them one last time before crossing to the rear entrance and knocking.

For a minute, nothing happened. Then footsteps approached from inside. The door opened a crack, revealing a sliver of light and a weathered face.

"We're closed. Come back ... Jasper?"

"Hello, Baric."

For a moment, Osric wondered if the man would send them away, close the door on them. Thankfully, he didn't. Instead, the door swung wide revealing a thin, gray-haired man, who gestured urgently.

"Inside, quickly!"

As soon as the last of the group had filed in, Baric looked down each direction of the street outside before shutting the door behind him. The shop's front room was cluttered with shelves packed with cloth, dyes, and various imported wares. A single candle burned on the counter, casting long shadows across the merchandise.

"Baric, it's good to ..." Jasper started to say, before Baric shushed him.

"Keep your voices down. Never know who might be listening these days."

"That bad?" Jasper asked, much quieter this time.

"Worse. Folk disappear for asking the wrong questions."

"What happened here?"

Baric settled onto a stool behind the counter. "Where do I start? The baron, he's made himself almost invisible. No one's seen much of him in months. Around the same time, the First Counselor Ranulf started making himself quite visible. Daily proclamations, new regulations, inspections. Feels as if he's running the city now. With him came the increase in guards. They've got us all walking on eggshells."

"Any idea why he disappeared?" Osric asked.

"Not really, but how would I know? It's not like he comes in to buy my goods, is it? There's been talk, of course. Marketplace gossip that he's under the first counselor's control, that his wife was poisoned and he's been caring for her, you know how it is. When people are in the dark, they make up their own stories."

"Someone mentioned that. We heard she died."

"She did. There was a big funeral yesterday. A procession and everything. That everyone knows, it's how she died that has the rumors of poisoning starting up. Some say the baron killed her, others that the counselor did it. You know how these things go."

"What about this Ranulf?" Rowan asked.

"He's been busy, that's for sure. Proclamations of all kinds, including one putting him in control of the daily tasks of the baron. Others about threats to the baron and his family, which were used to justify all the new security measures. One even blamed the Rangers, which is why they were disbanded. Accused them of treason. Nonsense if you ask me."

"We need to reach the baron," Jasper said. "We have important information for him."

Baric actually laughed. "Reach the baron? That would be hard, even in the best of times. Now? Impossible. Who would you even talk to about that? Several longtime city officials have vanished. Others were replaced overnight. Everything goes through Ranulf's people now."

"There has to be someone."

"Getting any kind of official business done means dealing with Ranulf's bureaucrats. And handing out coin."

"What about people who used to work in the keep? Before Ranulf started making changes?" Osric asked, frustrated.

"Well. Maybe. There's Hale. He used to be one of the guards up at the keep until they sacked him. Cleaning house of people not loyal to the first counselor, to hear him tell it. Could be he's just bitter since instead of a life inside the keep, he's now working down at the lumber yard and spending his nights at the Hollow."

"The Hollow?"

"A run-down little tavern, definitely not the finest establishment, if you take my meaning. But the food is cheap, and the drink is cheaper."

"You think he'd talk to us?" Jasper asked.

"He might. He talks a lot once he gets some drink in him, but that's mostly complaining. Actual information, I don't know. He's real quiet when he's sober."

"Where exactly is the Hollow?"

"It's in the Lower Ward near the lumber yard. Head north from here, past the old brewery. Turn left at the cooper's shop. You'll smell the sawdust before you see the tavern."

"We appreciate this," Jasper said.

"You were always a good man, Jasper. I'm happy to help. Be careful, though. This city's changed. People I've known for years won't meet my eyes anymore. Everyone's watching everyone else, wondering who might turn them in for a few coins," Baric said, standing and walking them toward the rear door. "He should be there already. If you're lucky, it was a good day and he's going slow on his drink. He usually sits at a table in the back corner. Big man, thick beard, missing part of his left ear."

The merchant opened the door a crack, peering out into the darkness. "Coast looks clear. Take the alley behind the weaver's shop. Follow it west until you hit the main thoroughfare."

They filed out into the night. With one last look, Baric's door clicked shut behind them, the sound of multiple locks sliding into place following immediately after.

"Well, that wasn't helpful," Grace said once they'd moved away from the shop.

"No one said this would be easy," Osric said. "Let's go."

Baric wasn't wrong when he'd described the place as 'not the finest establishment.' The Hollow squatted between two larger buildings like a forgotten afterthought, its weathered sign hanging at an angle that suggested no one cared enough to fix it.

The smell of stale ale and unwashed bodies hit him as soon as he walked through the front door. The interior lived up to its name, a hollow shell of what might once have been a respectable establishment. Mismatched tables and chairs filled the cramped space, most occupied by men who looked like they just wanted to forget their day.

"There," Grace said quietly, tilting her head toward a corner table.

Osric followed her gaze. A man sat alone, hunched over a tankard. His broad shoulders and the way he positioned himself, back to the wall, clear view of the door, marked him as someone accustomed to watching for trouble. The patched leather jerkin and worn boots fit Baric's description of Hale.

"Let's grab that table," Osric said, gesturing to an empty spot close enough to observe but not obviously so.

They settled in, ordering watered ale from a serving girl who looked too young to be working in such a place. Jasper leaned forward once she left.

"We need to be careful. A dismissed guard might be desperate enough to sell information about us to Ranulf's people."

"Or desperate enough to help us," Osric countered.

"How do you want to approach this?" Rowan asked.

Osric studied the man for a moment longer. Hale took another pull from his tankard.

"Rowan and I will talk to him directly. The rest of you keep an eye out and be ready to run if this goes south."

Grace frowned. "And if it does?"

"Then we deal with it."

Talia touched his arm briefly. "Be careful."

Osric nodded and stood; Rowan followed behind him as they crossed the tavern. It only took a moment for the man to clock them headed in his direction. The former guard's eyes tracked their approach, his hand shifting slightly toward his belt where a knife handle protruded.

Osric pulled out a chair and sat down without invitation. Rowan remained standing, positioned to watch both Hale and the room.

Hale's bloodshot eyes narrowed. "This table's taken."

"We're not here to cause trouble," Osric said.

"Then find another table."

"We're looking for someone who might be interested in some work."

Hale took another drink, studying them over the rim of his tankard. "Work's scarce these days. Especially for strangers who don't know when they're not welcome."

"We heard you used to work in the keep. My name's Robert, used to be with the Rangers before ... well, before they decided we weren't needed anymore," Rowan said, providing a false name.

"The Rangers. Another one of Ranulf's improvements. Tell me, Robert, how's unemployment treating you?"

"About as well as you'd expect."

"Then you should know better than to bother honest folk trying to drink in peace."

"We're not here to bother anyone," Osric said. "My name's Owen. We just need someone who knows their way around, knows the right people."

"The right people. And what kind of people would strangers be looking for?"

"The kind who might help with a business opportunity," Rowan said.

"You are being awfully careful with your words for a simple business opportunity, and you two don't look like merchants to me."

"Appearances can be deceiving," Osric said.

"Not as much as you'd think. See, when strangers come asking questions about the keep, about the 'right people,' it usually means one of two things. Either they're working for Ranulf, trying to flush out anyone who might still be loyal to the old ways. Or they're fools about to get themselves arrested."

"We're neither," Rowan said.

"That remains to be seen."

Osric decided to shift tactics. "We've heard things have changed in Wolfridge. New policies, new management. Some people might not be happy with those changes."

"Lots of people aren't happy. Doesn't mean they're stupid enough to talk about it with strangers in taverns."

"Even if those strangers might be able to help?"

"Help how? You going to give me my position back? Going to make it so a man can walk the streets without being harassed? Going to bring back the Rangers and the old guard?"

"We can't change the past," Osric admitted. "But we might be able to affect the future."

"Pretty words. I've heard plenty of pretty words lately. Usually right before someone gets hauled off to the dungeons."

"We're taking the same risk being here," Rowan pointed out.

"No, you're not. You can walk out that door anytime you want. Me? This is my city. My home. I've got nowhere else to go. You want my advice? Leave. Get out of Wolfridge while you still can."

"We can't do that."

"Can't or won't?"

"Both."

Hale studied them for a long moment. "You're not merchants."

"No."

"And you're not just passing through."

"No."

"Then you're fools." He signaled for another ale. They waited while the serving girl refilled his tankard and left. Hale took a long pull before continuing. "So, fools, what exactly is this business opportunity you mentioned?"

"We need to reach certain people," Osric said carefully.

"Talking to anyone is dangerous, but it sounds like you're asking me to take a real risk."

"We're willing to take that risk with you," Rowan said.

"Are you now? And what makes you think I'd help strangers take such risks?"

"Because you're still here," Osric said. "Still drinking in this tavern where anyone could recognize you. A man who was truly beaten would have left the city by now."

"Maybe I've got nowhere else to go."

"Or maybe you're waiting for something. Or someone."

Hale's expression hardened. "Careful, boy. That kind of talk could be considered treasonous."

"Only if someone reports it."

"And how do I know you won't?"

"Because we need your help," Osric said simply. "And because we're risking just as much by asking."

Hale was quiet for a moment, then shook his head. "You still haven't told me what you really want."

Osric glanced at Rowan, then made a decision. He leaned forward, lowering his voice. "We need to reach Baron Blackthorn. We have important information for him. People's lives depend on it."

"Lots of people's lives depend on lots of things. Doesn't mean ..."

"We have something the baron needs to see. Something that could help with the troubles plaguing the region."

Hale stared at him. "The troubles plaguing the region. You mean the complete breakdown of law and order? The dismissal of anyone who shows a hint of loyalty to the old ways? The baroness dying under mysterious circumstances? Those troubles?"

"Among others."

"You're either brave or stupid. Possibly both."

"Will you help us or not?"

Hale drained half his tankard in one long pull. "Even if I wanted to help, which I'm not saying I do, there's no way to reach the baron. No one sees him except Ranulf and his inner circle."

"There must be some way."

"Must there? The baron's own guards can't reach him. His advisors have been replaced or silenced. Even the servants who've worked in the keep for decades are kept away from him."

"What about before?" Rowan asked. "People who knew him personally?"

Hale's laugh was bitter. "You mean the people Ranulf had dismissed? Arrested? Made to disappear?"

"Not all of them disappeared."

"No. Some of us were just thrown out like garbage." He took another drink. "Look, even if someone wanted to help you reach the baron, it would be suicide. Ranulf has informants everywhere."

"We're not asking you to take us to the keep," Osric said. "Just to connect us with people who might know another way."

"Another way." Hale shook his head. "You really are fools."

"Maybe.

Hale finished his ale and set the tankard down carefully.

"You know, I wasn't the only one Ranulf decided was no longer suitable for service."

"Others were dismissed?"

"Dismissed. Arrested. Some just vanished one night. Good men who'd served the baron faithfully for years."

"Rangers, too?" Rowan asked.

"Especially Rangers. First Ranger Grange himself barely escaped ahead of the arrest order. Others weren't so lucky."

"I'd heard rumors, but ..." Rowan said, his voice trailing off.

"These other dismissed guards," Osric said. "They must be angry about what happened."

"Angry? Try furious. Men who dedicated their lives to serving the baron, thrown out like they were nothing. Their families threatened if they speak out."

"Sounds like people who might be motivated to help."

Hale studied them again. "You're determined to do this."

"We are."

"Even knowing it's probably suicide?"

"Even then."

"Why? What could possibly be worth that risk?"

"The truth," Osric said simply. "And a chance to fix what's broken."

Hale was quiet for a long moment. Then he stood, swaying slightly. "There might be some people willing to talk to you. Might be."

"Where?"

"Not here. Too public." He glanced around the tavern. "There's a warehouse in the Merchant Quarter. Belongs to a merchant who's sympathetic to those of us Ranulf cast aside. Some of the former guards meet there. Quietly."

"When?"

"Most evenings. About now, actually." He pulled on a worn cloak. "I could take you there. Introduce you."

Rowan caught Osric's eye, warning clear in his expression.

"That's generous of you," Osric said carefully.

"Not generous. Practical. If you go blundering around asking questions, you'll get yourselves arrested. And probably anyone you talk to, which means me."

"So you'll help us?"

"I'll take you to people who might help. What happens after that is between you and them."

Osric stood. "That's all we ask."

"No, boy. You're asking for a lot more than that. You just don't know it yet."

Hale headed for the door without looking back. Osric glanced at their table where Talia, Grace, and Jasper were already rising. They followed Hale out into the darkening streets. The former guard led them through twisting alleys and side streets, avoiding the main thoroughfares where guard patrols were more common.

The warehouse wasn't as far as Osric worried, relieved when Hale slowed down after only a few minutes' walk, approaching a side door to a warehouse. He knocked. Three quick raps, a pause, then two more.

"Old signal from our guard days," he explained.

The door opened, revealing darkness beyond. Hale gestured for them to enter.

Grace hesitated. "After you."

"Guests first. That's how we do things."

It was clear he wasn't going to go in first. Osric looked at his companions. Something felt wrong, but it wasn't like they had much of a choice. They'd come this far. He stepped through the doorway.

The warehouse interior was dimly lit by a few scattered lanterns. Crates and barrels created a maze of shadows. Osric took another step forward, letting his eyes adjust. As soon as the last of them was in and Hale moved behind them, movement erupted from behind the stacked goods. Armed figures emerged from concealment, surrounding them with practiced efficiency. Crossbows and swords pointed at them from every direction.

"Nobody move," a harsh voice commanded.

Osric counted quickly. At least a dozen men, all armed, all positioned with clear lines of fire. No cover nearby. No room to maneuver.

"Sorry about this. But like I said, nobody can be trusted these days. Not even a ranger," Hale said behind them.

Beside Osric, Talia's hand twitched. Three crossbows immediately swung to target her.

"Don't," Osric said quietly.

Grace's hands hovered near her weapons, fury clear on her face. "You bastard."

"Drop your weapons. All of them," Hale said.

Osric raised his hands slowly. "Everyone stand down."

"Osric ..." Talia started.

"No. We can't fight our way out of this."

He unbuckled his sword belt, letting it fall to the floor. After a moment, Rowan did the same with his bow. Grace was the last to comply, throwing her short sword down with obvious disgust.

"The staff too," one of the armed men said, pointing at Talia.
She reluctantly set her staff on the ground.

"Bind them," Hale said.

As the armed men moved forward with rope, Osric caught Rowan's eye. They'd been in bad situations before, but as the rope tightened around his wrists, Osric wondered if they'd finally found one they couldn't escape from.

Rebels

Instead of going out the way they came in, Hale and his men pushed Osric and the rest through the rear of the warehouse, into an alley. Rough hands yanked a rope tight around Osric's wrists as they were corralled into the alley, the coarse fibers biting into his skin. Another man forced a strip of cloth between Osric's teeth, pulling it tight behind his head. The musty fabric tasted of old sweat and dirt.

Part of Osric wanted to fight, resist as they had done before, but they were outnumbered and in tight confines. It was likely that one of his companions would be killed if he tried.

That was emphasized when Grace struggled briefly before a crossbow arrow pressed against her ribs convinced her to stop.

"Get them moving," Hale said.

The captors shoved them toward a slightly more open area where the alley connected with another, forming an almost intersection. Osric stumbled, his balance thrown off by his bound hands. Someone caught his elbow and pushed him forward again. At the intersection, a large wagon waited, stacked with crates. Several were pulled out to reveal a false interior hidden by the stacks of crates pushed against a wooden frame.

It wasn't perfect camouflage but a guard would have to pull a lot of heavy boxes out of the way to find it. Two draft horses stood in the traces, their breath forming small clouds in the cool air.

"Inside."

Osric climbed in first, awkwardly pulling himself up with his bound hands. His companions followed, pushed and prodded by their captors. Grace landed hard on her knees. Rowan helped her sit upright. The space barely held all five of them, forcing them to press against each other in the darkness.

The wood panel slammed shut, and the boxes were put back in place, causing total darkness to surround them.

After some muffled shuffling and the shifting of the wagon, maybe as someone climbed on the board seat up front, the wagon lurched forward. Osric's shoulder collided with the wall as the wheels found a rut. He shifted, trying to find a position where the rope didn't cut so deeply into his wrists. Beside him, Talia made muffled sounds.

This was a predicament. He just hoped that Jasper's friend Baric was right and this Hale wasn't working for the baron after all. It would be just their luck that this was some kind of trap. A double-blind to capture them.

The baron surely knew about them. The knights they'd fought had their descriptions, so it was possible.

The wagon turned left. Then right. Another left. Osric tried to track their path through the city, but after the fourth turn, he lost all sense of direction. The wheels clattered over cobblestones for what felt like hours, although almost certainly wasn't.

It was hard to gauge time without being able to see the sky.

The sounds changed. Rough city streets were replaced by a much smoother road, this one, maintained cobblestone. The wagon picked up speed. They'd left the city, almost certainly, and were on the Great Road itself. Through the stacked boxes, Osric heard the faint sounds of other traffic on the road. Horses passing. The creak of other wagons. A dog barking somewhere in the distance.

No one tried to stop them. Why would they? Just another merchant wagon heading out of Wolfridge on business. Nothing suspicious about that.

Time crawled by in the darkness. Osric's legs cramped from sitting in the same position. His jaw ached from the gag. The rope had rubbed his wrists raw. Beside him, someone shifted. A knee pressed into his thigh. An elbow jabbed his ribs.

The wagon slowed. Turned off the main road onto something rougher. The wheels bounced over roots and rocks. Branches scraped the boxes stacked above the hidden compartment. They'd left the Great Road entirely and were on a hard-packed dirt path, maybe.

He wasn't sure, even if he was familiar with this area, which he was not, he would have been able to figure out where they were.

Finally, the wagon stopped.

Light flooded in as the doors opened. Osric squinted against the sudden brightness. Forest surrounded them. A narrow dirt track led back into the distance, disappearing into the trees.

"Out."

Hands grabbed Osric's arms and hauled him from the wagon. His legs, stiff from the ride, nearly buckled. He caught himself and stood upright, blinking in the afternoon sunlight.

They were on a hunters' track, the kind that branched off the main roads and led into the forest. The trees pressed close on both sides. No buildings. No signs of civilization except the track itself.

One by one, his companions emerged from the wagon. Osric knew, out in the woods, Cinder was almost certainly following them. The wolf seemed to almost always know where they were, but he was too smart to come out of hiding now, while there was this much danger.

Osric tried to speak through the gag. The words came out as meaningless noise, but he tried to put a questioning tone into them. Where were they taking them? Why bring them out here?

"Shut up." One of the armed men shoved Osric forward. "Start walking."

The man's voice shook slightly. Not with anger. With nerves. Osric studied him more closely. Young, maybe twenty. His leather jerkin had been patched multiple times. The sword at his hip looked like it had seen better days, the blade nicked and the leather wrapping on the hilt coming loose. Not a professional soldier. Just someone caught up in whatever was happening.

"Move."

The men shoved the group toward the tree line. A game trail opened between two massive oaks, barely wide enough for them to move single file. Hale led the way, his broad shoulders brushing the undergrowth on both sides.

Someone produced a length of rope. They threaded it through the bonds on each prisoner's wrists, connecting them in a line. Osric ended up at the front, followed by Talia, then Grace, Rowan, and finally Jasper. Like a string of pack animals being led to market.

The trail wound deeper into the forest. Roots caught at Osric's feet. Low branches forced him to duck. Behind him, he heard Grace stumble. The rope tightened as she tripped, then Rowan's steadying hand went to her shoulder, keeping her upright.

Osric watched the sun through the canopy, trying to gauge their direction. Southeast, moving away from Wolfridge and into the Great Forest itself.

Their captors spread out along the line. Two in front with Hale. Three walking beside the prisoners. Four bringing up the rear. Ten men total, not counting Hale.

Osric studied them as they walked. Most of them had farmers' hands. Rough and calloused from working the earth. One had the burns and scars of a blacksmith, those he knew well. These were regular people, not fighters. Their weapons reflected that. A few proper swords, but mostly tools. A wood axe. A pitchfork with the tines bent straight. A sledgehammer that belonged in a quarry, not a forest.

They were so afraid.

They kept glancing over their shoulders. Checking the trees. Listening for sounds of pursuit. Whatever had driven them to this, they weren't comfortable with it.

The trail turned, following the curve of a small valley. Water gurgled somewhere nearby. A small stream, maybe.

An hour passed. Maybe more. Osric's wrists had gone numb where the rope cut off the circulation. His mouth felt like he'd been chewing cotton. Sweat soaked through his shirt despite the cool forest air.

Something happened that he couldn't see because Hale raised his hand which stopped everyone in their tracks.

Hale waited for a minute, head cocked like he was listening for something.

A bird called. Three short whistles.

Hale whistled back. Two long notes.

A moment later, figures emerged from the forest, dressed just like the men who'd captured them.

Those new men all held back as a broad-shouldered man with dark hair going gray at the temples moved forward, his eyes moving across the five of them bound and standing in the middle of Hale's group.

"What is this?"

"They found us in the city and were asking about the baron and drawing a lot of attention. I thought it best to get them out of the public view."

"We don't have enough problems without you abducting people like Ranulf does?"

Hale's jaw tightened. "They could be spies."

"You don't know that. That man's a ranger, for gods' sakes."

"We can't take chances."

"We can't take everyone who asks about the baron prisoner either. Do you want to be like them?"

The two men stared at each other. Then the leader of the new group gestured for Hale to follow him. They walked several paces away, far enough that their voices became just indistinct murmurs. Osric could read their body language clearly enough, though. Hale gestured at them and the other man shook his head repeatedly, pointing back the way they'd come.

The argument grew more heated with Hale raising his voice, though not enough for them to make out the words. The other man seemed much calmer. Back and forth they went, neither giving ground.

Finally, Hale threw up his hands and stalked away, finding a tree to lean against. Whatever the argument, he'd lost.

The new man just shook his head and approached the group. "Cut them loose and remove those gags."

The men hesitated.

"Now."

Hale's men looked in his direction, but it was clear their leader wasn't going to help them. Reluctantly, they pulled their knives and sawed through the ropes binding them, removing the connecting rope and coiling it back up. Blood rushed back into Osric's hands, bringing stabbing needles of pain as he reached up and pulled the gag free.

Osric worked his jaw, trying to get moisture back into his mouth. Grace immediately launched into a string of complaints that would have made a sailor blush as soon as she could speak again.

"I apologize for this," the man said, sounding genuinely regretful. "My name is Kestran. Hale is … well, these are difficult times and we've all lost much to Ranulf's rule. His fear makes him see enemies everywhere."

"We understand."

"Though going into Wolfridge and asking about getting in to see the baron makes you either courageous or foolhardy," Kestran said.

"Probably a little of both."

A slight smile touched Kestran's lips. "Could I ask why you were trying so hard to get in to see the baron?"

Osric considered how much to reveal. On one hand, these people opposed Ranulf, making them potential allies, but trust came hard when crossbows had recently been pointed at your head.

"The baron has something we need. Something important. Not just to us, but to everyone."

"That's rather vague."

"These are dangerous times," Osric shrugged and said. "You just said so yourself."

"Fair enough, but I'm afraid reaching the baron is nearly impossible. Ranulf keeps him fairly secluded. He hasn't been seen in public in several months."

"There must be some way to get to him."

"If there is, I don't know it." Kestran paused. "Paulin might."

"Who?"

Rowan spoke for the first time since they'd been freed. "He's a ranger, or was. One of the best that ever served. I'd heard he'd retired, though."

"Retired." Kestran's mouth twisted. "That's one way to put it. Built up a farm, took a wife, and then Ranulf's men burned it all to the ground when he wouldn't turn over more taxes."

"He survived? The Paulin I met would have fought them to the death."

"He fought them alright, got a fair number of them too, but in the end, he and his wife were struck down. One of his neighbors found him hours later and dragged him out of there, nursing him back to health. Man is tougher than he looks. He's been organizing people like us. People who want things back how they were."

"And this Paulin," Osric broke in. "He might be able to help us?"

"Like I said, he's the one organizing all of this. If anyone knows how to get to the baron, it would be him.

"Then I think we need to see Paulin."

It took them an hour of walking along the game trail before the path finally broke into a clearing that opened wider than he expected. More than a clearing, a small village, of sorts, although not one of the established ones around the city. Much of the cleared land looked newly raised to Osric's eyes. Three farmhouses in the center looked long-established, perhaps an old farmstead, but the rest ... they looked newly built. Two dozen smaller cottages, some barely able to be called that, spread out from the farmhouses to the edge of the forest.

What land didn't have small homes on it was filled with plots turned in neat beds that ran to the trees. The area was very crowded, even for as large as the clearing was.

There were signs everywhere of habitation. Smoke thinned above cookfires, carts sat with wheels propped, straw packed against spokes. Someone had hung laundry on lines strung between posts. Two goats stared at the newcomers and bleated once before wandering off with the arrogance only goats could manage.

Kestran raised a hand as they left the forest and entered the edge of the makeshift village. People had started to notice them. Children squealed and ran up to see them.

They must be a sight. Kestran had returned their weapons and armor to them, which made the five of them stand out even more surrounded by farmers turned revolutionaries.

"Wait, before we go further," Osric said. "I need my companion."

"Companion?" Hale asked.

Osric cupped his hands to his mouth and called out, a throaty whistle not that different from one Master Ironhand had used to get his attention. For a heartbeat, the men all looked around, unsure of what was happening.

Brush parted near the tree line as Cinder stepped out of the shadow of birch trunks. Dark gray with pale streaks along his flanks, head low, tail just above his hocks, he cut toward Osric and stood by his side. The children who had begun to crowd in on them jumped back, forming a ragged half-circle, trying to get a view of the animal.

"Thestra keep us," someone said behind Kestran.

Kestran's hand went to his knife.

"It's all right," Osric said. "He's with me."

"What do you mean, with you?"

"This is Cinder. He's my friend and travels with my group. We'd left him outside of the city, for obvious reasons, and he has been shadowing us since you brought us out here.

The wolf's amber eyes flicked up to Osric, then to the men, as he huffed at their stares.

"Does he … eat children?" a girl asked.

"No," Osric said. "He eats worse things."

Grace leaned toward the girl. "Like little boys who pick on their sisters."

The girl grinned before being tugged back by her sleeve. A boy nearby, maybe her brother, blanched. Grace must have seen something in their interaction and figured out their relationship. She had an interesting knack with children, something he wouldn't have guessed from her outward demeanor.

The crowd swelled as they moved further into the makeshift village. Women came from kitchens, and men with hoes and wooden clubs inched closer. The children broke through their fear before the adults did and fell in behind the group, trailing like ducklings.

Osric studied the men who held themselves like they mattered here. As with Hale's men, these weren't warriors or soldiers. These were more farmers and shopkeepers. Refugees, not rebels.

"Make way," someone called from the porch of the largest, central farmhouse.

An older man stepped out and set his palm on the rail.

"That's an interesting group."

"Paulin. You were right. Hale grabbed the people from the wanted poster," Kestran said.

"I didn't …"

"No one said you did anything wrong, Hale," Paulin said, before looking at Osric and the others. "You should all come inside."

Osric followed Paulin into the farmhouse with the rest of the group on his heels. The room they entered was fairly Spartan, although stacks of clutter on chairs and a small table off to the side suggested it had been cleared in anticipation of their arrival.

A long table sat in the center, scarred by knives and hot pots. Cinder padded in and curled up near the threshold, facing the room. He kept his ears aimed toward the outside.

Paulin closed the door. He did not sit. "You have quite the bounty on your heads."

"We don't know why," Osric said. "This is mostly our first time in Wolfridge."

That wasn't entirely true. Osric had a good idea why the baron, or at least this man Ranulf in the baron's name, wanted them arrested. He was involved with the Brethren, who had made it clear since Osric found the ring that they wanted him dead.

"Whatever you did, it must have been big, because there are wanted posters up not just in the city, but in many of the surrounding villages. You were foolish to go into Wolfridge at all, and lucky you made it as far as you did without being arrested. Why would you go back there?"

"We need to talk to the baron."

"Why?"

Again, Osric wasn't sure he wanted to answer that question. Paulin seemed like a good enough sort, and Rowan seemed taken with him, but the knowledge of the Blackstar, and that it was loose in the world, wasn't something Osric wanted to let be known.

After how hard the Brethren had fought to keep the document out of people's hands, it was safe to assume they would want the artifact for their own uses.

"We need something he has," Osric said.

"What?" Paulin asked.

"It's hard to explain, but it's a very old artifact that we believe could stop some of the ... unusual events that have been happening over the last few years. We think they are a sign that the world is in trouble, and we think we can use it to help fix things."

If Paulin was a ranger, he would know what Osric meant by unusual events. The creatures released on their world hadn't been recent and had been seen in enough areas that even people in his own village had talked about them. A ranger would know of them for sure.

"Why do you think the baron knows about this artifact?"

"Because when we went to retrieve it, we learned that the baron and a large party of knights had beaten us there and left with it."

"Where was this?"

Osric paused a beat before he said, "The Claws."

Paulin blinked. "You went into the Claws."

"We did," Rowan said.

"And you came back?" Paulin asked. "Never mind. Obviously, you did. That is very impressive. I have never heard of anyone going there and coming out safe again. That does explain where the baron went though. We knew he had left the city and that many of his knights left with him, and that even after he was seen in public again, many of those knights remained missing, but we could not figure out where he went or what they were doing."

"Many of them died. As far as we can tell, most of the men who went into those mountains with him did not make it back out."

"Well, the ones that did come back had an artifact, the one we are seeking," Osric said, steering the conversation back. "It could pose a serious threat if it is not handled correctly. It is critical that we get it from the baron."

"The baron never goes out in public. You're going to need to get into the keep if you want it."

"Yes, that was what we were trying to do. We'd looked for your men because we understood they might know a way in."

"Into the city, perhaps. We have ways. But the keep itself?" Paulin shook his head. "That's another matter."

"We were told that the rebellion against the baron had people on the inside," Osric said.

That wasn't entirely true. It had been implied, and Osric just hoped those implications were true and not just wishful thinking.

"We do. Servants, a few guards who remember better days. They can get us information, even open certain doors, but the keep is full of Greenwood Guard and the baron's sworn knights. I can't make them disappear."

"But we have to get in to see the baron. This is critical."

"I wish I could help, but we have our own problems. People are suffering under Ranulf's policies, families are being torn apart, livelihoods destroyed. It is all we can do to keep our people free and fed. I can't abandon them for some artifact with nothing but vague warnings about it."

That was what Osric had been worried about. He didn't want to say too much, but he had to give them something.

Before he could start explaining more, Jasper suddenly spoke up, saying, "What if we could solve both problems?"

"What do you mean?" Paulin asked.

"We deal with Ranulf. Free the baron from his control, get what we need, and restore proper leadership to the barony. What if we could do it all?"

"Deal with Ranulf?" Paulin laughed, but there was no humor in it. "He has the entire Greenwood Guard backing him. The sworn knights follow his orders. You survived the Claws, which speaks to your capabilities, but you can't fight an army."

"We won't need to fight all of them."

"How do you figure that?"

Jasper looked toward the door, toward the settlement beyond. "You have been doing more than just feeding people and hiding them. I saw other wanted posters. Posters for bandits robbing tax shipments, warnings about aiding the rebel elements. Unless I miss my guess, that is you. Your goal can't just be holding on, can it? If you are resisting, then ultimately your goal must be to free your barony."

"Yes, but we are a long way from that."

"A long way from taking the barony yourself, yes, but you have enough men here to cause a distraction. To create enough chaos to keep the guard and maybe even the knights busy while we are slipping through one of the passages into the keep."

"The void we will," Hale said from where he stood against the wall. "Look outside. Look at who we've gathered. Farmers. Shopkeepers. Good people, brave people, but not warriors. They'll be slaughtered."

"That's exactly my point," Jasper said. "These are not the people who will storm the city, defeat its guard, and retake the barony. You don't need them for that task. You need us."

Paulin's expression hardened. "You're suggesting we use these people as bait?"

"I'm suggesting we work together. These people don't need to defeat the baron's forces. Just keep them occupied long enough for us to reach Ranulf and the baron."

"And then?"

"Once Ranulf falls, his hold breaks. Without a leader, I don't think the guard will keep fighting, keep supporting the policies Ranulf has been pushing."

"You seem very confident about that."

"I know how these organizations work. Cut off the head ..."

"It's not that simple. Even if you could reach Ranulf, even if you could defeat him, the chaos would ..."

"Bring in the Rangers," Rowan said.

Everyone turned to look at him.

"What?" Paulin asked.

"The Rangers. Yes, they have been disbanded and First Ranger Grange arrested, but that doesn't mean they've given up on the barony. They're still out there."

"You haven't been around since the Rangers were disbanded. I have been and I've spoken with many of them. They're angry, but there's a reason they haven't made a move. They see this for what it is, they know the odds. They don't want to throw their lives away on futile gestures."

"This isn't futile," Osric said. "We can deal with Ranulf and reach the baron. We just need the chance."

Paulin stood and walked to the window, looking out at the settlement. Children still played outside, the excitement of the visitors forgotten for more immediate entertainment. Life persisted despite everything.

"I served with Grange for fifteen years," he said quietly. "Good man. I was pleased when he was named First Ranger. When they arrested him, claimed he was a traitor, it was when I knew things would never be able to go back to the way they had been, peacefully."

"Then help us fix it."

"You really think you can stop Ranulf?"

"I know we can."

"And the baron? What makes you think he'll listen? The man's been acting strange for months."

"We'll make him listen," Talia said. "Or we will deal with him."

"I hope it doesn't come to that. That's not what I want."

"Neither do we," Osric said. "But this barony is our home too, and we also want this to end. One way or another."

Paulin turned from the window. "The rangers ... some will answer the call. Not all, but maybe enough. If they see a real chance for actual change."

"How many?" Osric asked.

"Forty, perhaps fifty."

"That would be enough."

"It would. But I need to know you're serious about this. That you won't abandon these people once you have what you came for."

"We won't," Rowan said.

"Your word on it?"

"I'm a ranger."

Paulin nodded slowly. "Then I'll reach out to those I trust. It will take time. A day, maybe two, to gather them, explain the situation."

"We can wait that long."

"Good. Kestran, find them quarters," Paulin said, moving toward the door. "I'll send riders immediately. If enough rangers answer the call, if we can coordinate properly ... this might actually work."

"It will work," Osric said.

"For all our sakes, I hope you're right."

A Plan

Osric shouldered the last of their bundles into a vacant hut and set them down by the wall. On the surface of it, the place was clean and well-kept. Cut wood filled a corner in a neat stack near the cooking fire, and someone had swept the dirt floor, pushing the grit into a thin line along the threshold.

Someone had lived here, but the place hadn't been packed up as if they had moved. No, a pot remained on the fire, empty and collecting dust, blankets still hung on a peg against one wall, but personal effects were missing. There were no mementos. The things that people kept and would not leave behind easily.

Whoever had lived here hadn't just moved. They would have taken the blankets and the pots, things they needed, with them. No, those keepsakes had just been cleaned out, removed by someone making this hut livable for a new tenant.

This suggested that the rebels were having more losses than they cared to admit.

He began to unpack the simple things they would need for a few days: rations, things to clean their weapons and armor. Talia helped him and started to prepare food for them, as it had been some time since their last meal, but Grace, Rowan, and Jasper had simply dropped their things and left again, to wander the village.

It worried Osric. In the wilderness, they were a single body, living and fighting together. Now that they were in some kind of civilization again, they quickly fragmented.

They still had a long way to go, and he was worried that if they could not stay together, they would not be able to see this quest to the end.

"I'm going to check on the others," he said to Talia.

"Bring back some water. I think we have enough to make one last stew."

"Sure," he said, taking the jug that had been left behind near the cooking fire and stepping out the door.

He assumed the well was somewhere near the farmhouses, which would have been the original buildings here, set up with purpose rather than as temporary dwellings to hold the influx of people.

Near a wide patch of open ground, children ran with sticks. Not far down the way, he saw Jasper standing at the edge of the play area, apart from the bustle, his hands folded in front of him, watching the children with a still face.

Osric walked to Jasper and took a place beside him. He did not greet him at once, simply joined him in watching the children.

The children split into two sides, then three, then none at all when a pair broke off and argued about whether the center log counted as the base. A small boy with a red scarf tied on his wrist proposed that anyone who touched the log owed a forfeit, which set off howls. Someone suggested that new arrivals could claim amnesty for one count. Then a taller girl declared that you could only tag with the flat of the stick, not the tip. The little ones cheered the new rule because they could manage the flat.

Another pair ran up and changed the teams with no quarrel. The game bent to fit them. It made Osric smile. Even in times like this, children always seemed to find each other for a little comfort and fun.

"They are so resilient," Jasper said, echoing Osric's thoughts.

"That's good. It's how things ought to be. The laughing and the playing."

"How it ought to be," Jasper said, his mouth flattening.

They were quiet for a minute longer before Osric broached the subject. "Are you thinking about her? The girl?"

"Nora, and yes. I never stop thinking about her. Every day I fall asleep and see that cellar again, the ring of them around her in the lamplight. Me sitting there useless, my hands bound in front of me. I cry and beg for them to stop, to leave her alone."

The children surged toward the log in a clump. Sticks knocked. A boy went down and rolled to avoid being trampled. Laughter rose, untidy and harsh.

"It's like I'm standing outside myself, watching. Sometimes I break free of my bonds and throw my body over her, taking the blow meant for her. Then I wake up and the truth remains. I didn't stop them. The blood remains on my hands."

"I don't think that's true," Osric said. "As I understand it, they gave the job of killing her to you, and you refused. Not only refused but tried to get her away from there. You put your life in danger to protect hers."

Jasper's eyes tracked a boy who chased two girls with a whoop. "It did not change her end."

"Maybe not," Osric said. "But it set your path for you. It showed what side you stood on. That matters for what comes next. Doing the wrong thing for the right reason matters as much as doing the right thing for the wrong reason. The gods judge us on our intent, on what's in our heart. You failed, but you tried."

Jasper swallowed and set his jaw. "Her last sound was my name. Did you know that? She called out to me one last time."

"You were her protector. You were the only one who'd tried to save her, so of course it was. And I know you tried to save her. She would not want you blaming yourself for how it ended."

"She doesn't want anything. She's dead," Jasper said angrily, and then fell silent again for a long moment. "When I pray, I do not see her at peace. I see her out of reach, dying in front of me. Again and again."

A boy tripped on the root of a stump and popped up, dirty-faced and grinning. The game shifted again. Someone called out that the log now counted as safe if you hopped on one foot. Two older children, a lanky girl and a boy with a missing tooth, clapped, which had the littlies copying them. The field turned to a chorus of one-legged hops and wild swings. The balancing looked foolish and brave.

"That is your guilt showing you those things, not your heart. You were taken as a cleric by Heathus who watches over the family and the homestead. Do you think that was a coincidence? Does a god of healing and community take a man who murders children as one of his acolytes?"

Jasper didn't answer, his eyes never leaving the playing children.

"Something for you to think about," Osric said, taking a step back. "Talia is going to make stew; if you're hungry it will be ready in a little bit."

Jasper nodded but did not turn.

Osric continued on to the center of the village, finding the well about where it should have been and filling up the jug. He was halfway back to the hut when he saw Rowan standing down a long dirt path that led into the trees. He was near some saplings at the edge of the forest, just staring into the darkness.

Osric sighed and diverted his path. They were so close to this piece of the Blackstar; he just had to hold them together.

"See something out there?"

"No. Too many people here, the animals will keep their distance."

"So ... just looking for some quiet then?"

As with Jasper, Rowan didn't answer right away. He just stood there, staring, lost in his own thoughts.

"What are you doing way out here? Talia's making food."

"Thinking."

"About?"

"About all of this. Everything we've seen recently. I cannot make peace with Wyndra and the Claws. I stood in those canyons and saw what that place does to her beasts. The trees there grew wrong, where any lived. The earth bled sand where it should have fed roots. We closed a rift, and I know that matters, but the range still sits there like a wound that never scabs. She rules the wild. How does she allow that place to stand?"

"She isn't doing nothing. She's working with the other gods, the members of the Veilguard. They are trying to fix what is happening, but they can't come into our reality, or so I understand it. They can't do anything about the Claws, not directly. Those were pulled into our reality by the people abusing magic on this side of the Veil. It's why they have us, to fix it."

"If she cannot act, what is worship then? Where are her clerics? She has people in this world to do her will, where are they? If she cares for the wild, why not gather more together instead of sending us out alone with vague visions? Where are the others of the Veilguard? Jasper stands here because we found him along the road and he needed to run from his past, not because Heathus sent him to aid us."

"I don't know. We don't know everything that is happening. Maybe there are other places that need them. The Veil is thin all over, and people who need help are everywhere. I only know that they are sending someone. Us."

"It still seems wrong. People here are paying a price while they sit in their kingdoms, watching us."

"Maybe, but we don't know that. All we can do is keep pushing, keep searching for answers and doing what we must. The gods aren't here, but we are, and these people are counting on us. You saw those people, farmers, women, and children. They can't survive this without us, so we have to do what we have to do."

Rowan made a low sound that might have been a laugh. "You are consistent. Hammer, nail."

"Tell me I'm wrong," Osric said.

"Of course you aren't," Rowan said. "But it doesn't mean you're right, either. Or at least you're not giving me the answer I need. Sorry, I think I need some time alone."

"I understand."

"Thank you," he said.

Rowan turned into the green growth and slipped through the first line of trunks. He did not move fast, but he vanished all the same, one step, then another, and then he was gone.

Osric walked to the tree line and stopped. He listened for any call or break of branches that sounded like a fall. Nothing came. The man was a wonder, but he gave Rowan the space he requested, turning and retracing his way back through the village.

Osric cut across the open ground and returned to the hut. He pushed the door open and stepped inside. Talia and Grace had set their bedrolls in the far corner and hung two blankets over the pegs to make a thin wall for warmth and modesty. The hearth sat ready with tinder and fine splits of wood. Talia had their small cookpot set on a flat stone and a few herbs in a twist of cloth lay near it as Osric handed her the jug of water.

His people were fracturing, feeling the weight of their mission. For now, it was Jasper and Rowan, but Talia wouldn't be far behind. He'd already seen the signs; she was under stress. Even Grace, who always seemed unaffected by everything, seemed to feel the weight, which is probably why she put so much pressure on Jasper.

It worried Osric, and he knew it would only get worse.

Paulin lifted a hand, and the talk around the large campfire set up in the center of the village thinned. As conversation died down, riders threaded through the trees at the village's edge as a dozen rangers, green cloaks muddied from the road, appeared out of the darkness.

One by one, they slung their horses' reins over the hitching rail near the main farmhouse and joined the rest of the people gathered around the fire.

"Is this all?" Paulin asked.

"No. There are more, we were just the closest. The rest will be here between tomorrow and the next day."

"Good. Very good."

Osric sat back and watched, knowing this wasn't really the place for him to take action. Rowan, however, jumped to his feet as several more men appeared in the firelight.

"Fenn? By the goddess, is that you?"

A bearded man looked up, then broke into a grin. "Rowan. I heard you were headed south toward Eldamar."

"Never got that far. Hooked up with this lot and have been running ever since," he said, pointing at Osric and the rest.

Several others slapped Rowan on the shoulder when they saw him, each greeting the other as long-lost friends.

Which apparently they were.

"I know my messages were short, but I had to be careful with what I said. I think we should head to the farmhouse and talk about what needs to be done and let the rest of these people enjoy their night. Grab some food if you need it."

The rangers nodded and began to peel away. Some led horses toward the rough rope corral, others went to help lift water from the covered well, while still others grabbed bowls and filled them from the large pot of stew on one side of the fire.

Rowan turned to Osric. "Come on."

He waved Osric and the rest of their group toward the cluster of new arrivals. "Everyone, this is Osric, Grace, Jasper, and Talia. They're with me."

"So what's this all about? The message said something about needing men to take the fight to the baron to end the tyranny once and for all. Looking around, though, I'm not seeing much in the 'men' category. No offense."

"None taken," Paulin said, coming out of the shadows. "But let's go in the house to discuss it."

Osric and the rest followed him into the farmhouse. Some of the rangers joined them while others were busy getting food and tending to their mounts. Osric assumed they would get caught up on what was happening from the others.

"So what's this plan to bring sanity back to Wolfridge?" one of the rangers asked as they all settled down around the farmhouse table.

"It's bigger than just Wolfridge," Rowan said.

"What do you mean?" the ranger Rowan had called Fenn asked.

"The baron has come into possession of something dangerous," Osric said. "An artifact that could cause far more chaos than what he's already causing, which is why we came looking to talk to him, but what is happening here, around Wolfridge, is not isolated. We have proof that Ranulf has been infiltrating other cities and has been in direct contact with people there, trying to overturn their local leaders as well. Farvale for sure. The corruption runs deep."

The rangers exchanged dark looks. Gareth spat on the ground. "We knew Ranulf was behind the changes. The way the baron turned, the policies that came out of nowhere, it all stank of him."

"You knew and didn't stop him?" Osric asked.

"Suspected is more like," another ranger said. "Didn't have no proof, but rangers talk, which is maybe why he wanted to tear us apart, so we couldn't put it together."

"Well, we have the proof," Osric said. "And we can get the baron to listen, make him see what Ranulf truly is."

"How?" A ranger someone had called Mara asked.

Rowan gestured toward Talia and Jasper. "For one, we have outside authority on our side. We have a mage who can explain why the artifact is dangerous, and why we think Ranulf sent the baron for the artifact. And we have a cleric of Heathus to corroborate that."

The rangers studied Talia and Jasper with new interest.

One of them, a younger man with sandy hair, said, "You're young to be in the Conclave."

"I studied under a particularly talented teacher," Talia said.

That was one way to put it, Osric thought. Also, a good way to divert the questioning from her.

Any further questions were interrupted when Hale and several of the villagers that Osric had come to recognize as their leaders joined them.

"It's your plan, you go first," Paulin said, gesturing to Osric.

"Paulin says his people know a way into the keep. The plan is that we will sneak back into the city, the same way we were taken out, and take that path into the keep. It was rightfully pointed out that inside the keep are enough guardsmen and knights to make it unlikely we'd ever reach Ranulf, let alone the baron, which is where all of you come in. We need someone to pull as many of the guards and knights as possible away from the keep."

"You want us to attack the city?" One of them asked in horror.

"No, just make it look like you are. It has to be convincing, but we are not looking for you to take or hold the city. Your goal is to keep the casualties to a bare minimum while making your attack real enough that they stay focused on you while we do what needs to be done."

"There's only thirty or so of us, maybe forty if we're lucky. How do you expect us to make it seem convincing?" Fenn asked.

"That's where the people here come in. They will join you."

The rangers all looked at each other with expressions somewhere between bewildered and horrified at the idea.

"I know, I know. Many are not soldiers, but they have been raiding the baron's tax collectors and causing general mayhem. And they have as much at stake in this fight as you do, otherwise they would be back with their families in the villages they grew up in."

"And as he said, you don't need soldiers, you aren't looking to take the gate," Rowan said. "You're just looking to make enough noise to keep them busy. That's it. Just make it look real."

"It'll still be dangerous," Fenn said.

"They know that," Osric replied. "And we have another day or two until the rest of your people arrive, so we can train them the best we can."

"In a few days! Impossible."

"Not if we're only training them to be believable. They just have to put on a good show of it. We can give them basic instruction. How to hold a weapon, how to move together, how to protect themselves."

"And how sure are you that you can get into the keep?" Mara asked.

"While you're distracting the knights and guards, I can lead a small group through the sewers," Hale said. "There's an old access point behind the tannery that connects to passages under the keep."

"You know the route?"

"Used it myself when I worked in the keep. It's how some of us would sneak out for a drink after our shifts. The baron never knew."

"Can you get us all the way to the baron?" Osric asked.

"I can get you to the keep's lower levels. We have people inside who can help you get about halfway up through the keep. Once there, though, you're on your own."

Grace, who had been silent until now, spoke up. "That's a lot of ifs. If the distraction works, if the sewers aren't blocked, if we can navigate the keep without being caught."

"It's the best chance we have," Rowan said.

The meeting broke up, rangers and villagers filtering out to spread the word and begin preparations. Osric caught Rowan's arm as they left the farmhouse.

"You trust these men?"

"With my life. Some of them I've known since I first joined the Rangers."

"And they'll follow through, even knowing people will die?"

Rowan's expression grew somber. "They're rangers. They've sworn to protect the innocent. If that means risking their lives to stop whatever evil has taken hold of Wolfridge, they'll do it."

The next morning dawned clear and cool. Osric found himself in the main clearing with Rowan and Grace, surrounded by nearly fifty villagers who had volunteered to fight. They ranged from young men barely old enough to grow beards to fathers with graying hair, all united by desperation and determination.

The available weapons had been gathered and laid out: pitchforks, scythes, wood axes, hammers, kitchen knives, a few rusty swords that had been family heirlooms, and a fair number of bows. If they had been somewhere else, bows might not have been as numerous, but in the forest, nearly everyone knew how to use a bow to one degree or another.

Osric picked up a pitchfork and began by demonstrating the basic grip.

The morning progressed with Osric, Rowan, and the rangers moving between groups, adjusting grips, correcting stances. A young woman struggled with a heavy wood axe, and he helped her find a smaller hatchet that better suited her frame. An older man with a farmer's strength proved surprisingly adept with a sledgehammer.

By midmorning, they had progressed to working on makeshift shields. Wooden boards, pot lids, even thick leather aprons were pressed into service. Rowan demonstrated how to overlap them, creating a wall that could withstand arrows and deflect blows.

The rangers who had arrived the previous day assisted, mostly helping those who could shoot to be able to shoot a little better, although they also corrected footwork and demonstrated proper techniques to avoid exhaustion.

As the day wore on, more rangers arrived. First, a group of six, then eight more an hour later. Each new arrival was quickly briefed and integrated into the training effort. By mid-afternoon, thirty-eight Rangers had assembled, and that looked like all they would get.

It was much better than what they'd had just the day before, however.

The training continued through the afternoon. It wasn't pretty, and it wouldn't fool any real soldier able to get in close and see them, but it would work for people hiding in the woods, shooting at a walled city.

It was better than the chaos that would have ensued without preparation.

As the sun began its descent toward the western horizon, Paulin called a halt to the training. The villagers dispersed to eat and rest before the next night's action. The rangers gathered in small groups, discussing tactics and assignments.

Osric found himself standing with his companions near the edge of the camp, watching the preparations.

They would all get a good rest tonight and spend tomorrow preparing and moving toward the city, with the attack planned for nightfall.

Osric just hoped it would be enough.

The Keep

Hale kept the wagon steady through the ruts and broken stone, but to Osric, each jostle felt like he was being kicked in the side. He lay under the false floor with his knees jammed against a brace. The grinding sound of the wheels over the cobblestone drowned out most sound.

"Gate coming up," Hale called down.

A moment later, the wagon pulled to a stop, and Osric could hear a new voice. Now that the wagon had stopped, he could hear them well enough.

"Delivery for the keep kitchens," he heard Hale say from above them.

"Bit early, isn't it?" The guard sounded tired.

"Cook wants it before the morning rush. You know how she gets."

There was the sound of coins clinking, probably being handed to the guard, who said, "Okay, go on. But tell your friend he still owes Rolf a jug for last time."

"I'll remind him."

The wagon lurched forward. Osric counted to fifty before allowing himself a proper breath. Beside him, Grace shifted her weight off his arm.

Hale took a slow turn, then another and another, moving along for almost five more minutes. It was late, but there were still voices around, people out drinking. Or on their way back from it.

After one last turn, the wheels bumped over a lip or curb before the wagon rolled to a stop. The whole thing shifted as Hale climbed down and then there was silence for a moment before the false side slid open, revealing Hale and the walls of an alley.

"Clear," he said.

Osric heaved himself up, the cold boards scraping his forearms. He pushed through the layer of sacks and slats and rolled onto the alley floor. His legs prickled after being stuck in that position for so long. He stood and dragged Talia out by the wrist. She landed lightly and reached back without a word. Grace hooked her foot on the edge and popped out next, grinning as usual.

"Cozy trip," Grace said. "I'll be sure to recommend it to my friends."

"What friends?" Rowan said as he came out behind her, followed by Jasper. "We're the only people you talk to."

"I have friends," she said, still grinning.

Cinder wriggled free last, belly to the floor to slide out. He shook his fur out and froze, his ears forward. Hale slid the plank into place and kicked a tarp over the seam.

"This way," he said, waving them after him.

This way wasn't very far. Maybe a hundred feet down to the end of the alley where three buildings met to form a dead end. A pallet and other debris leaned against the wall. Hale rolled it aside to show an iron-ringed hatch half-hidden by the splintered slats and trash.

"Patrols rarely come down here, but still, we should be quick."

Rowan unshouldered a coil of rope. Osric crossed to a thick beam that stretched out over the hatch, tested it, then looped the rope over the wood. He put his weight into a knot and pulled until it bit. Hale crouched and worked the ring. The hatch lifted with a dull scrape to show a stone lip and a black throat below.

"This drain drops twenty feet to the underworks. We'll take the east run, then the north drift. Third turn puts us under the keep's storage rooms," Hale said.

Osric dropped the secured rope into the hatch.

Grace already had the rope in hand. "I'll go. I like surprises."

Osric wrapped his hand around the rope above hers. "Two tugs if clear," he said.

"Or one if I fall and die?" She flashed a look over her shoulder and dropped.

Rope hissed over the beam. The line went slack, then jerked with two quick pulls.

The others started to follow after her. Osric tapped his shoulder, and Cinder climbed around his neck, wrapping himself over his shoulders. He was incredibly heavy, but it was the only practical way to get the wolf down there, and only worked because Cinder held himself very still, knowing what they were doing.

Osric lowered himself into the hole and descended the rope hand over hand, lowering himself slowly. It was cold in the sewer, several degrees colder than above. Reaching the bottom, he stepped onto the stone there, letting Cinder jump off his shoulders onto the stone floor.

The tunnel ran in both directions, waist-high at the sides and deeper in the middle channel. The walls had the look of old work with mortar crusted between uneven stone. It was small, with the roof of the tunnel almost touching his hair. The air had a fetid, stale tang to it. Not a place Osric wished to ever be.

"No rats. Disappointing," Grace said.

He ignored her. She made quips when she was nervous.

"Torch?" Rowan asked.

"No flames," Hale said. "Slats above us pull air up to keep build-up from happening, and it'll take smoke with it. Someone will see it."

Talia lifted both hands. She pressed the tips of her index fingers together to form a triangle and drew them apart slowly. A soft blue orb budded between her hands, grew to the size of a melon, and floated up to hover behind her shoulder. The light washed the tunnel in a pale blue glow, hard shadows chewed at the angles.

"Stay off the center flow," Hale said. "Slime looks like stone from above. Step wrong and you lose your footing."

"Fun," Grace said.

Osric took the lead with Rowan at his shoulder. He held his sword down along his leg and kept it clear of the stone.

They made the first turn left at a junction where the water split around a pile of fallen brick.

Hale pointed with two fingers. "Straight here. The next branch to the right will look good. Ignore it. It silts up in twenty feet."

They passed a collapsed spur where the ceiling had broken and spilled rubble into a half-assed dam, the water changing pitch as it passed the obstruction.

They kept up a good pace. Turn and then another turn, following the path as it curved in what felt like a northward direction. They passed a silted culvert where brown muck had swallowed the channel.

Hale lifted his chin toward the bend beyond. "That is the ladder shaft up to the keep's lower stores. The grate above is loose. I greased it in the spring."

"Let's pray it takes," Jasper said.

Osric moved to the base of the shaft and looked up. A square of black metal sat flush with the stone at the top. It looked heavier than it had any right to look. He climbed up, set his hands and pushed. The grate clanked and refused to budge. Osric craned his neck and saw what looked like a lock looped around two of the rungs, holding the grate in place.

"There's a lock," he said.

"What? That wasn't there before," Hale said.

Grace brushed past his shoulder.

"Allow me," she said, putting her boot on a rung and climbed above him, producing a short tool with a half-hook at the end. "This is a pretty new lock. Bad workmanship, though."

Above him, Osric heard a tool clinking against the lock. Grace paused, listened, then nudged again, a metal click answered. She sucked in a satisfied sound and slipped the cylinder free with her fingers.

"Got it," she said, sliding down to him. "Go put your muscles to use and lift the damn thing."

Osric climbed the ladder, planted his feet, and pushed up on the grate, feeling it give. It rose a few inches. Stone grit fell past his face. He shoved it higher with a grunt and held it against the side of the shaft. Grace slid up past him and out. Osric followed. He laid the grate over the edge so it would drop back into place without a crash.

A dimly lit storage room spread around him. Barrels stood stacked to his left, a line of sacks lay to his right. The air held a dry smell of grain and old wood. Talia popped her head through the hole. Osric caught her forearm and hauled her up. She flicked her fingers and the hovering orb winked out. Darkness folded in and

Osric let his pupils adjust to the weak spill of light from a distant sconce.

Rowan came up next, Cinder around his neck. Osric reached down and lifted the wolf up and into the room before taking the ranger's wrist and pulling him the rest of the way up. Once they were through, Jasper climbed up with Hale behind him. Hale swung the grate into place and lowered it slowly until it was seated without a clatter.

A door at the far end of the room opened. A short woman stepped in with a sack over her shoulder. Seeing everyone gathered in the room, she froze. Osric turned lifting up his sword at the possible new threat.

"Wait," Hale said quickly, lifting both hands. "She's with us."

The woman's eyes moved over their faces and settled on Hale. She gave one curt nod. "You cut this one close."

"You said the path would be clear," Hale said. "When did they lock this?"

"A few days ago. The baron is getting paranoid, but you made it, so what's the problem?" She said, tossing the sack aside. "I can take you through the service corridors to the main level. After that, you're on your own. I can't risk going further with you."

Osric studied her face. Lines cut at the corners of her mouth. Her hair bound in a scarf.

"What's your name?"

"Aka."

Osric nodded and turned to Hale. "Stay here. Keep the hole clear in case we have to run. If we do not return, pull out and get word to Paulin."

Hale looked like he wanted to protest, but he swallowed it down and nodded.

Aka jerked her chin toward a narrow door beside a bin of onions. "Come on."

They slipped through the door. The corridor was tight, with the occasional door that led to other storage rooms. Second left, immediate right, then straight.

Osric was just behind Aka with Rowan behind him. They turned into another corridor and came face to face with two guards who looked bewildered to run into anyone down here, but especially an odd group of armed adventurers.

One was leaning against the wall, a wineskin in his hand, while the other was laughing at something, the laugh dying on his lips when he saw them. Both men had red faces. The one leaning against the wall wore a dented helm pushed back on his skull, while the other had his laces loose and his surcoat untucked, a skin hung loose from a cord at his belt. Both had swords on their hips.

"What the ..." The first guard started to straighten, fumbling for his sword.

Rowan moved faster than Osric would have thought possible. He crossed the distance in three strides and drove his shoulder into the first guard's chest. The man flew backward, crashing into the wall. Osric was right behind him. He seized the guard's sword arm before the blade cleared its sheath and slammed him against the stone again.

The guard's eyes went wide. Osric's sword punched through leather and cloth, into his chest. The man, desperate, punched Osric, but he ignored it and pressed harder, feeling muscle and sinew give way as the sword slid up between the man's ribs. He twisted the blade and pulled it free. Blood spread across the guard's tunic as he slid down the wall.

The second guard had his sword half-drawn when Grace appeared behind him, almost as if by magic. Her boot connected with the back of his knee. The drunk guard, only being held up by the wall, cried out as he fell to his knees. He opened his mouth to shout, but nothing came out as Grace's dagger opened his throat instead. Blood sprayed across the corridor floor. The guard clutched at his neck, gurgling, then toppled forward.

It was all over in less than five seconds.

Aka stared at the two men. Her mouth pinched.

"I told them they shouldn't be down here. Fools."

Osric squatted and dragged the blade of his sword over the hem of the dead man's surcoat, wiping the blood away

"Any more down here?" he asked.

"There shouldn't be," she said. "Guards rarely come down here but the sergeant stashes keys in a bucket above the kitchen door.

They visit here sometimes after they've been drinking to get an extra wheel of cheese or bread."

"Then we were early or they were late," Rowan said. He flexed the fingers of his right hand. His shoulder had a numb spot where he struck the guard.

They dragged both guards by the boots across the corridor and through a half-open door into a side room. It smelled like onions and old meat, with shelves lining the walls with cheeses and jars. Jasper took one of the guard's shoulders and lifted while Osric grabbed the legs. They pushed him under a table with a cloth that hung to the floor. Rowan lifted the other by the wrists while Grace took his boots to guide his legs, tucking him into a corner behind a stack of crates.

Not perfect, but it would hide them long enough. Once they got above the main level, the odds of an alarm being sounded were high anyway.

They slipped out and moved on. The next run led to a stairwell that went up to the next level of the keep. Aka stopped them at the foot of the steps and put two fingers to the wood, tilting her head. No one moved above. She set her foot on the stair and took them up to the passage at the top, which cut across another row of storerooms to yet another stairwell.

"We are near the main hall. I cannot go further," Aka said.

Now they had to wait for the diversion. As if on cue, the sound of bugles cut through the air. On the floor above, beyond the opening of the stairwell, they could hear raised voices followed by boots slapping on stone and then further off muffled shouts. More trumpets answered.

Rowan slipped past Osric to the top of the stairwell and peeked out.

After a moment, he returned and said, "That's it. The attack has begun. It looks like most of the keep is moving out."

"The baron's chambers are on the fourth level. Good luck," Aka said.

She turned and hurried back the way they'd come.

Osric listened at the stairwell as the sounds of guards streaming past continued. Rowan snuck back up and watched, staying in the shadows. As the sounds of running feet ended, he waved to them.

This was it.

"Let's go," Osric said.

They hurried from the main floor up the staircase that led to the upper floors of the keep. From Hale's description, it wasn't a continuous set of stairs, but staggered up different corners of the keep, presumably to slow down attackers trying to get to the upper floors of the keep.

It didn't take them long to find the next staircase, and thankfully, they did not encounter any more guards on the way across the first floor. Most of the guard was outside of the keep, so only a small number of men had deployed from here to the front.

The sounds of the diversion, the distant cry of horns, and the muffled shouts of men grew fainter as they climbed. Osric had switched out with Rowan for now, as it was unlikely they would be able to sneak the rest of the way up, and he wanted himself in front if they ran into any danger, although the ranger followed close behind.

They emerged onto a landing that opened into a wide corridor, tapestries of faded hunts and forgotten battles hanging between iron sconces.

Rowan pointed to a hallway on the left which would lead to the next stairwell. They had turned and made it halfway down the narrow passage when a figure in polished steel plate covered by a decorated surcoat bearing the black wolf of Wolfridge came around the far corner, blocking their way to the stairwell.

Behind him, more men filed into the corridor clad in leather armor and simple helms marking them as members of the keep guard. Seven in total. Each of the men pulled a sword as soon as they saw Osric and the rest.

While they weren't trapped, they could turn and run, that would not take them where they needed to go.

"Halt. Throw down your weapons."

There was no negotiation here. They already knew they'd have to face off against knights of the realm, who would almost certainly be guarding the baron, and that they would probably have to kill some of them.

Even though the decision had been made, Osric did not like it. He'd already killed several of the baron's men, but these were knights dedicated to the realm. It was not their fault their loyalty to Baron Blackthorn put them in the grips of a member of the Brethren.

For a moment their groups just looked at each other, everyone frozen in place. The lull didn't last. When it was clear Osric and the rest were not going to lay down their arms, the knight signaled his men, and they began to move forward.

"Move back," Osric ordered, his voice low and urgent to those behind him as he made way for Rowan to step up next to him.

Behind him, he could hear Talia begin to move her arms around, casting something. He looked back in time to see her finish the gesture and shimmering, translucent layers of force materialize around her, protecting her.

Good. She'd been injured enough in their fights, and he didn't want her in any more danger than she had to be.

As the guards reached them, the man directly in front of Rowan lunged first, quicker than Osric expected. The man's sword darted forward, a simple but effective thrust aimed at Rowan's exposed side. Rowan twisted, his own blade coming up to parry, but the guard's angle was good. The tip of the longsword scraped past Rowan's defense, biting into the leather armor on his arm. A line of red bloomed on the ranger's sleeve. Rowan grunted, his footing solid, but the first blow had been struck.

Simultaneously, the knight surged forward, his entire body behind a powerful, cleaving slash aimed straight at Osric's head. Osric braced himself, planting his feet and angling his shield to meet the assault.

The impact was immense, resulting in a deafening clang of steel that vibrated through the metal, jolting his entire arm from wrist to shoulder. The force of the blow drove him back half a step, the edge of the knight's longsword screeching as it slid off his shield's rim, carving a fresh scar into its surface but finding no purchase.

The knight's strength was considerable, but his attack left him momentarily overextended.

Seeing his opening, Osric ignored the tremor in his shield arm and pivoted on his back foot, all his weight shifting from defense to offense. He didn't use a wide, sweeping arc, but he made a tight, vicious thrust of his own sword. His longsword hammered into the knight's shield, the blow aimed not to cut but to batter. The knight grunted, his shield arm driven back by the focused impact.

Before the knight could recover his posture, Osric's blade was already moving again. He twisted his wrist, the sword now free, and brought it around in a swift, horizontal slash. The blade cut through the air and bit deep into the knight's side, just below the ribs where the plate armor gave way to mail. The knight roared in pain and surprise, staggering back a step, his shield dipping.

Osric could hear Jasper saying a prayer behind him, followed swiftly by a subtle warmth that settled in his bones, sharpening his focus and pushing strength through him. He felt surer, faster as Jasper called his god's blessing down on him and the rest of their group.

Rowan, ignoring the wound on his arm, struck back at the guard who had drawn his blood. Bolstered by Jasper's divine aid, his short sword was a blur of motion. It slipped under the guard's clumsy parry and punched through the leather jerkin covering his chest. The guard's eyes went wide, a wet gurgle escaping his lips as he stumbled backward, his longsword clattering to the stone floor. He was not dead, but the fight was gone from him.

Osric didn't let that distract him from the life-or-death struggle he was in, but he almost lost his concentration when Cinder, who had darted between Osric's legs, launched himself at the wounded knight, planting his paws on the front of the man's chest plate and knocking him over backward.

The wolf rode him to the ground, his fangs finding the knight's now exposed throat, as his head leaned back into the fall, and tearing.

The man, a sworn knight, was dead before he hit the ground.

The knight's fall created a void, a momentary vacuum in the guards' line. Grace exploded from her position as soon as there was an opening. She didn't run through the gap; she vaulted into a low, twisting tumble that carried her past Osric and Rowan before coming up on her feet with cat-like softness behind the guard Rowan had wounded.

The man had been trying to stumble back, to find a wall to lean against, and never saw her coming. Osric caught the motion from the corner of his eye, a flash of Grace's arm, the upward thrust of her short sword, the blade sliding between the guard's ribs.

There was no cry, only a final, shuddering exhalation as the man's soul left him. He collapsed, a discarded puppet whose strings had been cut, slain before he even had the chance to register the new threat. Grace was already spinning away from the falling body, knowing she had placed herself in the middle of the fight.

Two enemies down, but the corridor was still a press of bodies. Another guard, face grim and determined, shoved his way forward to close some of the gap left by their deceased comrades. As soon as he got into place, he lunged at Osric, his sword straight.

Osric, his attention momentarily pulled away by Grace's actions, reacted a fraction too late. He brought his shield down, but the guard's attack was quick, slipping under the shield's rim. The blade's point bit into the muscle of his thigh, a sharp, searing pain that shot up his leg. It was not a deep wound, but it burned like fire.

Ignoring it, he refocused on the man in front of him. Osric's first strike was not a slash but a blunt, brutal blow with the flat of his longsword against the man's shield. The impact was a dull thud, staggering the man and causing his shield to dip from the force of the blow.

That was the first step of Osric's attack. Before the guard could reset his defense, the second step of his attack flowed from the first as he twisted his wrist, bringing the sword's edge to bear. The longsword swept across the top of the shield, connecting with the guard's neck, just above the collar of his leather armor. The man's eyes widened in disbelief, a choked sound bubbling in his throat. He dropped his sword and shield, his hands flying to his throat as he went down on one knee, and then pitched forward, lifeless.

Three down.

Before Osric could do anything else, Talia's hands shot between himself and Rowan, her left hand raised, fingers splayed, and her right hand thrusting forward. Three bolts of pure, white energy shot past his head leaving shimmering trails in the air for a heartbeat before slamming into the chest of the guard closest to Grace. Each missile knocked the man back a step as they struck.

Staring down in horror, the guard screamed, a high, thin sound, dropping his sword and clutching his smoking chest.

Rowan took advantage of the opening Talia had created and moved to exploit it. He stepped forward, his short sword held in a reverse grip, stabbing deep into the man's chest while his defenses were down. Rowan twisted the blade and pulled it free in a single motion, sending the guard crashing to the ground.

The press of bodies thinned again. Four guards remained standing, all of their initial confidence gone as their number had been cut in half.

Cinder gave a low growl and launched himself forward, a gray streak moving low to the ground. The targeted guard, already unnerved, tried to fend him off with a clumsy kick. Cinder dodged it with ease, his powerful jaws snapping shut on the man's sword arm. Teeth sank through leather and into flesh. The guard howled in pain, his sword arm rendered useless as Cinder shook his head violently, worrying the limb like a captured rabbit.

Grace didn't allow him the chance to figure a way out of Cinder's grasp, swinging around behind the man, she drove her short sword upward, piercing through his armor and into the man's kidney.

Three men remained, and Talia wasn't done. Her hands had continued to move even after the bolts left her hand, this time, she pinched her thumb and index finger together, then drew her other hand toward her in a clawing motion. She touched the two hands together, then thrust one forward.

A pair of sickly green arrowheads hissed through the air, two of the three remaining guards taking them to the chest. When they hit, they splashed as if liquid before the energy disappeared, and both men began screaming as if doused in flaming oil.

A faint smoke rose from their mail shirts, accompanied by the acrid smell of dissolving metal and burning flesh. Both men staggered, trying to rip off their mail shirts as the smell of burning flesh wafted up from them.

Osric didn't hesitate, using the opportunity to thrust his sword into the chest of one of the men who had obligingly pulled his mail away, exposing the soft, and bubbling, skin underneath.

Rowan followed his example a second later, his sword taking the same path and ending the second life.

215

The last guard had had enough. He stood among the bodies of the seven other men who had come down the hallway with him and wanted no more of this. He turned to flee, throwing his sword down to free himself of any encumbrance, so he could move faster.

He made it only a few steps down the hall before a twirl of silver chased after him and one of Grace's daggers embedded itself just at the base of the man's neck, in the very center of his back, above the mail protecting him.

He dropped and skidded to a halt, his spinal cord was severed, his feet twitching slightly, but otherwise very much extinguished like a torch that had been suddenly doused. There one moment and gone the next.

For a moment the five of them just stood there, looking at each other.

"We need to move," Osric said. "Everyone in the keep had to have heard that."

"Your leg ..." Talia said, looking at him, worried.

"I'll live," Osric cut her off.

They raced for the stairs, Grace bending to retrieve the dagger from the last guard's back as she went past. They took the stairs two at a time, leaving the carnage behind. The third level was eerily quiet. The sconces on the wall flickered, casting long, dancing shadows down an empty hallway. Doors stood ajar, leading into empty rooms.

If any men had been stationed here, they must have fled their posts in a hurry.

"Where is everyone?" Grace said, peering into several of the empty rooms.

"Maybe they all went to protect the gate," Talia suggested. "If they were up here, we would already be seeing them after all the racket we made."

"Maybe," Osric said, but he didn't believe it.

That thought turned into a certainty when he turned the corner and saw a shape sprawled on the floor at the far end of the corridor. He motioned for the others to halt, looking around with his sword up.

They were on the third floor and had just passed a group of guards, so whoever had left that body here had to come from this level or higher.

Which was a problem.

Osric approached with caution. It was a guard, one of the Greenwood Levy by his livery, but there were no sword wounds, no arrow shafts protruding from his back. Instead, his leather armor was blackened and melted in several places, as if he had been struck by searing heat. Around the burns, the flesh was blistered and raw.

"What did this?" Jasper murmured, kneeling beside the body. He pointed to the man's throat. "And look here."

Long, deep gouges were carved into the man's neck and face, as if he had been savaged by some great beast. The cuts were too deep, too wide to be from a wolf, but were definitely from an animal of some kind.

They found two more bodies further down the hall, both bearing the same horrific injuries. One man had been thrown against a wall with such force that the stone behind him was cracked. The other had been torn nearly in half.

Osric had an instant flashback to the tower in the Claws. To some of the things that they'd seen there, and his blood ran cold.

Worse, there was a sound that wasn't coming from outside. It came from above, from the floors of the keep yet to be explored. It was a deep, resonant roar, a sound that vibrated through the stone floor and into Osric's bones.

He exchanged a look with his friends. Jasper's face had lost a little of its color. Had they done something with the piece of the Blackstar? Brought a part of that cursed place back with them?

Osric hoped not, but they couldn't stop now. If they were going to get the piece back and stop this, they had to keep going.

Ranulf

The next floor proved quieter than the last. Clearly, this was a more important part of the keep. The walls were decorated with tapestries or even art in places, and the corridor was wider. They continued along the edge of the building, looking for the next set of stairs going up.

When he saw it, he also saw a set of double doors near it, partly open. Unlike the other open doors they had seen, they could hear voices coming from beyond this one.

Voices that sounded distraught. Agitated.

"I don't care what you were told, take the key, get your men into the baron's quarters and secure everything before he brings the whole keep down around us!" A man's voice was saying.

If they needed a key to get in, the baron must be locked in his quarters. Also, it struck Osric that there was only one man who might give an order like that.

The man they needed to deal with.

Osric didn't hesitate. He charged through the doorway, his companions close behind him. The office they entered was richly appointed, heavy furniture of dark wood, shelves lined with leather-bound books, and a massive desk that dominated the room's center.

Behind it stood a man in fine dark clothing, his graying hair neat and well-kempt. He held a brass key extended toward one of two knights in Blackthorn house livery. Four additional guardsmen stood in the room, closer to the walls, although if they were guards for the man behind the desk or with the two knights, Osric didn't know.

"Where's the baron?" Osric demanded, sword already in hand. "Does he have the Blackstar?"

The man, who had to be Ranulf, froze. At first, his eyes were on Osric, at his sudden appearance. Ranulf opened his mouth, as if to give a command, when his eyes slid from Osric and locked on Talia.

His mouth hung open, the color draining from his face as the key slipped from his fingers to clatter on the floor.

"That's not possible. She died when their experiment went wrong. But you ... you look exactly like her. How is this possible?"

Talia went rigid beside Osric. "What?"

"They had a child, but I was told it died with them."

"Who?" Talia said, seemingly having forgotten what they were even doing here.

"It doesn't matter," Ranulf said, almost shaking himself back into the moment. "Kill them."

Grace reacted first, whipping up her short bow from where she stood in the doorway. The bowstring snapped, and an arrow hissed across the room. It struck the guard farthest to the right, punching through the chain on his shoulder. The man grunted, his sword faltering as he staggered forward a step.

The other men in the room, hearing the order, were already moving before the arrow hit. The knight closest to Osric had closed the distance, his sword coming down in a brutal, overhand arc aimed at Osric's collarbone. Instead of blocking it with his sword, Osric chose to catch the blow, turning his shoulder to take the impact on his pauldron. The half-plate held, but the force of the strike was immense, a hammer blow that drove a spike of pain deep into his bones and sent a jarring shock down his arm.

Osric's own sword was moving, free to attack. He swung his longsword in a wide, horizontal slash. The blade bit into the knight's side with a screech of tortured metal, the edge scoring a deep gouge in the plate. The knight grunted, momentarily un-balanced, but the blade did not puncture his armor.

Osric pressed the attack, reversing his swing with a quick back-hand cut, but the knight recovered quickly enough to interpose his shield, deflecting the blow.

A second guard, seeing Osric engaged, scurried around the knight's flank. He lunged with his short spear, a low, opportunistic thrust. Osric felt a sharp pain in his thigh as the spearhead slid under the rim of his shield and punched through the leather of his breeches. He cursed but stayed standing.

From the doorway, a second arrow and then a third flew into the room, this time fired by Rowan. Both shafts struck the guard Grace had wounded. The first punched through the mail over his chest. The second took him in the throat. The man dropped his sword, his hands clawing at the wooden shaft protruding from his neck as he collapsed, a gurgling sound escaping his lips before he fell silent.

Another guard, positioned near the far wall, raised a light cross-bow, leveling it at Grace, who was still framed in the doorway. A bolt shot past her head, thudding into the wooden frame with a solid *thwack*, causing her to flinch and duck.

Next to her, Cinder exploded into motion, weaving through the crowded room. He ignored the towering knight and launched himself at the guard who had speared Osric, his powerful jaws closing around the man's calf.

The guard screamed as Cinder's teeth sank in. With a savage twist of his head, the wolf ripped the man's leg out from under him. The guard crashed to the floor, his head hitting the polished stone with a sickening crack.

Behind his desk, Ranulf raised a hand, his voice low and reso-nant, speaking words in a language Osric didn't recognize. The pattern of it felt like a litany. Like one of the prayers Jasper might say. A palpable weight settled over Osric.

He felt slow, like he was wearing a thick, heavy cloak.

Jasper stepped forward, his hand raised.

"Be blessed in your duty!" he called out, his voice a warm coun-terpoint to Ranulf's chilling chant.

Strength seemed to flow back into Osric, clearing some of the unnatural fatigue from his mind.

The guard nearest Ranulf flipped his spear into one hand, pulled it back to his shoulder and hurled it at Rowan, who twisted away at the last second, the blade cutting through a part of his leather armor before embedding itself into the door frame.

An odd twin to the arrow next to Grace.

The other knight seemed to have the same idea, charging to-ward Rowan, shield forward. Rowan barely had time to drop his bow as the knight crashed into him, pinning him against the wall next to the door.

Talia had been weaving her hands around in complex gestures since the fight started. She finally finished, pulling her hands apart and then slapping them back together again.

The air shimmered, and time itself seemed to warp around them. The effect was weird, and Osric's stomach did a kind of half flip. More of the sluggishness that had set in when Ranulf made his blessing, or whatever he had done, seemed to vanish.

It must have affected all of them, because Rowan, locked in combat with the second knight, made an almost preternaturally quick step to the side, his short sword appearing in his hand as if from nowhere.

He lunged, a low, reverse-grip slash aimed at the knight's thigh. The blade bit deep into the less-protected joint. The knight bellowed. Rowan followed with a rapid flurry of strikes, a riposte and an inside stab, but the knight's heavy plate and shield turned them aside, sparks flying from the impacts.

The crossbowman dropped his weapon and drew a short sword, rushing Grace. He swung wildly, but she slipped back, the blade cutting empty air. She was a blur of motion, tumbling under the guard's clumsy attack to come back up behind him. She drove her own blade forward in a quick, vicious stab that slid between the links of his mail armor at kidney level, dropping him.

Ranulf had begun to chant again in that same odd language, tracing some kind of pattern in the air. A golden trail flowed from his hand before streaming across the room into the knight squaring off against Osric.

Osric ignored Ranulf for a moment. He had the opportunity to remove one of their threats easily, and he was going to take it. He brought his sword down in a brutal, two-handed chop that smashed into the man's chest. Without pausing, he pivoted into a swing against the knight, the blade crashing against the knight's torso, driving him back a step.

With its target dispatched, Cinder wheeled and charged across the room. The wolf launched itself at the guard standing in front of Ranulf. His jaws clamped onto the man's shin, and with another violent wrench, he pulled the guard down. The man landed hard, his spear clattering away.

The knight Osric had pushed back, brought his arm down hard on Osric's already bruised and hurting shoulder, staggering him back. The knight's follow-up was slower, a backhand swing with his now freed sword that Osric easily turned aside with his own blade.

Before Osric could do something to counter the man, Talia's hands thrust out again and three shimmering darts of pure energy shot from them. Surprisingly, they did not all go to the same target. Two slammed into the knight fighting Osric, punching through his armor and into his chest, leaving smoking holes as the man toppled over. The third went across the room and smashed into the wounded guard's chest, sending him sprawling.

Rowan, bleeding and battered, danced away from the guard Talia had just taken down, turning and dipping, coming up on the other knight's shield side, his sword lashing out to slash the knight's hamstring. The knight stumbled, his leg buckling.

As the knight fell, Rowan pressed his attack with a flurry of swings. His first caught the man in the collar, clear of his armor, the second had the hilt knocking the knight's shield away, clearing the way for a third swing that would have been a killing blow had the man not gotten the armor on his forearm interposed, sending the blade off target, just missing his body.

Freed from fighting the knight in front of him, Osric turned and charged the one who was down on a single knee struggling with Rowan, crossing the room in three long strides, plunging his longsword into the distracted man. The knight looked up, surprised, grasping the blade before he fell to the side in a clatter of metal.

With nearly all of the men in the room except Ranulf down, Grace ran at him, vaulting over the massive desk and stabbing at the chancellor, hoping to end this fight. Instead, she and her sword ricocheted off of him, bounced off the corner of the desk and fell to the floor.

"He's warded!"

Jasper, standing over the body of the last guardsman, his mace still in the man's skull, held up his hand and said, "Heathus, help us! End this fiend's evil spells."

For a moment, nothing happened. Then there was a bluish shimmering around Ranulf that began to melt like a ball of ice on a warm day.

The chancellor looked stunned that his protective field had gone. He, however, didn't have time to consider that, as Cinder leapt at him, jaws clamping on Ranulf's arm and tightly holding onto him. Ranulf shook his arm but couldn't dislodge the wolf.

Grace pushed herself off the floor and came at the chancellor again, pulling a dagger. This time, she wasn't thrown aside by a magical shield; instead she plunged the dagger into Ranulf's side.

Ranulf was vulnerable, one arm trapped, unable to call forth any more of his vile magics. Or so Osric had thought.

But he uttered a few words and a wave of force exploded out from him, sending Cinder, Grace, and everyone else flying across the room, bouncing off walls.

"Enough!"

Talia got up on one knee, her hands whipping through the air and said, "Not nearly enough."

As her hands finished their pattern, a brilliant bolt of lightning, a white-hot lance of pure energy, erupted from her hands. It cracked as it crossed the room, slamming into Ranulf. He screamed, his body convulsing as the raw power coursed through him. His fine clothes were charred, his skin blistered. He staggered, but incredibly, did not fall.

He was, however, stunned.

Osric pushed himself off the floor and charged, sword first, screaming. The chancellor seemed to get a hold of himself just in time for Osric's sword to punch into his chest, the force of Osric's charge pushing him over, the sword pinning him to the floor.

A bloody laugh escaped his lips, a rattling, wet sound. "You think this stops anything?" he choked, blood flecking his lips. "You are just ... pawns ..."

"Pawns for who?" Osric demanded, leaning on his sword.

Ranulf just laughed again, a final, defiant sound that ended in a rattling sigh, and then he went limp.

For a moment, the entire room was silent as they gathered themselves. Osric pulled his sword free, saw the brass key lying on the floor where Ranulf had dropped it, and scooped it up.

"We need to get to the baron," he said.

The brass key felt cold in Osric's hand as he led the way up the final flight of stairs. The sounds of battle from the city below had faded to distant shouts and an occasional crash. Time was running short.

Ranulf was dead, but no one could call off the guards and release the city from the grip it was under except the baron.

"Getting colder," Grace muttered behind him.

She was right. He'd just thought the key felt colder, but it wasn't just the key. The temperature dropped with each step they climbed, much colder than it had been outside the keep, or even just one floor below them.

Osric's breath began to fog in front of him as they reached the top landing.

That wasn't the only indication that something was wrong. He could feel a low vibration running through the stone floor beneath his boots. Not quite sound, not quite shaking, but something that made Osric's teeth ache and set his nerves on edge. The sensation grew stronger as they turned toward the corridor leading to the baron's private chambers.

The hallway stretched before them, lit by wall sconces that flickered in the disturbed air. At the far end stood a set of ornate double doors, their carved surface hidden beneath a thick coating of frost that spread across the wood and onto the surrounding stone.

Between them and those doors stood six knights in Blackthorn colors, their armor dented and streaked with dark stains.

Osric was tired and didn't want to fight his way through any more men if he didn't have to. But they were too close to turn back.

They weren't the only knights on this level, however.

Four more knights lay scattered across the corridor floor, their bodies torn apart, much like the bodies they'd seen lower down in the keep. One knight's chest plate had been ripped open from the inside, the metal peeled back like the petals of some terrible flower. Another's helmet had been crushed inward, smashing his skull.

The surviving knights stood with swords drawn, but their attention remained fixed on the frosted doors. They didn't even notice Osric and the others at first. Their faces, what Osric could see beneath their helmets, were pale and drawn with exhaustion and fear. One knight's sword hand trembled visibly, and two of the others looked ready to bolt at any moment.

The knights must have heard them, because as they approached the knights all whirled around. One of the men, maybe their leader, raised his free hand to halt them. He was an older man with graying hair visible beneath his helmet and deep lines carved around his eyes.

"Stop there."

"What happened here?" Osric asked, though he suspected he already knew at least part of the answer.

At first, Osric wasn't sure the man would answer. After all, he and his friends were trespassing here and there was a rebellion occurring outside. The other knights they'd run into had been much more hostile. Whatever these men had seen, though, had shaken them enough that they didn't seem to question why Osric would be asking.

"Baron Blackthorn sealed himself inside four days ago. Said no one was to enter, no matter what we heard." The man's eyes darted to the frost-covered doors, then back to Osric. "Then the sounds started and those ... things began appearing."

"Things?" Rowan asked.

"I ... I can't describe them. They were like nothing I've ever seen. Like something from a story I might tell my children to scare them. They didn't even come through the door. They just appeared, right out of the air itself without any warning at all."

From beyond the frosted doors came a sound that made everyone in the corridor tense. Words, or something like words, whispered in a strange language. This wasn't like the language Ranulf had spoken. That, at least, sounded something like a language a person would use. This sounded more like if a warped animal could talk.

"Started getting worse a few hours ago," the knight continued. "Right when the attack on the city began. Two more of those things appeared and headed down into the keep."

Talia moved past Osric, her attention focused entirely on the doors. She raised her hands, fingers spreading wide before she swept them slowly apart.

Blue light flared around the doors, so bright that several of the knights stepped back in surprise. The magical field pulsed and writhed, revealing patterns of energy that twisted through dimensions the human eye couldn't properly perceive. The frost on the doors seemed to move in response.

"Gods above and below," Talia breathed. She turned to face the others, her face pale. "The magical distortion in there ... it's massive. And I've felt it before."

"Where?" Osric asked.

"At the bottom of the buried temple, where we found that document. Where that beetle thing was."

Osric and the others exchanged looks. They all remembered that giant creature they'd fought to get the other half of the document. Osric still saw it in his nightmares. There had been a massive rift down there, which meant there might be one on the other side of this door.

But the Blackstar was supposed to absorb the energy and repair the rifts. It made no sense that one of its fragments would do the opposite.

"The baron took something he shouldn't have," Osric said, addressing the lead knight directly. "An artifact. An ancient and powerful artifact."

For a moment, he thought he might be able to reason with the shaken knight, but training and loyalty took back over.

"The baron's business is his own."

"Not when it threatens everyone in this keep, maybe everyone in this entire barony. The baron can't control it. No one can, not anymore."

"You're lying."

"Are those creatures you fought a lie? If we don't get in there and contain it, the energy will consume your baron. Then the keep. Then it will spread outward until there's nothing left of Greenwood but nightmares."

The knight's resolve wavered for a moment, uncertainty crossing his features. Then his jaw set again.

"The baron gave us orders. We follow them."

"Even if it means dying for nothing?" Grace asked.

"Especially then. We swore oaths. We don't abandon them because things get difficult."

The other surviving knights nodded, standing a little straighter, holding their swords up to make it clear to Osric and the rest that they weren't leaving. They were exhausted, terrified, but they would fight if commanded. Their loyalty, even in the face of horror, was absolute.

"Your loyalty is admirable," Jasper said, moving to the front of the group. "But there are oaths higher than those sworn to mortal lords."

"There are no oaths higher than a knight to his lord."

"There are. The oaths we take to the gods and to our families. I'm a follower of Heathus. I speak with the authority of the Provider, the Guardian of the Hearth, the Father of the Family."

Several knights made reflexive gestures of respect at the mention of the god's titles. Heathus was one of the more popular gods in rural baronies like Greenwood and Southwatch. More than half of the people here worshiped him.

"The thing beyond those doors is not your baron anymore," Jasper continued. "It's an abomination. A violation of everything Heathus stands for. Family, community, home, all of it will be destroyed if that evil is allowed to spread. You took other oaths. Oaths to defend the realm and its people. They are in danger."

"The baron ..."

"The baron was deceived. Manipulated by those who sought to use him for their own ends. You've seen what happened here, heard the orders given. You know this is true. You've seen how he's changed these past months. The paranoia. The isolation. That wasn't natural."

"Counselor Ranulf said ..."

"Ranulf is dead," Osric said bluntly. "He was using the baron. Using all of you. The artifact he convinced the baron to retrieve is killing him, and it will kill everyone in this city if we don't stop it."

The whispers from beyond the doors grew louder, more insistent. The frost spread further along the walls, and the vibration in the floor intensified. Something scraped against the inside of the doors, a sound like claws on stone but somehow worse.

"Your duty is to protect the people of this barony," Jasper said, raising his voice to still be heard over the racket. "Not to follow orders that will see them all dead. The choice before you is simple. Stand aside and let us try to save your people, or stand your ground and condemn them all."

The lead knight looked at his men, saw the fear and uncertainty in their faces. One of the younger knights spoke up, his voice barely steady.

"Sir Avery, perhaps we should."

"Quiet," Avery snapped, but there was no real force behind it.

He looked back at the bodies of his fallen comrades, at the unnatural wounds that had killed them. His shoulders sagged slightly.

"If you're wrong about this ..."

"Then you can arrest us afterward," Osric said. "But if we're right and you stop us, there won't be an afterward."

Avery stood frozen for a long moment, the weight of the decision visible on his face. The other knights watched him, waiting for his command. The whispers from beyond the doors grew more urgent, and another scraping sound echoed through the corridor.

Finally, slowly, Avery lowered his sword completely.

"Stand down," he said, and then looked back at the door. "It's locked from the inside. Even with a key, I don't know if you can ..."

"We'll manage," Osric said, hefting the brass key.

The knights moved aside, forming a corridor for Osric's group to pass through. As they did, Avery grabbed Osric's arm.

"Save him if you can," the knight said quietly. "He was a good man once. Before all this madness began."

Osric nodded. "We'll do what we can."

Avery released him and stepped back with his men. They kept their swords drawn but pointed at the floor.

The Baron and the Blackstar

Even with the key, it took a moment to get the door open. Osric had to put his shoulder into it to break the hold the frost had on it, with a cracking sound traveling up the door frame as the ice released.

If it had been cold in the hallway, it was frigid in the antechamber itself, colder than any winter Osric had ever experienced, biting at his skin through his armor. The walls and floor were covered in ice and frost like a powdery moss covering every inch of the space, making it hard to cross the room. Only the fact that it wasn't thick made it possible for Osric to stamp his feet hard, breaking through the layer and getting some kind of traction.

Across the large room was another, more elaborate set of doors. These were almost completely sealed in ice and frost.

There was no time for finesse or to wait to see if it was locked. Osric lowered his shoulder and charged, his heavy boots skidding slightly on the slick floor. He hit the frozen door with the full force of his weight. Ice shattered with a sound like breaking glass and groaning wood as the door gave way in a percussive crack. They flew open, sending Osric stumbling into the chamber beyond.

The difference between the chamber beyond and the antechamber was stark. Where the first had been freezing, this chamber was boiling hot. On one side of his body, he still felt the frigid chill, while the other was sweltering. The air was thin, tasting of ozone and something almost metallic. At the far end of the chamber, a rift like Osric had not seen since the bottom of the temple was shimmering and pulsing.

Unlike other rifts, where he could almost see something on the other side, this one was a range of oranges and yellows that shimmered in waves that made it impossible to tell what was on the other side. More frightening were the sounds. From somewhere deep inside the rift came a ceaseless, low whispering that crawled into his mind, the sounds unintelligible but also undeniably not of this world.

And in front of that stood Baron Blackthorn. Or what was almost the baron.

The man was a warped caricature of his former self. His limbs were elongated, his body unnaturally thin, as if stretched on a rack. His skin was the color of old bone, pulled taut over the distorted frame. He only had one hand, which was in a gauntlet, and the other had twisted into something almost animal-like, several fingers fused together and ending in a dark claw.

In the still-gauntleted hand, he clutched a shard of absolute blackness that seemed to drink the very light from the room; there was only one thing that could be. The Blackstar fragment, although seemingly too small to make up a third of the object Osric had seen in his vision.

At first, Osric wasn't even sure the man had heard them enter, even with Osric smashing through the door. He seemed completely unaware of their presence.

And then he turned. Slow and menacingly, like he was being distracted from something of extreme importance. His eyes were hollow pits, the pupils lined in an almost orange light that he fixed on Osric. It was impossible to read anything in the deep, pitch-black pit inside the orange rings that surrounded his irises, but even still, Osric knew the man was looking at him.

He did not speak, but a low growl rumbled in his chest as he took a step forward, deliberately tucking the fragment into a pouch that he wore around his neck.

The artifact stowed, he reached to his waist and pulled a long sword with his more human-like appendage.

Whatever this thing in front of them was, it wasn't the baron any longer.

Osric did not hesitate. They came for the fragment and now that he knew where it was, he was going to get it. He lunged forward, closing the distance in three long strides, although he knew this would be no easy fight. Even in Eldham, everyone knew how ferocious a fighter the baron was. Master Ironhand had told a story of seeing the baron fight as a young man in a tourney, before he'd returned to the forest.

He'd been fighting for longer than Osric had been alive. Not that he was going to let that stop him.

Osric wasn't trying anything fancy, simply coming in hard with a diagonal strike. As Osric's sword began its descent, Blackthorn's own blade lashed out. It was not a parry but a direct strike, a perfectly timed counter that slid under Osric's attack. The steel bit deep into Osric's side just below his breastplate, a line of fire tore through mail and leather. A grunt of pain escaped Osric's lips, but he didn't divert his own attack.

His sword never connected.

Just as the steel was about to bite into the baron's shoulder, it struck what felt like a wall, stopping his blade before it could touch the paper-thin skin below it. As soon as his sword touched the invisible wall, Osric was struck by a wave of concussive force. It was like being struck by a battering ram.

The impact threw him backward, his feet leaving the floor as he was hurled through the air, crashing hard into the splintered door he had just broken through, the wood digging into him before he crumpled to the ground, prone and breathless, the air driven from his lungs. Pain flared in his side and his back, and a dizzying confusion washed over him. *What was that?*

He wasn't the only one moving.

He saw Grace blur past him, her short sword aimed at the baron's flank. She was fast, a whirlwind of motion meant to catch their foe off-balance while he was focused on Osric. She lunged, a low thrust at his ribs.

Then it happened again; she hit the same wall Osric had and was in turn hit by the same invisible force. Grace gave a sharp cry as she was flung backward, tumbling end over end before landing in a heap on the floor, her sword clattering away from her hand.

From the doorway, Rowan had an arrow nocked. He took a quick step to the side for a clear shot, his movements fluid as he drew and loosed in a single motion. The arrow flew straight and true, aimed high, just above where the baron's breastplate ended. It should have been a perfect shot. Instead, the arrowhead struck at the baron's unnaturally pale skin and deflected with a brilliant shower of blue sparks.

The man was clearly protected by some kind of ... energy, perhaps.

Behind him, Jasper was praying, calling down the favor of the gods to aid them.

If their swords couldn't touch the man, they were going to need it.

The baron ignored the others and moved to Osric, who was struggling to rise, stalking toward him in a jerky, unnatural way. He stood over Osric, his distorted shadow falling across him. His longsword rose and fell, a brutal downward chop aimed at Osric's head. Osric tried to roll, managing to get halfway over, forcing the blow to land on his breastplate, denting it but not cutting through. The force was still enough to rattle him, jarring his bones and taking more of the wind out of him.

The baron was about to strike again when he stopped, looking up and past Osric to where Talia stood in the doorway, her hands waving through the air. The results of her magic weren't readily understandable at first, as there was none of the accustomed blasts of energy, fire, or acid.

The baron, however, acted perplexed, his motions suddenly becoming painfully slow and stiff, even seizing up for a beat as if he was trapped in an invisible mud.

Osric used the distraction to roll away and push himself up. It was clear his sword was useless unless they could figure out some way to get through the baron's protective force. It was time to try something else.

Planting his feet, Osric took a deep breath and drove forward, channeling all of his strength into his shoulder, trying to knock the baron down, although he wasn't sure it wouldn't have the same result. Osric braced himself as he slammed into the baron's chest.

Thankfully, it did not elicit the same response. He wasn't picked up or thrown back by whatever the force protecting the baron was. It surprised the man, who grunted as he gave ground, his boots scraping across the stone floor, knocking him a full ten feet back in the chamber, toward the rift.

The baron, slowed by Talia's spell and pressed by Osric, still tried to counterattack, bringing his longsword around in a short, brutal crosscut aimed at Osric's arm. The blade bit deep, and Osric cried out, his grip on the baron almost failing.

Already injured from their earlier fights, Osric was now bleeding freely from a half-dozen wounds and his strength was starting to fade as he weakened, allowing the baron to take a step away from Osric, freeing himself from the grapple-like hold.

Even though the first arrows had bounced off of the energy field protecting the man, Rowan hadn't given up. He fired another arrow, this one aimed low. It struck the baron squarely in the knee joint and made it through. The mad lord screamed as his leg buckled, enough to make him stumble, but not take him to the ground.

Rowan's arrow and Osric's successful rush of the baron, gave Osric an idea.

"Grace, go for the stone!" Osric yelled as he pushed forward against the baron again.

He redoubled his effort, putting every last ounce of his waning strength into restraining the baron. He wrapped his arms around the man, pinning his arms to his side. The baron struggled, the bottom sections of his elongated limbs thrashing, but Osric held on, his muscles screaming in protest.

Grace moved as soon as Osric had the man in a bear hug, coming behind the baron and jumping up, wrapping her arms around his neck and hanging off him, shimmying over his shoulder, her hands going to the clasp on his breastplate to start loosening it enough to get her hands inside.

The baron roared, trying to break free as she got a little slack in the plate, but Osric continued to squeeze, holding the baron's arms tightly as the man twisted violently. She didn't get a lot of slack, but enough that her arm could fit between his breastplate and his chest. Her arm snaked through the gap and grabbed the pouch hanging down inside of the protective shell provided by the plate when she screamed as the baron twisted enough to cause the breastplate to pin her wrist hard, the metal edge pinching into her skin.

The baron gave another roar, this time making a noise that sounded like something no man alive could make. It didn't even sound bestial. It reverberated in Osric's head, shaking him to his very core.

Osric felt the man's muscles bunch and twist under his hold, a horrifying strength that threatened to snap his ribs. He squeezed tighter, his own wounds screaming in protest, the feeling of the metal edge of the breastplate digging and pushing against Grace's arm from the other side, but he couldn't let go to help her.

Then Rowan was there, putting a hand on the breastplate, trying to pull it back to make room for her arm.

"Pull!" Osric grunted.

He shifted his weight, trying to use what was left of his strength to create a fraction of an inch of space for her. He almost shifted too much, feeling the baron start to pull loose, almost freeing himself before Osric clamped his arms back down.

Rowan braced against Osric's shoulder, pushing him into the breastplate as he pulled the plate away from the baron's skin.

Grace's arm moved out another fraction of an inch and then stopped again. She tugged. Once. Twice. Pulling hard against whatever the strap seemed to be caught on the inside. She gave a third tug, and something seemed to give way, her hand shooting out of the cavity behind the breastplate and coming free, clutching a very large drawstring purse in her hand.

Osric's relief lasted less than a breath.

The baron went rigid. The animalistic thrashing stopped, replaced by a stillness that was far more terrifying. For a moment, Osric thought maybe he was giving up, or maybe the artifact was the thing that had some kind of hold over him. And then he felt something like the deep rumbling of an overladen cart rattling across a wooden bridge, but it was coming from inside the baron, seemingly from deep in his body.

A low hum started in the man's chest, a vibration that Osric felt travel through his own body. The metallic taste in the air seemed to grow. And then the world seemed to explode around him.

Explode wasn't really the right word.

It was like the force that had happened when he'd hit the baron with his sword, a sweep of concussive force that felt like he'd been smashed by a staff, but across his whole body without a sign of any actual contact being made.

The world went white for a second, the humming sound becoming a deafening crack. Osric was torn from the baron, his grip broken as if by a giant's hand. He was thrown sideways off his feet. He managed to twist in the air enough to get his feet under him when he landed and to pop back up.

Grace went flying off in the other direction, thankfully well to the right of the rift, landing much more gracefully than Osric had. Rowan, who'd been next to Osric, landed right next to him, but took a bad tumble, going head over heels backward and landing hard.

The one who hurt the worst was Jasper, who'd just come around to try to help Grace. The wave of force caught him full on, lifting him from his feet and slamming him into the far wall. He hit with a sickening thud and collapsed to the floor in a heap, motionless.

The baron looked like he was about to charge, make his next attack, when a bolt of lightning cracked, tearing across the now open space, smashing into him, sending tendrils of electricity wrapping around his body and scorching his breastplate.

He convulsed, his elongated limbs jerking spastically as the electricity coursed through him, as the force of the strike drove him back until his heels were inches from the swirling, chaotic colors of the rift. He teetered there, smoke rising from his wounds, his hollow eyes wide with a new kind of fury.

"Knock him in!" Osric shouted, pushing himself up.

Rowan was also up and charged from the side before Osric could move, a low, powerful sprint that ended with him driving his shoulder hard into the baron's side. There was no finesse to it, just desperation.

The baron, however, was unmoved, pushing Rowan off and sending the ranger stumbling back a few feet as if he'd run into a stone wall.

Osric was right on Rowan's heels, closing the distance quickly. The ranger was more experienced than Osric would ever be, but he would never be able to match the weight and strength Osric had built from growing up hammering over the forge. This wasn't a test of skill but one of pure strength, which Osric was built for.

As he got close to the rift, the whispers grew louder, worming their way into his thoughts with their strange language that still somehow felt enticing and almost hypnotic.

He blocked it out, focused on his target.

He lowered his shoulder and hit the man with every ounce of strength he had left. The impact was solid, and unlike with Rowan's charge, the baron gave way.

There must not have been any floor on the other side of the rift because as soon as the baron was through, he dropped five feet, just catching his arms on the "ledge" made out of the floor on this side of the portal.

Osric was just gathering himself to push the baron a final time when tendrils of orange light, thin and fast as striking snakes, lashed out from the rift, wrapping around Osric's leg, his waist, his arm. They were insubstantial but immensely strong, and they were cold, a deep, draining cold that seemed to suck the very life from him. He cried out as the tendrils tightened, pulling him off balance. His feet slid out from under him, and as he hit the ground he felt himself being dragged into the rift with the baron.

"He's talking to me," the baron said from next to him.

Osric twisted, fighting the pull of the tendrils, turning to look at the baron. The man was looking at him, and for the first time, there was something other than madness in his eyes. The orange rings and pure black centers in his eyes were gone, replaced by the hazel eyes of a man. They were filled with a terrible, soul-deep agony.

"I can't block him out," Baron Blackthorn said. "He took her from me."

Across the room, Sir Avery and the other knights charged in, drawn by the sounds of the fight, skidding to a stop next to Talia, their faces masks of shock and horror at the sight of their master, a monster half-devoured by a hole in reality, and Osric being dragged in with him.

"Osric!" Jasper's voice called.

He was on his feet, rushing forward with Grace at his side. They grabbed Osric's arms, trying to pull him back. Rowan, recovering, joined them, adding his strength to theirs. They pulled, and the tendrils pulled back, a horrifying tug-of-war on the edge of the world.

"The baron! Pull him out!" Osric yelled.

If the man could be saved, if the insanity had left him, then they needed to do so.

"No," the baron said. "You must stop me. Before it's too late. Save my people."

There was one last, pleading look, begging, then his eyes clouded over and returned to the orange rings and deep black centers.

The man was gone, replaced once more by the monster. With a guttural roar, it lashed out, its clawed hand slamming against the stone floor at the edge of the rift. The impact sent a shockwave through the ground, knocking Grace and Jasper back. The momentary weakness in their grip was all the rift needed.

Thankfully, Rowan managed to maintain his footing, pulling his sword and cutting through the tendrils holding onto Osric. As soon as they released, Osric scrambled away from the rift, desperate to get out of their reach in case they tried again. Behind him, the baron tried to claw his way out of the rift, his twisted body heaving itself back into their world.

"Talia!" Osric screamed.

She'd been the only one able to really affect the monster this whole fight.

She didn't need to be told. As soon as he was free, a volley of glowing white shards flew across the room, striking the baron in the shoulders and upper chest, one after another. They stopped his forward progress, then drove him back, back into the swirling vortex. This time, there was no stopping his fall. He disappeared completely, his final, inhuman roar swallowed by the rift.

The portal pulsed violently. The whispers rose to a shriek, and a powerful suction erupted from its center. Rugs were torn from the floor, tapestries ripped from the walls, all pulled into the swirling maw. The knights cried out, digging their swords into the floor for leverage. Grace slammed her dagger into the floorboards, anchoring herself. Everyone braced against the sudden, violent wind.

"The fragment! Grace, give it to me!" Osric yelled over the roaring gale.

They had closed a rift once before, and Osric thought he had an idea of how to close this one.

Pulling her dagger free, Grace began to crawl toward him, fighting the pull of the vortex, her body low to the ground. She reached him and pressed the small, heavy pouch into his hand.

He clutched it. The fragment inside felt cold, a piece of absolute nothingness. The Blackstar had been made to draw and repair tears in the void. Osric's only hope was that it could still do that, even when in pieces.

He closed his eyes, shutting out the chaos, holding the fragment in one hand he placed his other over it, just as he did when he reached for the quiet place inside himself, that he found when he laid his hands on a wound and healed it, except this time he focused not on a wound, but on the screaming tear in the world in front of him. He pushed, pouring all his will, all his exhaustion, all his hope into the tiny piece of darkness in his hands.

For a moment, nothing happened. The wind howled, the whispers clawed at him.

Then there was a deafening crash, a sound like the world splitting in two, that seemed to come from inside the room, from inside his own head.

Osric's eyes snapped open.

The rift was gone. It had collapsed in on itself, the swirling colors vanishing into a single point of light before disappearing entirely. The whispers were cut off mid-shriek, like a screaming horse suddenly silenced.

The wind died. The pulling stopped.

The chamber was plunged into a sudden, shocking silence, broken only by the ragged breathing of his friends and the terrified knights.

Epilogue

The inn was quite the change after marching through the keep with all the opulence that was there. They could keep that. Osric felt much more at peace somewhere like here, with its modest furniture and simple walls.

It was much closer to home and what he grew up with. Osric wasn't sure he'd ever get used to finery. Although, this inn was a step better than sleeping on hard dirt, in caves or hollowed-out trees.

Plus, it gave him privacy to do what he needed to do.

He was sitting cross-legged on the wooden floor, the Blackstar fragment resting on a cloth before him. The crystalline shard seemed to absorb all the light in the room, pulling the light toward it. The surface gave off no glints and had no shine. It was like staring into a deep, empty pit.

For the third time that evening, he closed his eyes and tried to quiet his thoughts, reaching for whatever connection he had to the gods and the visions they had given him.

Again, no visions came. No mountains or landmarks were shown to him. No hint of where the rest of the fragments of the Blackstar might be. Osric had stared at its multifaceted surface until his eyes watered, traced its jagged edges with his fingertips, prayed, hoped, wished, and every other damn thing he could think of to get some kind of answer, but the gods remained silent.

He couldn't believe they'd stopped now. They'd given him the vision to find this first piece, the vision to find the document, why would they suddenly give up now?

But gods were gods, and they lived by their own whims, not by the wishes of mortals.

With a frustrated sigh, Osric wrapped the fragment in its cloth and rose from the floor. His knees protested after sitting so long. Jasper and Rowan were up at the keep with Grange, Paulin, some of the remaining knights, and the city leaders, trying to figure out what the hell to do now. Grace was who knows where, which left only him and Talia in their rooms at the inn.

Well, him, Talia, and Cinder, he thought, looking over at the wolf lying on its side. As if in response, the animal opened one eye to consider him.

"I'm just going to Talia's room for a minute. Go back to sleep," he said.

The wolf huffed once and closed its eye again.

Osric hoped that Jasper and Rowan were at least successful in getting the warrants for their arrest removed, or the rest of their quest would be at an end anyway. They hadn't been arrested the moment the fighting had ended, and Sir Avery had even called for a halt in the fighting, opening up the city to Grange and the rest while they were figuring out what to do, so it seemed a good bet they wouldn't end up in a dungeon.

But Osric's luck had not been running well the last few months.

Still, there was nothing he could do about that now, and if they were allowed to leave, they needed to know where to go.

And there was only one person Osric could think of who might be able to figure out where that was.

Osric tucked the fragment into his pouch and left his room, headed down the hall to the room assigned to Talia. Candlelight spilled from under the doorway, telling him she was still awake.

He knocked gently on the door and waited.

No answer came.

He knocked again, this time saying her name. When again no answer came, he tried the knob, and found that it wasn't locked. Pushing the door open, he saw his friend sitting curled up in a high-backed chair, facing the window that looked out into the city.

He knocked lightly on the door's frame. "Talia?"

She didn't move, her focus fixed on something beyond the glass.

"Talia," he said again, a little louder this time, stepping into the room and closing the door.

Her head turned slowly, her green eyes finding him. They looked distant. It wasn't hard to figure out what was bothering her.

"Are you thinking about what Ranulf said? About your parents?"

She gave a slow, deliberate nod. Her gaze drifted back to the window. "I don't understand. All my life, Elder Miriam told me my parents died in the fire that swept through Torfen. Why would she lie about that?"

Torfen had been the village she'd grown up in, about a day's ride south of Eldham. He'd been there a few times and seen the burned-out remnants of their smithy, the forge still half standing. The town was never rebuilt all the way after the fire, which is why people used to place orders with Master Ironhand when they needed things from a smithy.

So the fire, at least, had been real enough.

"Ranulf could have been the one lying," Osric offered.

"No," she said, shaking her head. "You saw his face. It wasn't a lie. He was really shocked to see me, to recognize me. And he recognized me because I look like them, apparently, which means he knew them. And if he was telling the truth, then who were they? And who am I? You heard him, heard the language he was chanting and you heard the whispers from the rift when the baron ... when he was lost."

Osric nodded grimly. The memory of that was unsettling, to say the least.

"It was the same language. I'm sure of it. How could a man like Ranulf, a man here in Wolfridge, know a language that comes from whatever place that was? It was evil. You saw what it did to the baron. Before it regained control, he begged us to kill him. You saw what Ranulf did, probably in whatever was over there's name. How could my parents have been involved in something like that?"

"We don't know that they were," Osric said, stepping further into the room. "We don't know anything yet. For all we know, they discovered what the tears in the veil were doing and tried to fix it, or they discovered the Brethren and were fighting against them."

242

"How?" Talia's voice rose, a flash of her old self breaking through the despair. "They raised sheep. How would they discover anything or stop anything. It's not like they were mages."

"Do you still believe that's true?" Osric asked gently.

Her mouth opened, then closed. She looked away, unable to meet his eyes.

"Talia, there's a reason Miriam found you," he continued, taking another step closer. "There's a reason she knew about you and your parents. Power like yours, it doesn't just appear from nowhere. Miriam didn't have apprentices, hell, she didn't even let anyone know she had trained at the Conclave. She took you in for a reason and if you have gifts, then it's likely they had the same gifts you do."

"Then why didn't she tell me?" The question was a raw plea. "Why would she lie to me about everything?"

"I don't know, but there had to be a reason. A good one. You know Miriam. You know she's a good person. She loves you. She wouldn't be part of anything evil." He reached out, resting a hand on her shoulder. "Whatever the truth is, she was probably trying to protect you from it. Don't jump to any conclusions until we know more. We'll look into it. We'll find out what's going on, together."

Talia searched his face, her own expression softening just a fraction. "How?"

"I don't know how, but it all has to be connected, right? The Brethren, the rifts, your parents. All of this isn't just a coincidence; we just haven't seen enough yet to know what's really happening. But even if it's not connected, after we settle this and fix the veil, we'll keep looking. I won't let you go through it alone."

After a long moment passed between them, she let out a long breath and gave a small nod.

"Okay," she said, wiping her face before looking at him as if she'd finally realized he was there. "Did you need something? You didn't come here just to check on me."

"Well, I did want to check on you after everything that happened, but yes, I also needed something else. I've been trying to use the fragment to get another vision from the gods, but I'm drawing a blank and we don't know where to head next," he said, pulling the fragment from its pouch. "I was hoping you and Jasper could look at it. See if you can figure out where the next piece is."

She took the piece of Blackstar from him, her fingers brushing his.

"You got nothing?"

He shook his head. "No, and I really tried. I tried until my head ached, but ... nothing."

It was Talia's turn to look at him. He only shrugged.

"Sure, we'll look at it."

"Thanks," Osric said, heading back toward the door before hesitating. "Do you want me to stay? Keep you company for a while?"

She offered him a kind, if weak, smile. "No. I think I'd rather be alone for a bit."

"Alright. I understand. If you need anything, my room is just down the hall."

"I know," she said softly.

Osric gave her one last look, then turned and walked out, leaving her alone with the artifact, now worried about two things instead of just one.

About the author

Travis writes science fiction, fantasy, and thriller novels (and the occasional coming-of-age story), with the hope of transporting and enthralling readers. Publishing novels since 2015, Travis's passion is creating worlds and characters that live and breathe, and experiencing the joy of those stories with his readers.

When not writing, Travis enjoys connecting with readers and other writers, managing the popular Complete Marvel Reading Order website, where he works on his other passion for comics and graphic novels, and spending time with his family.

If you have enjoyed this book, please consider taking a moment to rate or review it wherever you found your copy, as it helps new readers find my works and ensures I can continue writing book into the future.

Find out more at:
amazon.com/TravisStarnes/e/B072YBDC3S/

Or visit
https://tstarnes.com

Maps available at

https://tstarnes.com/book-series/imperium/

Signup to get free previews and notifications of upcoming books at

http://tstarnes.com/preview-notification-newsletter/

Also by

John Taylor Stories

Rebirth
False Signs
The Wrong Girl
Burying the Past
Family Ties
Election Day
Danger Close
Extraction
Designated Target
Border Crossed
Desperate Rendition
Broken Ground

Country Roads Series

Playing by Ear
Fanfare
Dissonance
Elegy
From the Top
Center Stage

Imperium Series

Volume 1
The Sword of Jupiter
The Trumpets of Mars
The Sands of Saturn
The Depths of Neptune
The Fires of Vulcan
The Triumph of Venus
Volume 2
The Wings of Mercury
The Plains of Pluto
The Clouds of Caelus

Shattered Lands Series

In the Shadow of Lions
An Ending of Oaths
The Barons' War
Heavy Lies the Crown

False Start Series

Second Down
Scramble
Breakaway

The Veilguard Saga

Threads of Destiny
The Blackstar Legacy

Stand Alone

Going Home